THE STRANGE DISAPPEARANCE OF A BOLLYWOOD STAR

Also by Vaseem Khan

The Unexpected Inheritance of Inspector Chopra
The Perplexing Theft of the Jewel in the Crown

THE STRANGE DISAPPEARANCE OF A BOLLYWOOD STAR

Vaseem Khan

MULHOLLAND
BOOKS
HODDER

First published in Great Britain in 2017 by Mulholland Books
An imprint of Hodder & Stoughton
An Hachette UK company

1

A CIP catalogue record for this title is available from the British Library

Hardback ISBN 978 1 473 61233 4
Trade Paperback ISBN 978 1 473 61234 1
eBook ISBN 978 1 473 61235 8

Typeset by Hewer Text UK Ltd, Edinburgh
Printed and bound by CPI Group (UK) Ltd, Croydon, CR0 4YY

Hodder & Stoughton policy is to use papers that are natural, renewable
and recyclable products and made from wood grown in sustainable
forests. The logging and manufacturing processes are expected to
conform to the environmental regulations of the country of origin.

Hodder & Stoughton Ltd
Carmelite House
50 Victoria Embankment
London EC4Y 0DZ

www.hodder.co.uk

To my friends in India who welcomed me, all those years ago, with such warmth, friendship and generosity, that when I left a decade later it was with enough wonderful memories to write a thousand splendid stories.

A BOLLYWOOD CONCERT

On a sultry March evening, in the great hive-city of Mumbai, Inspector Ashwin Chopra (Retd) was once again discovering the futility of reasoned discourse with his fellow countrymen.

'He is an elephant,' he said sternly. 'Elephants do not eat hot dogs. They are herbivores. In other words: vegetarian.'

'Hah!' said the hot-dog vendor, snapping his tongs triumphantly in the air. 'These *are* vegetarian.'

Chopra looked down at the sizzling griddle. Then he looked at the heap of sagging hot dogs set beside it on the vendor's handcart. Flies circled amorously around the pyramid, like B-2 bombers on a raid.

He turned and fixed his companion with a stony look. 'Did you take the hot dogs?' he asked.

Ganesha blinked rapidly, then twirled his trunk in the air, rocking back and forth on his blunt-toed feet, ears flapping, as Chopra glared.

He recognised the signs.

During his thirty-year career in the Mumbai police service he had interrogated thousands of suspects, and in so doing had become intimately familiar with the language of tells, involuntary movements that gave the inexperienced dissembler away.

It seemed that similar laws governed the behaviour of one-year-old elephants.

'What have I told you about helping yourself?' he scolded.

Ganesha hung his head.

'What's going on here?'

Chopra looked up to see his wife Poppy powering down the road with young Irfan in tow, the boy's walnut-brown face split by an enormous smile. In his right hand he clutched a stick of candyfloss, floating above his head like an umbrella. Poppy, resplendent in a marine-blue sari, steered him through the crush of people moving towards the entrance of the Andheri Sports Stadium.

'This elephant here is a thief!' replied the hot-dog vendor primly. 'I have caught him in the act.'

Chopra closed his eyes.

Poppy's cheeks reddened. 'Is that a fact?' she said.

'He has consumed four of my finest hot dogs,' continued the vendor, oblivious to Chopra's shaking head.

Poppy stepped forward and jabbed the paunchy man in his chest. 'What proof do you have that he ate those hot dogs?' Jab. 'Who would want to eat such rubbish anyway?' Jab. Jab. 'Do you even have a licence for this cart? Look at the state of it! It is filthy!'

'But– but–' The vendor backpedalled into the traffic-clogged road. An auto-rickshaw with a cage of scrawny chickens strapped to its roof swerved around him, honking madly. A cloud of feathers trailed from the rick as it buzzed away.

'Chopra! There you are!'

Chopra turned to see a heavyset, grey-haired man with a walrus moustache bearing down on them, arms outstretched in welcome.

In the three years since Chopra had last met Bunty Saigal his old friend had gained weight, padding out a naturally generous frame that now strained the seams of a navy-blue safari suit. Saigal had left the Brihanmumbai Police five years ago – four years before Chopra himself had been forced into early retirement by an ailing heart. Saigal had made the change for financial reasons, moving into a lucrative role as a security consultant at the Andheri Sports Stadium. Now he organised security for major events, such as the Bollywood concert that Chopra and Poppy were attending this evening. A month ago Chopra had made the mistake of mentioning Saigal's new position to Poppy. Upon discovering that Saigal would be presiding over the upcoming concert featuring Bollywood's newest star, Vicky Verma, she had harangued Chopra to twist his arm for front-row seats.

Chopra had reluctantly obliged.

Bollywood movies were one of Poppy's enduring passions and, as the show was to take place at the nearby stadium, it seemed churlish of him not to at least enquire.

Saigal had been more than glad to help.

He had always been a gregarious and jovial man, the life of the party, whereas Chopra himself was of a more taciturn disposition.

A broad-shouldered man with a head of jet-black hair greying only at the temples, Chopra's most impressive feature was an imposing moustache that underlined the natural authority that emanated from his tall frame. For almost three decades he had served Mumbai's citizenry as a policeman; for three decades he had remained steadfast to the principles ingrained in him by his father: honesty, integrity and decency. This in itself made him something of an oddity, for such qualities were often notable by their absence in the venal sinecures of the Indian police service.

Saigal pumped Chopra's hand with his strangler's grip, then led them past the crowded turnstiles, through the packed outer courtyard, and into the stadium proper.

A wall of noise greeted them as they moved along the running track, past the cordoned mass of jostling, chattering concert-goers trampling down the field grass, to the front row where a string of security guards were holding back the crowd as it ebbed and flowed.

As they walked along, the great bowl of the stadium opened up around them.

Chopra glanced up.

Beyond the rim of the cantilevered steel roof, the iconic fifty-metre-tall Andheri water tower, with its conical tanks, loomed over the stadium like a praying mantis. He noted the many fans settling onto the rows of concrete bleachers curving upwards under the roof. He would have preferred to be up there, away from the chaos, but he knew Poppy wouldn't hear of it.

The day's heat had settled into the stadium. Chopra found that he was sweating inside his white cotton half-sleeved shirt and beige duck pants.

He glanced at Ganesha, happily trotting beside Irfan. Occasionally, Irfan would lower his candyfloss so that Ganesha could pluck some off with his trunk and insert it into his mouth.

As usual, the pair were as thick as thieves.

Irfan, a street urchin who had walked into the restaurant Chopra had opened after his retirement a year earlier, had become a bona fide member of the family. He continued to live at the restaurant, as did Ganesha, but there was no doubt the pair had slipped into the vacant space in Poppy and Chopra's lives, a space occasioned by the absence of children of their own.

Chopra recalled the fuss Poppy had made getting the boy ready for his first-ever concert. Smart new clothes, stylish shoes, fragrantly oiled hair parted with geometric precision. Even Ganesha had been given a bath and a sprinkling of Poppy's favourite perfume. There had been no question that the little elephant would not attend.

Thanks to Poppy, Chopra's young ward was now as addicted to the Bombay talkies as his wife.

On the day of his retirement the infant elephant had arrived at Chopra's home, a fifteenth-floor apartment in the Mumbai suburb of Andheri East, as a malnourished and despondent calf with barely the energy to lift his head. The elephant had been accompanied by a curious letter from Chopra's long-vanished Uncle Bansi, a notorious prankster from his childhood in the Maharashtrian village of Jarul. But this time Bansi's tone had been serious. Bansi had not explained why he was sending Chopra an elephant, nor anything about the calf's past, merely stating, cryptically, that 'this is no ordinary elephant'.

At first thoroughly at a loss as to what to do with the strange bequest, Chopra had eventually warmed to his role as guardian. And in Ganesha – as he had named his young ward – he had ultimately discovered a sensitive and adventurous soul. The little elephant possessed depths that Chopra had yet to fully fathom; what was certain was that he was a highly intelligent creature, and an emotional one. As each day passed Chopra discovered new facets to Ganesha's talents. He had yet to solve the mystery of the elephant's past, but his appreciation of his ward's extraordinary abilities continued to grow.

Saigal ushered them to the front row, parking them before a group of singing, chattering youngsters.

'Sir!' A brisk young security guard pointed at Ganesha with his baton. 'There is an elephant behind you!'

Saigal rounded his eyes and held his hands to his cheeks in dismay. 'Where?'

'There!' said the guard.

Saigal turned and made a horrified face. 'An elephant! I must be getting old. I thought it was my shadow.'

The guard, realising that his boss was making fun of him, coloured.

'Chopra, I shall leave you to it.' Saigal bid them farewell and lolloped off back the way they had come.

Chopra's eyes wandered over the crowd jostling around them, comprised largely of teenagers and young women wearing far too few clothes in his opinion.

But such was the modern fashion.

Occasionally the knot of girls behind them would squeal delightedly as canned pictures of Vicky Verma were flashed onto the giant screen erected above the stage. Verma leaping from a moving train; Verma bashing up an assortment of villains; Verma romancing a sultry, pouting leading lady. There was even a surreal shot of Verma in an astronaut's outfit sipping from a can, a particularly cheesy ad campaign for a major soft drinks company.

He glanced at his watch, tapping it furiously. The watch was nearly a quarter of a century old, a memento of his departed father, the schoolmaster of the village in interior Maharashtra where both Poppy and Chopra had grown up. A congenitally temperamental timepiece, but he would not dream of parting with it.

Beside him Poppy licked a thumb and wiped a smear of sugar from Irfan's mouth. Ganesha trumpeted happily. He was receiving a great deal of attention from the girls behind them, who kept crowding around him to take photographs. Chopra knew his ward enjoyed the limelight, though sometimes he wished Ganesha would be a little more retiring.

His thoughts were interrupted by a loud klaxon, and then a cavalcade of fireworks erupted from the gantry above the stage. Smoke billowed from the stage floor and then, as it cleared, an overweight man in a bright red suit with a matching tie and black fedora jogged forward, holding a mike.

Chopra recognised the well-known Bollywood comedian Jonny Pinto.

Pinto lifted off his fedora, bowed to the crowd, bellowed a welcome, and immediately launched into a fusillade of cheap jokes – some that seemed to Chopra to skirt the boundaries of good taste – before introducing the first act, a fusion dance troupe marrying traditional Punjabi bhangra dance with modern street dance.

Chopra found himself shaking his head, even as howls of delight rocked the stadium.

He knew that such concerts were an integral part of the industry. Bollywood films were, almost without exception, musicals – indeed, movie music was an industry all by itself, and audio sales an important source of revenue. Concerts such as this were vehicles for promotion: for the movies, the stars, and the music. Producers pumped millions into them; they became miniature productions in their own right, microcosms of the glamour and spectacle that was Bollywood. Chopra, however, found them gaudy and coarse, lacking the refined artistic sensibility that appealed to him.

The concert proceeded apace, with each energetic act following closely on the heels of the one before, punctuated with comedy skits from Jonny Pinto. A succession of ageing stars and up-and-coming starlets – in costumes ranging from swirling saris to shimmering miniskirts – performed dance numbers, and another well-known comedian brought the house down with a send-up of the state's much-maligned Chief Minister.

And then the lights dimmed.

Finally, it was time for the main event.

Pinto launched into a gratuitous introduction – 'Bollywood's newest sensa-*tion*! The kid that's taking the industry by *storm*! More super than *Superman*! Mumbai's own bad boy, the one, the only, Vicky *Verma*!' – then back-pedalled offstage as fireworks erupted around him. More smoke engulfed the stage.

When it cleared, a tall figure stood silhouetted against a colossal movie poster. The roving spotlight sprang onto the solitary figure dressed in shimmering silver trousers and a stylishly cut black jacket above a white vest. Designer stubble and twin earrings. A quiffed and gelled mullet of dark hair, barely held in check by a red bandana.

Vicky Verma, enfant terrible of Bollywood, and superstar in the making.

The crowd went wild. Chopra had to hold his hands to his ears as the gang of cheerleaders behind him hurled themselves forwards on a tidal wave of noise.

Verma launched into a dance routine, gyrating about the stage while lip-syncing to a raunchy number from his last movie. When he was joined onstage by a troupe of dancers, the gyrations became even more suggestive.

Chopra stole a glance at Poppy. His wife was clapping away, as engrossed as any of the teenagers around her.

After the first number Verma paused for breath. His dark eyes swept the front rows with an imperious gaze. He suddenly caught sight of Ganesha and did a double-take. As accustomed to the extraordinary as Verma was, it gave Chopra a small measure of satisfaction to think that he had probably never seen an elephant in the front row of one of his concerts before. Particularly an elephant trumpeting as loudly in appreciation as Ganesha was.

The concert proceeded with three more numbers from Verma, interspersed with incoherent addresses to the audience, before the final dance act.

Verma and a cast of dozens congested the stage in gaudy historical costumes from the set of his latest movie, a big-budget blockbuster slated for release later in the year. A hypnotic beat from the movie's soundtrack pounded from the stadium's speakers.

And then, abruptly, the music stopped, and a curtain of ringing silence fell over the audience.

All the lights cut out, save a single spotlight focused on Verma. The compere began to count: 3 . . . 2 . . . 1 . . . Stage smoke erupted from beneath Verma's boots, engulfing him, and then was just as swiftly blown away by powerful fans . . .

The audience gasped.

Verma had vanished.

The crowd waited with breathless anticipation. Suddenly, the spotlight swung halfway down the stadium to a spot just above the highest bleachers on the stadium's eastern side.

Smoke erupted, then cleared . . . and there, impossibly, was Verma!

The crowd doubled their screams of delight.

Chopra blinked. Incredible! How could Verma have got up there in a few seconds, not to mention changed into a new costume?

He was given no chance to find out as smoke billowed forth again to consume the star. Now the spotlight swung over to the far side of the stadium, again to a spot above the highest bleachers. More smoke . . . and *there* was Verma once more, again in a new outfit.

More bellowing from the crowd.

Yet more smoke, and Verma vanished for a third time.

Now the spotlight moved to the rear of the stadium, and the whole act was repeated. This time, when Verma vanished, the spotlight swung all the way back to the stage. Another flurry of smoke whooshed over the dancing girls who remained frozen, awaiting Vicky's return.

The crowd roared in anticipation, counting off the seconds with the compere: 3 . . . 2 . . . 1 . . .

Emptiness.

For a moment there was a stunned silence, as if a wrong chord had been struck during a familiar piece of music. Everyone had expected Verma to be on the stage when the smoke cleared.

Yet he was not there.

The music started up again, and the dance troupe awkwardly began the closing number. But Chopra could tell their movements were off. Clearly, they had been expecting Verma onstage.

A few minutes in, the compere froze the dancers. Smoke billowed, passing a veil over proceedings; when it cleared, moments later, there was Verma again.

The crowd released a sigh of relief.

The dance was completed, and then, without even a goodbye to his loyal followers, Verma vanished backstage. Within moments the security personnel were herding everyone towards the exits.

It was an abrupt and strange end to proceedings, Chopra thought.

On the way home something continued to nag away at him. It wasn't until later that night that he finally realised what it was.

The Vicky Verma who had reappeared at the very end moved differently. If Chopra had been asked to swear to it he would have said that *that* Verma wasn't the one who had begun the concert. But he couldn't be sure, and no one else seemed to have noticed. Perhaps it was just his old policeman's instincts making a nuisance of themselves, looking for something that wasn't there.

It probably wasn't worth worrying about.

THE CASE OF THE MISSING HELMET

Chopra regarded the tall, thin, bespectacled man in the leather biker's jacket seated before him.

It was the morning after the concert and they were sitting in the office at the rear of Poppy's Bar & Restaurant, the air-conditioner thundering away in the corner.

Chopra had arrived early.

He had a number of case files to look through and then a busy afternoon ahead, planning activity on open investigations with his associate private investigator Abbas Rangwalla.

Rangwalla – once Sub-Inspector Rangwalla – had served for twenty years as Chopra's second-in-command at the nearby Sahar station. Now he had become an invaluable member of the Baby Ganesh Detective Agency, the second venture that Chopra had embarked upon since retiring. The truth was that the restaurant largely ran itself, left in the capable hands of Chef Lucknowwallah and Chopra's bilious mother-in-law, Poornima Devi. As a consequence,

Chopra found that he had time on his hands, time that he wished to put to good use. He had retired from the police force, but how could one retire the experience and instincts honed over an entire career? The detective agency provided an outlet for his need to put to use those hard-won skills, and his even greater need to pursue justice, a cause ingrained within the folds and hollows of his heart.

But Chopra's morning routine had been interrupted by the arrival of an unexpected visitor.

By day, forty-six-year-old Gerry Fernandes was a stock-market trader, a man who had made millions on the Bombay Stock Exchange. Under normal circumstances, Chopra and Fernandes' paths would never have crossed – they came from different worlds. But there was one point where their lives *did* intersect: their passion for motorcycles. Specifically, their passion for one particular motorcycle: the Royal Enfield Bullet.

Chopra and Fernandes had met at the local chapter of the Bombay Bullet Club, which Chopra had joined despite Poppy's strenuous objections. His wife made no secret of her disapproval of his penchant for tearing up the streets on the back of the 500cc beast. Chopra was new to the club but Fernandes was an old hand, having served as ride captain on many an outing of the Bisons, as the group styled themselves.

But today Fernandes was not here to discuss motorbikes. A shadow lay over his gaunt features. In the leather jacket emblazoned with the Bisons logo he looked like an accountant who had wandered into a costume shop and inadvertently walked out in the wrong outfit.

'I've come to settle our account, Chopra,' said Fernandes, reaching inside his jacket for his chequebook. 'How much do I owe you?'

'You don't owe me anything,' said Chopra. 'We are friends.'

'Business is business,' said Fernandes primly. 'Everything in its place.'

Chopra shifted in his chair. He knew that Fernandes was a very particular fellow, meticulous about money and notoriously ruthless in his business dealings. As a consequence, he had a very narrow circle of friends, and many detractors. It was only in the Bullet Club that Fernandes was able to relax his guard. Chopra had seen a side of the man that few had glimpsed. His careworn appearance belied his spirited demeanour when out on the open road.

Two weeks ago Fernandes had approached him for help.

It appeared that Fernandes' father, a retired civil servant, had misplaced a valuable family heirloom. The fact that the 'heirloom' was a motorcycle helmet was neither here nor there. The leather helmet – complete with goggles – had belonged to the legendary motorcyclist Erwin 'Cannon Ball' Baker, who had worn it during his record-breaking transcontinental ride across America in 1914. Fernandes, who idolised Baker, had purchased the helmet at an auction in California. Not long afterwards, his father had smashed the display case in which the items had been housed, donned the ensemble, and departed for a joyride on Fernandes' beloved Bullet.

He had been discovered some hours later in a roadside ditch on the outskirts of the city, naked, incoherent, and with a small goat strapped to the back of the bike.

Of the prized helmet there was no sign.

Fernandes had been beside himself at the loss of his Baker memorabilia. In desperation, he had turned to Chopra for help.

Having interviewed the senile paterfamilias, Chopra had asked an acquaintance specialising in hypnotherapy to examine him.

The results had been impressive.

Under hypnosis, Fernandes Senior not only led them to the lost helmet, but also on a tour of half-a-dozen previous lives, ranging from a junior miniaturist at the court of Emperor Jahangir to a famine-stricken farmer who had walked beside Gandhi on his legendary Salt March.

These revelations had greatly perturbed the Fernandes household. Three maids had already quit, and the head-man was walking around on eggshells lest he be once again belt-whipped by the old man while in the throes of his incarnation as prison-master of Calcutta's Fort William dungeon, known to history as the Black Hole.

Perhaps this explained Fernandes' haggard appearance, Chopra thought, as his friend tore off a cheque and held it out.

'If I take that cheque,' said Chopra, 'we are no longer friends. You needed help; I did what I could. That's what friends do.'

Fernandes stared at him, then tucked the cheque back in his pocket. 'Thank you,' he said with genuine emotion.

After Fernandes had left, Chopra considered how lonely the pedestal of wealth and power could be. He had met many privileged individuals in his life and so often their lives were shadowed by unhappiness, contrary to the belief of the average man on the street. Sometimes this misery was self-inflicted, but at other times it was simply the toll that fate demanded.

The noise of the television broke into his thoughts.

It was a news item on last night's concert. It appeared Vicky Verma had overexerted himself and was now confined to his south Mumbai home with a mysterious illness. This revelation was causing great consternation among his fans, as well as the Bollywood fraternity.

Chopra next spent an hour with Rangwalla going over the caseload.

Rangwalla's arrival at the agency had been fortuitous. Chopra had been steadily drowning beneath the mountain of work that had deluged the agency since its very public first case, which had exposed a major human trafficking ring in the city. Rangwalla – employing the street smarts that had made him so able a policeman – had immediately helped whittle down the load.

As they were winding up their meeting, Chopra's phone rang; glancing at the number, he saw that it was unlisted.

'Am I speaking to Chopra?' said a cultured, if somewhat dry, voice. 'Proprietor of the Baby Ganesh Detective Agency?'

'Yes,' said Chopra.

'The same Chopra who recently assisted in the reacquisition of the Koh-i-noor?'

Chopra was taken aback. 'How do you know about that?'

The details of his involvement in the return of the Koh-i-noor diamond – which had been stolen during a recent exhibition of the Crown Jewels in Mumbai – had been kept out of the public realm. Only a handful of people knew that he had been instrumental in tracking down the jewel.

'That is irrelevant,' said the voice curtly. 'I have been instructed by my client to request your attendance at her residence in Malabar Hill. It is a matter of the utmost urgency.'

'What matter? What client?'

'I am afraid I am not at liberty to discuss further details.'

'You can't expect me to drop everything and come running down to south Mumbai just on your say-so.'

The voice paused. 'Very well. My client is Bijli Verma, former film actress, and mother of noted actor Vikram Verma.'

THE LIGHTNING BOLT OF MALABAR HILL

The gilded Antakshari Tower had looked down from its precipitous eighteen-storey elevation atop Malabar Hill for the better part of five decades. Centuries earlier, Keralan pirates from the subcontinent's deep south had surveyed the fledgling city from these once-forested heights, planning pillage and plunder. Now the tower's lofty perspective provided expansive views over the nearby promenade of the Back Bay, the Hanging Gardens on the hill's western flank, and the ancient Banganga water tank, which legend said had sprung from the earth where Lord Ram's brother Laxman had fired an arrow into the ground. In the mid-nineteenth century the hill had been colonised by Mumbai's British overlords, after the demolition of their redoubt within Bombay Fort.

Now Malabar Hill was the city's most exclusive address, commanding real-estate prices that rivalled any metropolis on earth, home to business tsars, Bollywood superstars, and political VVIPs. The state's Chief Minister kept a bungalow there, as did the Governor. In the turbulent days before Partition the future Prime Minister of Pakistan Muhammad Ali Jinnah lived there in his sprawling bungalow South Court, plotting – with Gandhi and Nehru – the subcontinent's shimmering future.

As Chopra made the long drive down to south Mumbai he noted once again that Malabar Hill was not on the road to anywhere. One did not accidentally pass it on the way to somewhere else. To go to Malabar Hill, one must be invited. Perhaps this was what made it so exclusive.

In the rear of the converted Tata Venture van, Ganesha peered out from the windows.

Over the past months Chopra had discovered that his young ward enjoyed accompanying him on his travels around the city. In all good conscience, Chopra could not keep the little elephant cooped up interminably in the rear courtyard of the restaurant: as well as needing the exercise, Ganesha had shown that he had an adventurous streak. His naturally inquisitive nature had made him an able companion for Chopra, who could rely on the young calf to keep a vigilant watch on the suspect of the day. The arrangement had worked remarkably well and Chopra had all but stopped dwelling on just how strange it might seem that Ganesha was his 'partner' in his new life as a private detective.

This was India, after all, where the impossible became merely improbable.

Antakshari Tower was set within its own walled compound fronted by a bunker-like guardhouse and a row of parking bays. Unlike Bahadur, the scrawny and often forgetful guard who patrolled Chopra's residential complex back in Andheri East, the trio of guards who sprang from Antakshari's guardhouse were well built and smartly uniformed.

The guards rang into the tower and presently a tall vulpine man in a grey suit and tie materialised at the gate. To Chopra he resembled one of the many gargoyles adorning the Victorian-era buildings that were part and parcel of Mumbai's British legacy. His grey hair was swept back into a prominent widow's peak, his face was that of an ascetic, and rimless spectacles were perched uncomfortably on the end of an arrogant nose.

In spite of the day's oppressive heat he radiated a noticeable chill.

'Chopra, I presume? My name is Lal. Please come with me.'

Chopra recognised the voice from the telephone. 'One second,' he said.

He walked back to his van, opened the rear doors, and waited for Ganesha to trot down the ramp. 'I won't be long,' he said, patting the little elephant on the head.

In spite of Poppy's belief that he did not share her passion for Bollywood, the truth was that Chopra enjoyed a good movie as much as the next Mumbaiker. You could not spend thirty years in the city of dreams and remain uninfected by

Mumbai's virulent filmalaria. It was simply that Chopra considered himself an aficionado of the 'Golden Age' of Bollywood, generally considered to have begun in the late forties – encompassing enduring classics such as *Mother India* and *Aan,* or *Pride* – and peaking soon after the release of the towering *Mughal-e-Azam*, *The Grand Mughal*, in 1960.

Chopra also harboured a soft spot for movies from the seventies, particularly action flicks featuring his screen idol Amitabh Bachchan, who had reigned supreme at the time as India's 'angry young man'.

It was during this latter era that Bijli Verma – then Nandita Goyal – had burst on to the scene.

Exuding a raucous sex appeal, Bijli hit the industry like a one-woman earthquake. In the no-kissing world of seventies Indian cinema, she became the perennial other woman, the wet sari queen, the monsoon goddess dancing voluptuously against an alpine background as all around her the world fell apart. Volatile, raunchy, and excessive in personality, she singlehandedly turned the traditional Bollywood leading lady trope on its head. Bijli refused to play the demure, long-suffering foil to her leading men. Instead, she ad-libbed wild-eyed soliloquys, and would launch, without warning, into verbal assaults on her open-mouthed male co-stars.

Chopra recalled how shocked veteran critics of the time had roundly decried Bijli's antics. In spite of this, or perhaps because of it, Bijli had developed a cult following among younger movie-goers – including a smitten Chopra – a cult that ultimately grew into superstardom. Continuously at odds with the censors, her co-stars, and, seemingly, herself, her personal and professional life became the subject of salacious gossip, a grist to Mumbai's insatiable rumour mill.

Her birth name was soon forgotten as she was rechristened Bijli, 'the lightning bolt'.

The name appealed to her sense of self and stuck.

Bijli reigned supreme as Bollywood's number-one heroine for over a decade before marrying film producer Jignesh Verma. As with so many actresses in the industry, marriage and motherhood banked the fires of ambition, and soon Bijli Verma faded from the silver screen.

Though not quite from public life.

The former siren transformed herself into a socialite of the first order. The old fiery persona, too, had not altogether vanished, occasionally sparking a round of furious tabloid stories that Mumbai's first lady herself studiously ignored.

Chopra recalled some of those stories: Bijli publicly castigating the Chairman of the Indian Central Board of Film Certification for his 'medieval approach to censorship'; Bijli pouring a glass of champagne over the head of veteran thesp Raj 'Gunga' Ganesham after he had criticised her son's debut performance; Bijli denouncing religious demagogues following the burning of the Taj Palace hotel by terrorists in 2008.

This latter very public airing of her views had attracted considerable unwanted attention: she had been threatened by known right-wing organisations, though, ultimately, nothing had come of those threats.

In recent years the former starlet's energies had been consumed by her only child, Vikram 'Vicky' Verma, who had been launched with considerable fanfare into the Bollywood machine. As far as Chopra could make out, the young man had proved his mother's son, garnering a great deal of media coverage for his wild ways.

The elevator slid smoothly to a halt and disgorged them into a marbled antechamber on the topmost floor of the tower, hung with paintings of the Arabian Sea, dhows sailing into a red sunset.

Lal stalked past a turbaned doorman and marched stiffly into the apartment.

Chopra followed.

He was not sure what he had expected – a glamorous dusting of tinsel, perhaps, as befitted the home of a legendary Bollywood seductress – but what he was confronted with was a seemingly ordinary, if unusually spacious, apartment. Yes, the furnishings were exquisite: expensive leather sofas, twin sitars flanking a high-backed divan with Rajasthani bolsters, a sunken bar, an antique pianola, but there was nothing here that Chopra would not have expected to find in any wealthy Mumbaiker's home.

And then he took a second look.

On the walls, ensconced in various strategically placed niches, were framed posters of each of Bijli Verma's many films. Accompanying the posters were display cases housing memorabilia from those same movies, Bijli Verma's shrines to herself.

Chopra stepped towards the nearest display case. Inside were the golden bangles Bijli had worn in *Plaything of Emperors*, in which she had played a doomed courtesan destined to commit suicide by ingesting a vial of cobra venom; here was the revolver she had used to commit suicide in *Jilted Woman*, in which she had portrayed a doomed lover in yet another of Bollywood's eternal love triangles; here the jewelled dagger with which she had slashed her throat after murdering her cheating husband in *Modern Love Story* . . . Now that Chopra reflected upon it, Bijli had assayed more than her share of fatally troubled characters during her tempestuous career. He wondered if this had leaked into her volatile personality, whether it was true what they said about life imitating art.

Lal led Chopra out onto a vast balcony overlooking the Back Bay.

A stiff breeze blew across the balcony, rustling the fronds of the potted palm beside him.

Standing by the railing, clad in a richly filigreed black sari, hair pulled into a severe topknot, was Bijli Verma.

Chopra approached nervously behind Lal, who coughed to announce his arrival.

Bijli turned.

Chopra's stomach performed a cartwheel.

She was as beautiful as he remembered, a towering light undimmed by age.

Of course, the rational part of his mind knew that his vision was coloured by his own memories. The crow's feet around her eyes, the threads of grey running through her hair, the slight sag of her jawline all testified to the fact that ultimately no man – or woman – could prevail against the insidious corrosions of Father Time.

And yet, in the light of that liquid amber gaze, Chopra replayed moments of sheer cinematic magic; in those wide, full lips he relived the ardour of youth; in that delicate nose he recalled her ability to convey a gamut of emotion with a single twitch. For a moment he was eighteen again, a newly minted constable in the big city, watching this goddess beguile the leading heroes of her age. A haughty glance, an icy stare, a sashay of that incredible figure across a carpeted hotel floor . . . What man could resist?

'Inspector Chopra, I presume?' said Bijli.

Chopra shook himself back to the present. 'Yes, madam.'

'I see you have already met our family lawyer, Lal. I trust he explained the need for discretion?'

'To be frank, Mr Lal has explained very little.'

Bijli tapped a manicured fingernail against her thigh. 'In that case, let me enlighten you. Last night my son did not come home. You know who my son is, don't you?'

'Yes, of course. In fact, I saw him last night.' Chopra hesitated as Bijli stared at him. 'What I mean is that I attended the concert in Andheri,' he stumbled out.

'Then you have seen him more recently than I. Vicky was due to return home last night. He did not. Usually this would not concern me. He is a wilful young man. He is often out till late. But I have a rule: when a big shoot is due the following day he must spend the night here.'

'Surely, it is too early for alarm?'

'He has not telephoned me or any of his circle of friends since yesterday evening. No one has seen or heard from him. This morning he was due for a critical shoot at Film City. He would not miss it.'

Chopra chose his next words carefully. 'Forgive me for saying this, but how can you be sure he is not simply sleeping off a wild night somewhere?'

'I am well aware that my son has gone out of his way to earn a certain *reputation*,' snapped Bijli. 'But he is no fool. He would not jeopardise his career by missing this shoot.'

'What's so important about it?'

Lal spoke up. 'It's no secret that Vicky's current movie, *The Mote in the Third Eye of Shiva*, is the most expensive production ever undertaken in our industry. Many people have invested a great deal of money. Yet the film is well behind schedule and over budget. Today was to mark the beginning of a critical sequence that has taken months to set up. If he does not appear, the producers will be extremely unhappy. They can push back the shoot at most a few days. After that, the costs will escalate to a point where the whole venture becomes untenable.'

'I understand,' said Chopra.

'I don't think you do,' snapped Bijli, her eyes suddenly blazing. 'When my son did not appear last night I called everyone. Once I realised I could not find him, I was forced to put out the announcement of his illness. It was the only way I could placate the movie's financial backers. Not that it did much good. I am being hounded by calls. They are after his blood. They demand to know how serious this illness is, whether he will make the shoot. They demand to see him, which, of course, I cannot allow. They have threatened to blacklist him. Do you understand what this means? If my son is blacklisted none of the major studios will touch him. Everyone thinks star power is paramount in Bollywood, but the truth is that the studios can make and break whoever they wish. They control the big-budget productions, the regional distributors, the foreign rights, the marketing. That is what makes a star these days.'

Chopra saw the shape of things. He was being asked to take on a missing-person case.

'If you truly believe your son has come to harm you should enlist the help of the police,' he advised.

'Don't be a fool, Chopra,' said Bijli irritably. 'I have just explained to you why no one must know of this. I have called upon you for two reasons. One, you are a private detective, by all accounts a good one. Secondly, you are a man whose discretion can be counted upon.'

Chopra absorbed these words. 'Who told you about my involvement in the Koh-i-noor case?' he said eventually.

Bijli glanced at Lal, then said, 'The British High Commissioner to India. He is a close personal friend. You may set your own fee, of course.'

The temptation to take the case was strong. What Chopra had to decide was whether he would be taking the case based on its merits or because of the undeniable glamour cast by Bijli Verma.

He sighed. When all was said and done, he was being asked to help a mother find her son. That was the essence of it, and for this reason he could not turn the former starlet down.

'I will do what I can,' he said. 'But first I require some information.'

'Lal will give you everything you need,' said Bijli. 'I must go and speak to the director of the Indian Global Bank. They have loaned a great deal of money to the production. I have some difficult questions to answer. Please excuse me.'

He watched her leave, a vision of immaculate fury in a sari.

RANGWALLA RECEIVES A SUMMONS

In the quarter of a century that he had spent as a policeman former sub-inspector Abbas Rangwalla had learned a great many things. For instance: when approaching an armed suspect it was best to rely on the old adage of shoot first and ask questions later (or even better, shoot first, then shoot again just in case, then ask questions if anyone was still left alive to answer them); to leave the unfathomable complexities of paperwork to those best placed to tackle such a responsibility, namely those who hadn't scraped their way through their matriculation exams; and, perhaps most importantly, not to approach a senior officer with a request for overtime when he was having his lunch.

But the one thing he had never learned was how to deal with an aggressive and authoritative woman.

As he sat in Chopra's office, listening to the strident harangue emanating from the phone, he felt his heart shrivel inside him.

Mrs Roy was angry.

Just a short while earlier, Mrs Roy had hired the Baby Ganesh Agency to confirm her long-standing suspicion that her husband, the president of the local Rotary Club, had reverted to his old drinking habits.

Rangwalla had been given the case.

He had diligently followed the old sot around and duly confirmed Mrs Roy's fears. Unfortunately, he had also discovered that Mr Roy was keeping a fancy woman in a nearby apartment in Marol. Each Wednesday afternoon, when his wife believed him to be studiously planning Rotary business with the club secretary, the old letch was instead canoodling with a woman twenty-five years his junior, and at least three ranks beneath his social standing.

It was this latter fact that had so incensed Mrs Roy.

Rangwalla was feeling deeply put upon; after all, he was only the messenger.

Suddenly, he heard raised voices from the restaurant floor. Sighing, he said, 'I must go, Mrs Roy.' He put down the phone, cutting off Mrs Roy's astonished protest.

In the restaurant he discovered Anarkali, the hulking eunuch he and Chopra had employed for many years as a part-time informant. Anarkali was standing in the entrance, her muscular arms folded, irritation and embarrassment enveloping her dark features. She was being roundly berated by a trio of constables Rangwalla did not recognise – they were new faces at the restaurant.

He looked around for Chopra's mother-in-law, Poornima Devi, who Chopra, against his own better judgement, had employed as the front-of-house manager. To universal astonishment the cantankerous old woman had proven singularly effective in the role. But today Poornima was not at her usual station – behind the marble counter with its electronic cash register, which she manned as though it were a gun turret.

Rangwalla moved towards the fracas. 'What's the problem here?'

One of the constables turned, hitched up his khaki pants with his thumbs, and said, 'This eunuch here just came marching in. Can't he see decent people are eating?'

Rangwalla had lived long enough in Mumbai to understand that prejudice was part of the complex equation of life in the subcontinent's most crowded city. Caste prejudice, religious prejudice, social prejudice, prejudice in all its myriad forms. In this great sea of antipathy, the city's eunuch population occupied a unique niche, simultaneously loathed and feared. Loathed for their manifest difference; feared for the generations-old belief that a eunuch's curse was a potent weapon. But he knew too that many policemen had long ago shed their ancestral terror, and treated them brutally.

Rangwalla also knew that Chopra had little time for such men.

'This is Anarkali,' he said. 'She is welcome here.'

The man goggled at Rangwalla. His thumbs slipped from his belt and his trousers fell back below his ballooning gut.

Rangwalla turned to Anarkali. 'If you are looking for Chopra, he is tied up.'

'Then *you* must come with me,' said Anarkali. 'This matter cannot wait.'

'Come where?'

'To see the Queen of Mysore.'

THE PEOPLE'S JUDGE

The offices of the Dynamite Global International Acting and Talent Agency were located on the fifteenth floor of the iconic Air India building in Nariman Point in south Mumbai. For decades, the grand tower had served as headquarters to the national airline. But in recent years, many major corporations had moved to swanky new offices in the suburbs, and the elite Bandra Kurla Complex. Acceding to the inevitable, Air India too had abandoned their once-feted HQ and upped sticks to New Delhi.

Now, the twenty-three-storey building, overlooking the bustling Marine Drive boulevard, was leased out to an assortment of companies, government organisations, and small independents.

Babu Wadekar, Vicky Verma's agent, was a round, loud man in a shimmering purple satin shirt and the worst toupee Chopra had come across in years. The offensive hairpiece, acting in concert with a moustache that itself appeared glued on, gave Wadekar the look of a hired extra in a low-budget comedy.

Wadekar's office was consumed by a runway-sized marble-topped desk, and a number of life-sized cut-outs of actors he claimed to manage. Pride of place was reserved for Vicky Verma, who stood at Wadekar's shoulder with a smouldering look in his eye, wearing his trademark red bandana and toting an enormous rocket launcher.

'So Vicky's missing, what's new?' said Wadekar grimly. 'That kid has been a pain in my backside since the day I took him on.'

'Are you saying this isn't the first time he has gone missing?'

'The boy is mentally unstable,' growled Wadekar. 'He fights with his directors; he refuses to rehearse; he turns up drunk, then leaves halfway through a shoot.' The agent threw up his hands. 'Actors these days are no better than camels! Worse. At least, if you lead a camel to water, it will drink.'

'Why do you represent him if he is so much trouble?'

'His mother asked me to. I have known Bijli for years. In fact, I represented her towards the latter part of *her* career. Besides, the boy has all the attributes one needs to be successful nowadays. He looks good in a vest, he can dance like a drunk being electrocuted, and he has a famous parent to promote him.'

Chopra thought that Wadekar was being somewhat unfair. Though Bollywood continued to be ruled by the ancient codes of nepotism, it was still an exacting business.

New faces – both the sons and daughters of yesteryear's stars and those who had come up on their own merit – were increasingly asked to stay afloat on the strength of their talent. Chopra was no expert but it seemed to him that the winds of change were finally being felt in the world's most prolific movie industry.

'Has he contacted you since yesterday evening?'

'Hah!' said Wadekar, slapping his desk. 'He only contacts me when he gets himself into trouble.'

'His mother believes she would have heard from him by now if all was well.'

Wadekar struggled to frame his next words. 'Look, Chopra, I'm going to save you some heartache by telling you something. Just don't repeat it in front of Bijli. That woman is part of the problem. She has been controlling her son's life since the day he was born. Is it any wonder he's turned out the way he has? The boy is a spoilt brat, a thoroughly nasty piece of work. That's the best I can say of him, and *I* actually like the kid!'

Chopra considered this revelation.

Wadekar seemed to be implying that Verma was simply acting the delinquent, that there was no real cause for worry.

'He'll show up,' added the agent confidently. 'Because he knows that if he doesn't his career will be deader than my hair.'

A tentative knock sounded.

Chopra turned to see a slender young woman enter the office. She wore blue jeans below a drab olive kurta, and a dupatta wound around her neck. Her dark hair was pulled back in a ponytail, and her eyes wobbled behind bottleneck spectacles. Her face was unadorned by make-up but Chopra could see that she was quite pretty. She clutched a worn red handbag and bit her lip nervously.

'Ah, Greta. Good of you to come,' said Wadekar. 'Chopra here is looking for our mutual friend. The idiot.'

'Please don't call him that, sir,' said the girl.

'What do you think I should call him?' snapped Wadekar, his dynamic hairpiece jiggling atop his head. 'Gandhiji? Shall I touch his feet and ask for his blessings? Do you know that fool is missing? Again!'

Chopra observed the girl as her hands agitatedly worked the straps of her handbag.

He knew that her name was Greta Rodrigues and that she was Vicky Verma's personal assistant. She was apparently the last person to have seen him before his disappearance. He had asked the Verma family lawyer, Lal, to ensure that the girl was present at Wadekar's office so that he might interview her.

'Is there somewhere we can talk?'

'Why can't you talk here?' asked Wadekar suspiciously.

'In private, I mean.'

Grumbling, the agent wandered off to make a call.

Alone now, Chopra asked Greta Rodrigues exactly what had transpired the previous evening. He could see that she was upset by the idea that something might have happened to Vicky.

'We were at the concert,' said Greta. 'Everything seemed to be going well. Vicky was his usual self. Full of energy. He looked very dashing. We had got to the end and it was time for the final set piece. The choreographer, Mr Gowrikar – have you met him? He is a very nice man – had planned that Vicky would disappear in a cloud of smoke, then reappear at three places around the stadium, before vanishing again and appearing back on the main stage. It was supposed to represent the fact that Vicky is performing a quadruple role in *The Mote in the Third Eye of Shiva*. It was part of the film's publicity campaign.'

'How was it supposed to work?' asked Chopra.

'Oh, well, Vicky couldn't possibly get around the stadium so quickly. It was all an illusion, you see. There was a trapdoor on the stage, and when the smoke came out, Vicky went through the trapdoor and into a dressing room below. In the meantime we had three doubles ready, to appear around the stadium. If you ask me, they didn't look very much like Vicky, but then he's so handsome, isn't he?' she added wistfully.

Chopra nodded. He had already concluded such a ruse had lain behind the set piece. 'And then?'

'I was waiting for him in the room below the stage. Vicky normally doesn't like anyone around for costume changes, but he keeps me there in case of an emergency.'

'How long have you been his personal assistant?'

'Ever since the previous assistant left three months ago.'

'Why did she leave?'

The girl chewed her lip and blushed. 'I believe they had a difference of opinion.'

'What opinion did they differ over?'

'Well, I believe Vicky, ah, asked the lady in question to, ah, go on a date with him.'

Chopra could tell where this was heading. He spared Greta any further discomfort by saying, 'I understand. Tell me, has he acted in a similar way towards you?'

Greta's blush deepened. 'No. Never. He has been a perfect gentleman.'

Chopra observed the girl's expression, the intense flush of embarrassment.

'Of course, I am not very pretty. Not like his previous assistant.'

He saw things clearly now. The girl obviously had an unhealthy crush on Verma, blinding her to his faults. The picture that was slowly building up of the vanished actor was not a pleasant one. A spoilt brat with the manners and appetites of a goat. An arrogant man-child used to getting his own way.

'So Vicky was supposed to go down into this room, wait for the doubles to do their bit, then go back up onstage?'

'Yes,' nodded the girl. 'It was all supposed to be seamless. No more than a few minutes for him to change while everyone was distracted by the doubles. Then he climbs back up through the trapdoor.'

'But something went wrong,' said Chopra, remembering the delay when Vicky had failed to immediately reappear at the end of the illusion, and the awkward-looking final act. 'Who took the stage? It wasn't Vicky, was it?'

'No. One of the doubles had to race around to take Vicky's place once we realised he had gone.'

'Tell me, Greta, if you were in the room below surely you must have seen him leave?'

The girl lowered her eyes. 'It's all my fault,' she said on the verge of tears, her voice cracking.

Chopra waited, patiently.

'Vicky came down through the trapdoor. I could see immediately that he wasn't happy. He was mumbling something, but he wouldn't say exactly what he was angry about. I had laid out a new costume for him. That's when I stepped outside. You know, so that he could change in private.'

'He asked you to step outside?'

'Oh no. Vicky doesn't . . . care if I am there or not.' She blushed furiously again. 'But it wouldn't be right for me to stay while he was, you know, undressed.' She paused. 'That's when I made my mistake. Instead of waiting I went to the bathroom. I was only gone a few minutes but when I returned Vicky wasn't there. I assumed he'd gone back up onstage, but then one of the doubles came rushing in. He told me he had to go onstage because Vicky hadn't come back up. I was shocked. That was when I realised he had probably walked out of the show.'

'Does Vicky often do things like that?'

'It's not his fault,' she said defensively. 'He just gets very angry sometimes.'

Chopra wanted to take the girl by the shoulders and give her a good shake. She was clearly besotted and this was clouding what he felt was otherwise probably an intelligent judgement.

'What happened when the show ended? Didn't anyone look for Vicky?'

'Yes, of course. But he was nowhere backstage. I tried phoning him, many times, but he didn't pick up. The concert producer was angry, but at least Vicky had completed most of the engagement. I have seen him walk out of events at the very beginning.'

'He sounds like a difficult man to work with.'

'He is a very good person once you get to know him.' She had the decency to look away.

'Does he have any enemies?'

Greta hesitated, then dug into her bag. 'When Mr Lal called me this morning and explained the situation, I fetched these from my files.' She handed over a sheaf of letters, scrawled in ink on cheap A4 paper. The letters, written in Hindi, had been crumpled, and then smoothed out again.

Chopra looked through them.

They were threats, presumably directed at Vicky Verma. They ranged from the predictably banal: YOU CANNOT ESCAPE YOUR SINS to the premonitory THE PAST ALWAYS CATCHES UP WITH YOU and THE DAY OF RECKONING IS COMING.

Each letter was signed by *The People's Judge*.

'How long has he been getting these?'

'For the last few months. One on the first day of each month.'

'Did you inform the police?'

'Vicky wouldn't let me. He thought the letters were a prank. He didn't take them seriously.'

'Does he get a lot of mail like this?'

The girl sighed. 'Yes,' she admitted sadly. 'He gets many letters from his fans, but also many that abuse him or threaten to harm him. But these were different. They were *persistent*. And the way the author signed himself as "The People's Judge". It bothered me. But Vicky just wouldn't listen.'

'Did you tell his mother?'

'No. Vicky asked me not to. He felt Bijli Madam would overreact. I wish now that I had ignored him,' she added miserably.

Chopra considered what he had heard so far. 'Doesn't Vicky have his own bodyguards?'

'Why, yes, of course.'

'Where were they while all this was happening?'

'In the canteen. Once we were backstage they weren't needed until the end of the concert.'

'Is there anything else you can tell me? Anything at all?'

She considered this, then said, 'There was one other small thing, but I don't think it's important.'

'Why don't you let me be the judge of that?'

'Well, as I was returning from the, ah, *facilities*, a man passed by me in the corridor outside the room below the stage. He was a porter – he was wearing a porter's uniform and he was pushing a handcart. But there's nothing unusual in that – there are plenty of porters moving things around backstage.'

'Then why do you remember him?'

'Well, for one, because that area was supposed to be off-limits during the performance. But he was a porter so I thought it must be okay. And, second, because he was quite striking. He was an older man, in his forties I would say, with a red beard, and wearing a Muslim prayer cap. He glanced at me as he went by and I think I said "good evening", but he just ignored me.' She fixed Chopra with a sorrowful look. 'He *is* all right, isn't he? Vicky, I mean.'

'I'm sure he is perfectly fine,' said Chopra, with more confidence than he felt.

CITY OF DREAMS

As Chopra pulled up at the gates to Film City he found himself automatically replaying everything he had learned about the place over the years. In Mumbai, a metropolis often described as the city of dreams, Film City was where many of those dreams found their ultimate expression. The five-hundred-acre complex sprawled over a verdant landscape of low rolling hills, and contained sixteen hangar-sized studios and innumerable sets, recording rooms, editing suites, and viewing theatres. Serving as a canvas to the unbridled creativity of legendary art directors and megalomaniac producers, Film City had played host to every manifestation of Indian life imaginable. There were lakes, hills, deserts, clifftops, fake villages, and miniature cities. Mughal palaces rubbed shoulders with modern skyscrapers and seedy dance bars. In these studios countless fallen heroines had slapped the moustachioed faces of leering villains; innumerable stars had bashed senseless a conveyor belt of cronies; untold pairs of twins

– separated at birth by divine circumstance to pursue lives on both sides of the law – had been tearfully reunited in bell-ringing temples.

Every trope of Bollywood had been set into stone in Film City.

Certainly, all the great stars of the industry had cut their teeth here; all the great movies had shot scenes here. A million careers had been born and a million just as quickly snuffed out. For many insiders, Film City had now moved into a bubble of its own making, a dome of glamour that somehow altered the air, so that all who entered became intoxicated with something akin to madness. It was even said that life was more authentic here: the fake slums were poorer than their real-life cousins; the swanky mansions plusher; the villages more rustic. In an industry that produced more than nine hundred movies each year, Film City – operating four shifts a day, three hundred and sixty-five days a year – was the engine room, the beating heart of modern Bollywood.

Vicky Verma's agent Babu Wadekar had called ahead. Chopra was quickly ushered through the gates and directed to Studio 15, where shooting on Verma's current movie was scheduled for the next few days.

As he drove along the winding road he couldn't help but glance out at the various monuments to Bollywood that whizzed by. Here, for instance, was the iconic gable-roofed façade that had so often been employed as a court – Mumbai's High Court, Supreme Court, every type of court – and within which impassioned stars dressed in lawyers' black robes had shaken their fists at whey-faced judges, demanding justice in an unjust land; here was a village complete with cartwheels, piles of dung, and cud-chewing bullocks, where salt-of-the-earth farmfolk had, time and again, felt the boot of oppression hard upon their throats. And here, the famous 'godless' temple, where filmmakers brought along their own deities; and Suicide Point, where car chases often ended with the villain's white Ambassador arcing over the cliff to explode in a dazzling display of stunt pyrotechnics.

Chopra pulled into the car park of Studio 15.

He climbed out of the van, then let Ganesha out, before walking on to the Black Maidan, a vast field used for outdoor shooting.

The little elephant trotted behind him into the midday sun, gingerly flapping his ears.

Together they faced the dazzling set looming before them.

If Chopra had not already known what to expect, he would have gaped.

Rising into the cerulean sky before them was a perfect replica of the subcontinent's most iconic building, the Taj Mahal.

Described as the ultimate monument to love, the Taj had been built by the Mughal emperor Shah Jahan as a mausoleum for his beloved wife Mumtaz. Twenty years in the making and requiring the services of some twenty thousand artisans – and two thousand elephants – the Taj was described by poets as a 'dream carved from marble'.

If that were the case, then the extraordinary edifice rising before Chopra and Ganesha was the dream magnified a thousand-fold.

For the first time he understood what people meant when they said that in Bollywood everything was more real. Chopra had seen the real Taj and, as heretical as the thought seemed, *that* Taj bore no comparison to this splendid apparition. Here the marble sparkled with an unholy lustre, there was not the slightest sign of wear or tear on each razor-straight edge or flowing curve and, in this serene setting with the fake Yamuna river flowing behind – the current powered by a series of generators – it seemed to him that he had truly been transported to the mid-seventeenth-century durbar of the Mughals.

Behind the Taj, scattered across the vast expanse of the Black Maidan, a horde of extras in Mughal costume were milling around, stretching into the shimmering distance. Horses, elephants, camels, cannon, and medieval siege weapons were prominent. A number of individuals with loudhailers patrolled the front ranks of this massed army, occasionally firing off bursts of instruction that were duly ignored.

To one side of the vast outdoor set Chopra spotted a line of parked trailers. Close by, a camera crew lolled by their equipment, some dozing in plastic chairs, others chatting and smoking or drinking cups of tea. Flies buzzed over the remains of a buffet. A lone crew member reviewed something on a video monitor.

'You're late.'

Chopra turned to see a short man in a baseball cap, grubby T-shirt and jeans bearing down on them. He braked to a halt and looked down at Ganesha. 'What is the meaning of this?' he snarled. 'This elephant is too small.'

'What?' said Chopra, nonplussed. 'Too small for what?'

The man waved his clipboard at the faux Mughal army. 'I asked for five hundred war elephants, and what do I get? Sixty-three circus elephants, six bullocks painted grey, a papier mâché mammoth from the museum . . . and this!' He jabbed his clipboard at Ganesha. 'Look at him! The armour won't even fit him.'

'I'm not here for your shoot,' said Chopra stiffly. 'My name is Inspector Chopra and I'm looking for Bipin Agarwal, the director.'

'He's in his office,' said the man, stabbing his clipboard at a temporary-looking building on the perimeter of the maidan, before stomping away in disgust, muttering under his breath.

Chopra entered the office to find a bored assistant sitting behind a plywood desk. 'I am looking for the director.'

'B.P.?' said the young man, not raising his eyes from his mobile phone. 'He's inside.' He jerked a thumb over his shoulder.

Chopra wandered into the inner room, following the strains of a harmonium accompanied by raised voices. Ganesha trotted after him, even the sight of the elephant failing to pry the young assistant from his phone.

The inner room appeared to have suffered a recent encounter with a tornado. Drifts of balled paper and Styrofoam coffee cups were littered about the place. A coffee table had been upended and tell-tale smatterings of glass evinced the recent destruction of liquor bottles. A number of young men – very similar in appearance to the anteroom assistant, Chopra couldn't help but notice, and each clutching at least two mobile phones – orbited around a pair of sofas upon which were settled a trio of older gentlemen. One of them Chopra recognised as the director of Vicky Verma's film, the legendary Bipin Agarwal.

Bipin Agarwal – nicknamed 'B.P.' or 'Blood Pressure' Agarwal, due to his notorious on-set intensity – had long been considered a visionary. A relic of the Golden Age of Indian cinema, he had cut his teeth on plot-driven period pieces, but had then lost faith with the industry as it began to increasingly cater for the 'cheap seats' with senseless storylines and raucous dance sequences. In the end, Agarwal walked away from Bollywood, serving a self-imposed five-year exile. Some said he had entered an ashram in the far north, others claimed he had returned to his native village in the Indian interior.

When he did return the great director launched a one-man crusade against the modern 'big-budget brainless blockbuster'. He established his own arthouse studio and an annual 'alternative cinema' festival. He spearheaded a new-wave 'realist' movement and began to churn out low-budget movies devoid of frills, stars, or dance numbers, focusing on the real lives of Indian citizens, from the slum-dwellers of Mumbai and Kolkata to the lives of drought-stricken farmers in the heartlands. These films, at first scathingly reviewed by the 'pye-dogs of the Bollywood machine' (as B.P. himself labelled the critics pouring scorn on his efforts), slowly but surely began to attract an audience of impressionable young urbanites keen to show off their modern sensibilities. His six-hour epic *1001 Uses for the Kerosene Tin* – detailing the myriad uses for which the humble Indian kerosene tin could be employed, from lamp-oil repository to well-water carrier to roofing tile and food tray – became a cult classic, garnering numerous awards around the globe.

Years later Agarwal was christened the 'third eye of Bollywood' by legendary film critic Zubin Mehroun. This was a reference to the third eye of the Hindu god Shiva, deemed to penetrate the illusion that is life, and see the reality at its heart.

Having built a reputation as the pre-eminent anti-establishment filmmaker, it was a considerable surprise to many when, two years ago, Agarwal revealed that he had agreed to direct *The Mote in the Third Eye of Shiva*, a blockbuster slated to be the biggest Bollywood production of all time. While the press had a field day – 'Third Eye directs Third Eye' – devotees of the great man howled with anguish and claimed that he had sold out his own movement. Others sniggered that he had finally come to his senses.

In Bollywood, they said, money is the juggernaut that ultimately overrides all pretensions.

The director himself had remained steadfastly silent, refusing to reveal the reason behind his decision. 'Wait and see,' he had simply said.

Chopra looked down at the stick-thin figure of B.P. splayed on the hidebound sofa, clad in a maroon kurta and white pajama, grey hair scraped back to the nape of his scrawny neck, eyes shut tight, as if in deep anguish. A half-full whisky tumbler was clutched in his right hand.

On the sofa opposite him an overweight man was sitting cross-legged with a teak harmonium balanced across his knees. His plump fingers worked the instrument, releasing a plangent melody into the room. Beside the musician another elderly gentleman in a white shirt and dark trousers was scribbling furiously in a notebook.

He suddenly sensed Chopra's presence and looked up. Then he saw Ganesha. 'That elephant is too small,' he remarked.

'So everyone keeps telling me,' muttered Chopra. 'I need to talk with Mr Agarwal. It is about Vicky Verma.'

The harmonium player's fingers slipped, causing a discordant wheeze to erupt from his instrument. The five orbiting youngsters froze.

And B.P. Agarwal opened his eyes, which were bloodshot and full of rage.

He arose from the sofa and, in one fluid movement, threw his whisky glass at the wall where it smashed into a million pieces. 'If I hear that name one more time today I swear I'll kill someone!'

Chopra waited for the director's fury to subside. 'I must talk with you. It is important.'

'Important!' Agarwal foamed with rage. 'Let me tell you what is important. Over the next three days I am scheduled to film the most expensive scene in the history of Indian cinema. A scene that is itself the climax to the most expensive movie in the history of Indian cinema, a movie that is now so far over budget that it will bankrupt the studio if there are any further delays. Do you think *Mughal-e-Azam* was expensive? This movie makes Asif's film look like a soft-drink commercial. The climactic moment involves the greatest war scene ever depicted. I have ten thousand extras decked out in specially designed costumes; I have the most lavish set ever created; I have elephants, horses, chariots, and cannon. I have fifteen camera crews set up to film the scene from fifteen different angles. I have every stuntman from here to Kodaikanal on station . . . And what do I discover? That my leading man is unavailable. *Unavailable!*' Agarwal brandished a fist at the heavens.

Chopra was momentarily taken aback by the director's fury. Even Ganesha seemed impressed by his histrionics.

One of the young assistants spoke into the coruscating silence. 'B.P., sir, please calm down. Here, take your tablets.' He shook two tablets into the director's palm, then handed him another glass of whisky.

When Agarwal had recovered his composure, Chopra repeated his request. 'I must talk to you alone.'

'All of you, out,' said Agarwal, clapping his hands. 'Except you,' he pointed at the elderly gentleman in dark trousers. 'This is Farukh Mehboob, my assistant director.'

Once the room had been cleared, Chopra informed the two men of Vicky Verma's mysterious disappearance, requesting their discretion, and explaining that Bijli Verma had asked him to investigate. As the news hit Agarwal, Chopra thought the director would begin to rage again, but instead he simply collapsed back on to the sofa.

He drained his whisky glass, but this time refrained from hurling it against the wall.

'You know, when I was young the stars had almost no power. The studios controlled everything. If anyone got too big for their boots, we made damned sure their career took a nosedive off the nearest cliff. Of course, even now we can make or break them – they just don't seem to realise it. It's the fault of the media, preening over every *next big thing*, making them believe they are God's gift to the film industry. I mean, some of them are so wet behind the ears if I didn't insert my hand into their backsides and make their lips move they would forget to breathe. And actresses? As long as they are willing to parade around in a skirt so tiny it may as well be called underwear they will fill the cheap seats at every cinema in the land. And what ends up on those seats after they have danced one of their so-called "musical numbers" doesn't bear thinking about.' He shuddered, then pointed at Ganesha who was listening round-eyed to the great director's monologue.

'Do you know, I worked on *Mughal-e-Azam*? I was sixteen years old, a boy with Bollywood dreams in my eyes. My uncle was the key grip and hired me as the assistant to the dolly grip. It was the greatest experience of my life. I watched Dilip Kumar in his finest role. Now there was an actor! A genuine thesp. We had to do fifty-two takes in one scene where all Dilipji had to do was nod his head. He was the ultimate perfectionist.' B.P.'s eyes shone momentarily before darkening. 'The industry has changed, and not for the better. My father worked in a kerosene tin factory his whole life – for fifty years he stamped out the embossed bases for two thousand tins a day, sitting hunchbacked in front of a stamping machine.

He lost four fingers over the years to that clattering heap of metal, but he never wavered in his dedication to his allotted task. My father was the ultimate realist, the high priest of authenticity. That's why I made *Kerosene* – not just to honour him, but to honour the authenticity of the common man.' He looked once again at Ganesha. 'An elephant: now *there's* something authentic. There's nothing realer than an elephant.'

Ganesha trumpeted softly, perhaps sensing the fondness with which the old man was regarding him.

'Has Vicky ever disappeared from the set before?' Chopra eventually asked.

'Not once, but a dozen times! He has been nothing but trouble since the day I was forced to hire him.'

'You were *forced* to hire him? By who?'

'The producer,' said Mehboob, speaking for the first time as thunder closed once more around Agarwal's face. 'P.K. Das.'

'Why did Das insist on casting Verma as the lead?'

'I believe he felt it would establish Vicky as a major star, and that, in future, this would be of great benefit to his studio. Vicky is under contract to him.'

'You say he has walked out before. Can you tell me why?'

'Every reason under the sun,' thundered Agarwal. 'Sometimes he turns up drunk and fights with his co-stars. Sometimes he hasn't bothered to memorise his lines and blames the scriptwriters. Sometimes he is simply "not in the mood". That boy is a spoilt brat and acts like it. If it were up to me he would never work in the industry again. And I'd break his legs for good measure,' he added.

Chopra was momentarily silent. 'What is the movie about?'

Agarwal gaped at him. 'You mean, you don't know?'

'I'm afraid I do not follow Bollywood much these days.'

'Hah!' said Agarwal, pointing at Chopra while looking at Mehboob. 'Here is a living example of what I was talking about! The true film fan is turning away from modern cinema. We are driving them away in droves, Farukh. Droves, I tell you.'

'*The Mote in the Third Eye of Shiva* is a historical epic,' began Mehboob. 'A romantic action adventure set in the great age of the Mughal empire.'

'With elements of comedy and satire,' interjected Agarwal belligerently. 'The satire is very subtle, but completely necessary.'

'It is also a musical extravaganza,' continued Mehboob. 'With dance performances full of riotous colour blending ancient and modern dance techniques.' His eyes had glazed over and he seemed to be reading from a teleprompter that only he could see.

'With an unprecedented degree of verisimilitude in its depiction of everyday life in that glorious epoch of Indian history,' added Agarwal.

'Not to mention ten thousand extras,' said Mehboob.

'Plus a healthy dose of philosophy, religious discourse, and a meditation on the nature of man's relationship to reality,' continued Agarwal.

'Don't forget the ten thousand extras!'

Ganesha bugled loudly, mightily impressed by this duet of exposition.

'Yes, but what is it actually about?' said Chopra.

The two men seemed to deflate.

'It is a fictional take on the story of Mughal emperor Shah Jahan and his sons,' supplied Mehboob. 'In our version, Shah Jahan's four sons are born as quadruplets, who are subsequently separated by the whims of fate. One of them is adopted by Hindu beetroot farmers and grows up in a village. Another is stolen by dacoits and grows up as a godless bandit. A third is taken in by a Sikh soldier in the Mughal army and grows up a cavalryman. The last remains with the emperor and grows up a Muslim prince. Eventually, as the Grand Mughal fades towards death, war looms between the four brothers as they are brought together by the tides of destiny.'

'And Vicky Verma is playing all four brothers?'

'Yes,' confirmed Mehboob. 'It is the first time that a fully fledged quadruple role has been assayed in Indian cinema.'

Chopra looked thoughtful. 'Why is it called *The Mote in the Third Eye of Shiva*? I mean, it's set in the Mughal era. It doesn't seem a very apt name.'

'The movie has a greater message than what you see on-screen,' replied Agarwal sharply. 'Shiva's third eye denotes the ability to see beyond the physical realm – with all of its illusions – and, consequently, divine the true nature of man. In *Mote* we see four brothers, born together – essentially they are one being – but, by virtue of their star-crossed fates, they reveal the multiplicity of realities at the heart of the human condition: greed, lust, anger, envy. These alternate manifestations reveal man as nothing more than a naked being – a mote in God's eye – capable of glory, but equally capable of destruction on a cosmic scale.'

Chopra found himself greatly impressed by this lucid disquisition. It went some way to explaining why B.P. Agarwal, champion of reality, had agreed to direct the all-singing, all-dancing blockbuster. 'And the pivotal scene?' he asked. 'The one Vicky is missing?'

'The final battle between the brothers. This will be a four-way battle, another first in Indian cinema. We have ten thousand extras out there – many of them hired from the Indian army at an extortionate rate. We have practically taken over Film City. I have had to pay a fortune to other producers to halt their shooting for a few days just so I can film my scene. And at the climax of the take we will see Vicky burn down the Taj Mahal.'

'A truly spectacular denouement!' enthused Mehboob.

'I wanted to set fire to the real Taj,' groused Agarwal, 'but those idiots in Delhi wouldn't give me permission.'

'Who were all the young men in the room when I entered?' asked Chopra.

Agarwal's face soured. 'I have many names for them, none of them printable.'

'They are the other directors on the project,' Mehboob explained. 'The art director. The set director. The stunt director. The music director. The casting director. Laldas. Kalidas. Tulsidas. Laxmidas. Ramdas. And sitting outside is Haridas, the marketing director.'

'Do you have a factory where you produce them?' said Chopra ironically.

'Those imbeciles are all nephews of our producer,' snorted Agarwal. 'Between them they have just enough brains to make my life a misery.'

'Let's be fair, B.P.,' said Mehboob mildly. 'They're full of bright ideas.'

'Bright ideas!' spluttered Agarwal. 'Those nincompoops have the sort of bright ideas that start wars.'

'Aren't they a little young for such responsibility?' asked Chopra.

'Tell that to our producer!' exploded Agarwal. 'He hired them all so he could have a gang of spies reporting to him day and night.'

Chopra looked thoughtful, then said: 'I must ask that you both keep the matter of Vicky's disappearance to yourselves.'

'Do you think we want to harm the production any more than it already has been by telling the whole world that Vicky has vanished?' said Agarwal sourly.

A noise behind Chopra made him turn.

A tall, broad-shouldered man in a dark grey Nehru jacket and smoked glasses strode into the room. He wore a gruff-looking moustache above hard lips and a square chin that looked as if it had been hewn from a slab of granite.

There was a shuffling behind Chopra, and he turned back to see that both Agarwal and Mehboob had straightened. Expressions of unease had drifted onto their features.

'Ram ram,' said the newcomer in a deep baritone.

Neither of the directors responded with greetings of their own.

'B.P. Sahib, how are things?' asked the newcomer. 'Everything is fine? We will soon be seeing Mr Vicky back on set, yes?'

'Vicky will be back on his feet in no time, Pyarelal Sahib,' muttered Agarwal.

Pyarelal turned to Chopra. 'And who is this?' he asked.

'No one,' answered Mehboob hurriedly.

'He is very substantial for a no one,' said Pyarelal calmly.

'My name is Chopra,' said Chopra. 'I am . . .' He hesitated, before brightening with inspiration, '. . . a film producer. I came to see if I could persuade B.P. to direct my next movie.'

'A producer?' purred Pyarelal. 'And which studio do you produce for, Chopra Sahib?'

'Ganesha Film Productions,' answered Chopra.

'I have never heard of it. Is it new?'

'Very new,' said Chopra, unblinkingly.

'Are you in need of financing?'

Chopra glanced at Mehboob, who was slowly shaking his head. 'No,' he said.

'That's a shame,' said Pyarelal. 'I am acquainted with some people who specialise in financing film productions.'

A silence passed as Chopra and Pyarelal eyed each other, then Pyarelal's face broadened into a smile. 'Perhaps we will bump into each other again one day. Many producers begin with big dreams but sadly they often founder upon the rocks of reality. When that day comes you may have need of someone like Pyarelal. Ram ram.' He clasped his hands together in farewell, and turned to leave, pausing at the door to stare at Ganesha. 'That elephant is too small,' he said, then left.

'Who, exactly, was that?' asked Chopra, noting how the two directors had sagged with relief at Pyarelal's departure.

'You don't need to know,' said Agarwal, walking to a steel cabinet and removing a bottle of Black Label whisky before splashing out a generous measure.

'He works for the producer,' supplied Mehboob.

'What does he do?'

Mehboob and Agarwal exchanged glances. 'He is . . . a consultant,' said Mehboob eventually.

'A consultant of what?'

'Does it matter?' snapped Agarwal. His face had set into a hard scowl. The topic seemed to be off-limits. It was a mystery Chopra would have to resolve at a later time. He focused now on another question. 'Does Vicky have any enemies that you are aware of?'

'Hah!' said Agarwal. 'The boy collects enemies like the rest of us make friends. I'd happily throttle him myself.'

'In that case is he particularly *close* to anyone on set?'

'Vicky doesn't have real friends. Plenty of hangers-on and sycophants, but that's not the same thing, is it? Of course, there's always Poonam.'

'Poonam?'

'Our leading lady. Poonam Panipat. You have heard of her, I presume?' the director added sarcastically.

Of course Chopra had heard of her. Panipat was one of the most famous actresses in the industry, once nicknamed the Queen of Bollywood, although it was his impression that she was now on the downslope of her illustrious career. 'They are close?'

Agarwal waved a dismissive hand. 'Close? What does that mean, nowadays? For what it's worth, the rumour mill says the pair of them are *exceptionally* close, if you catch my drift.'

Chopra considered this. 'Is she on set today?'

'The maharani is probably in her trailer,' muttered Agarwal. 'Just don't expect to get any sense out of her. She's as bad as Vicky. Shiva save me from prima donnas.'

Poonam Panipat's trailer was an elongated white box on wheels, parked beneath the wide-slung arms of a fig tree. As Chopra approached, he suddenly spotted the woman herself, stomping across the dusty field beneath a pink umbrella held above her by an assistant struggling to keep pace. Panipat was resplendent in a multi-hued and heavily brocaded silk Mughal dress. Jewellery jangled on her arms and ankles, and her maroon bodice, worked with topaz stones and gold filigree, flashed and glittered in the sun. As she swept along she held up the bejewelled gown in an unsuccessful attempt to keep it from trailing on the ground.

Arriving before the trailer she stopped, then turned in fury to her assistant, and shouted: 'I told you to get rid of those evil things! Look at them, just sitting there, staring at me.'

The bewildered assistant followed the direction of her ire.

Chopra looked up too.

A row of black crows ruffled their feathers from the roof of the trailer, cawing and bobbing, seemingly gathered to pay tribute to the Queen of Bollywood.

'But, madam, they are crows,' protested the assistant. 'How can I get rid of them?'

'I don't care how you do it, just do it! Shoot them for all I care!' Panipat reached down, wrenched off a mirror-worked slipper and flung it at the birds. The slipper missed them entirely and landed on top of the roof.

Panipat unleashed a howl of fury before storming into the trailer, leaving the put-upon assistant to stare bleakly up at the nonchalant creatures. Sighing, he turned and walked away across the maidan.

Chopra parked Ganesha outside the trailer, then rapped loudly on the door. He waited, but, when no reply came, opened the door and entered.

The interior of the trailer was plushly decorated, the walls papered with blow-up posters of Poonam Panipat in a medley of career-defining roles. Chopra thought the effect was somehow ghoulish. To surround yourself with glorified images of . . . yourself smacked to him of someone who had either begun to believe too fervently in their own conceits or someone in need of reassurance that they were still the person they thought they were.

He glanced around, but could not see Panipat.

A rustle of movement alerted him to a wicker screen set up at one end of the trailer.

'Do you usually enter women's quarters without permission?' came a voice from behind the screen.

Chopra blushed. 'I knocked but there was no answer.' He coughed. 'My name is Inspector Chopra. I want to talk to you about Vicky Verma.'

'Hah!' said Panipat. Her bodice sailed out from behind the screen and landed at Chopra's feet. Not knowing what else to do, he picked it up, carefully folded it, and set it down on a wooden sideboard. 'If that idiot doesn't show up soon I'll wring his neck. I won't let him ruin this for me, not after what I've had to go through on this production.'

Panipat emerged from behind the screen dressed in cotton slacks and a sleeveless shirt. Her hair had been pulled back into a ponytail, but the make-up was still heavy on her face, setting off her fine features and dark, smouldering eyes.

Quickly, Chopra outlined Verma's unexplained absence, again explaining that Bijli Verma had asked him to investigate, and requesting Panipat's discretion. 'His mother believes he would not have simply vanished.'

'She's right,' said Panipat. 'I heard from friends that she had been calling around, looking for him. I thought he'd got drunk somewhere, as usual, that he'd turn up, staggering out of some Mazgaon bar. But when the news came out this morning about his "illness" I suspected something was wrong. Vicky's pulled a lot of stunts on this picture, but even he's not so stupid as to miss this shoot.'

Chopra recalled that Panipat was somewhat older than Verma. Certainly, she spoke as if he were some insufferable child she had been forced to nursemaid.

'If he doesn't show up soon the whole production is in trouble. Have you any idea what it's costing to keep that army out there on set?'

'I'm beginning to get an idea,' said Chopra. 'Is there anything you can tell me about Vicky? Any idea where he might have gone?'

Panipat reached into her pocket and took out a packet of cigarettes. She lit one and offered the pack to Chopra. 'I don't smoke,' he said.

'Good. It's a filthy habit.' She drew in deeply and blew a cloud of smoke at him. 'Vicky's been a handful since the first day. Frankly, if it wasn't for his mother and the fact that he has a legion of teenage zombies following his every move, he would have been booted off this picture a long time ago. But he wouldn't have just vanished, not now, at this critical point.' She smiled grimly. 'Did you know that we're supposed to be embroiled in a passionate affair?'

'I have heard the rumours.'

'*I* spread those rumours,' said Panipat smugly. 'Bollywood is a nest of vipers, and what vipers feed on is the milk of scandal.'

'So you are not having an affair?'

'It's irrelevant whether we are or not. As long as *they* out there think we are. Haven't you heard? There's no such thing as bad publicity in the being-famous industry.'

'Does Vicky have a girlfriend?'

'No one permanent, if that's what you mean. I think he spends so long admiring himself in the mirror that he doesn't have time to actually get to know anyone else.' She sighed. 'Bollywood can be a lonely place. There aren't many people outside the industry who understand what we have to go through every day just to keep up the illusion.'

'I'm sure the millions living in our slums might say you were living the dream.'

'Every dream sours, Chopra. And there's a high price to pay for this particular one.' She grimaced. 'I can't afford for this movie not to be successful. You know, I grew up in a one-bedroom apartment in Dombivali. My father was a rickshaw driver, my mother a seamstress. We were just one step up from living in a slum. I had six brothers and they were all worthless. I promised myself I wouldn't end up like my parents. As dirt on the shoes of the rich and powerful. I studied hard in school, and as soon as I got out into the real world I worked. I took whatever job I could get, just so I could make enough money for acting classes, dancing classes, singing classes. Then I started auditioning. That's when I first understood how the world *really* works. You see, if you don't have a sponsor or a famous parent, breaking in is almost impossible. It was a bitter pill to swallow, to realise that it didn't matter how well I acted, how well I danced. My only real assets were this,' she pointed at her face, 'and this,' she waved her hands over her figure. 'And so I used what God had given me. If I told you the number of times I've had to close my eyes and let greedy hands paw at me . . .' Her face became still, lost in the past. 'But I don't regret it. I did what I had to. It got me my break, and once I was in, there was no stopping me. You hear nowadays that such-and-such a star was made by so-and-so a director. No one made *me*, Chopra. *I* made me. Some say I've had a good run, that I should get married and slide off into the sunset. But I'm not ready to lie down and die. I had to fight for this role. The producer wanted someone younger, but I convinced him. Oh, how I convinced him.'

Chopra heard many things in the actress's voice – a violin note of bitterness, with a side order of sadness; but beneath this there sounded the undying clarion call of her own future. He found himself admiring her tenacity, her ambition, her willingness to do whatever it took to achieve her goal. In some respects, she reminded him of himself.

He changed tack. 'Are you aware that Vicky was receiving threats? Through the mail?'

'So what's new? I get a dozen such letters a week. Mostly from men who think I'm a bad role model for their wives. A woman who thinks, a woman who isn't afraid of her sexuality, a woman who isn't afraid of being who she damn well wants to be.' She leaned forward, her face suddenly drawn. 'If you're asking me did Vicky have any enemies, then the only person I can think of who might have genuinely intended him harm was our beloved producer sahib.'

'P.K. Das?' Chopra was astonished. 'But he is . . . P.K. Das!'

P.K. Das was a living legend, one of the most powerful men in Bollywood, a visionary renowned for delivering hit after hit over the past thirty years through the auspices of his studio Himalayan Productions.

'Hah! Don't be fooled by his public persona. The man is a *goonda*, a thug.'

Chopra felt as if he had wandered into an alternate reality.

P.K. Das, recipient of the Kirti Chakra for services to film, noted humanitarian and all-round much-feted number-one gentleman . . . a thug?

'A few weeks ago I walked into Vicky's trailer. Das and Pyarelal were with him. Have you met Pyarelal? He's Das's muscle. Pyarelal had Vicky up against the side of the trailer, his forearm across Vicky's throat. Vicky's tough, but he's no match for Pyarelal. Now, there's a man who scares me, I don't mind telling you. You know, I don't think I've ever seen him without his sunglasses. Anyway, as soon as they saw me, they stopped. Das laughed and mumbled something about "rehearsing for a fight scene", and then they left. Afterwards, I asked Vicky what it had all been about, but he wouldn't tell me.'

Chopra considered this revelation. It seemed at odds with everything he had ever heard about Das . . . But then again, wasn't the whole of Bollywood a façade of smoke and mirrors? The ultimate manifestation of *maya* – worldly illusion.

'No matter how foolish Vicky is, I don't think he would have vanished of his own accord. He knows what's at stake, for all of us. He knows I would kill him if he ruined this for me!' Panipat blew out another cloud of smoke. 'You know, with the right lighting you could be an actor. You have the aura for it. A serious man. And you sound like you actually care. Unlike the rest of us, who've been faking it for so long we've forgotten what caring means.'

Chopra emerged from the trailer to discover that Ganesha had vanished.

A momentary panic gripped him until he located his ward among a crowd of adult elephants, mahouts, and extras dressed as Mughal warriors. The little elephant was staring round-eyed as they rehearsed, charging at each other, clanging fake swords and maces against round shields and studded breastplates. The elephants – gloriously decked out in brigandine steel plates and chain mail, tusk swords and skull masks – were urged into action by their overzealous mahouts, themselves masquerading as Mughal bowmen in the howdahs affixed to their mounts' backs.

The earth trembled as the elephants thundered up and down, bugling loudly and clanking their armour.

Chopra was impressed.

The elephants appeared to be better actors than the actors.

'Come on, boy,' he said, patting Ganesha on the crown of his head. His mind was still deliberating on the conversation with Panipat. Vicky's co-star appeared to have no idea where he was. Furthermore, Panipat seemed convinced something untoward had happened to the young actor.

Chopra himself was steadily moving towards that conclusion.

A knot of stuntmen in tattered chain mail and sporting bloodied wounds had gathered around the little elephant. 'He's a little small, isn't he?' said one, folding his arms around an arrow protruding from his chest.

'Maybe he's only got a *bit* part,' joked another.

Ganesha huddled closer towards Chopra, perhaps sensing that he was being made fun of.

'He is not part of the cast,' said Chopra stiffly.

'That's a pity,' said arrow-man. 'I'd rather a pipsqueak like him charging at me than one of those brutes.' He jerked a thumb at the war elephants. 'The mahouts keep telling me they're only acting, but has anyone told *them* that?'

'You can see why the Mughals prized them so highly, though,' mused his companion. 'Akbar was obsessed by all accounts. Had five thousand of the beasts. Used to wheel them out at any opportunity. Loved crushing the heads of his enemies under an elephant's foot. Squish.'

'Thank you for the history lesson,' said Chopra stonily.

He turned and led Ganesha away.

THE QUEEN OF MYSORE

The building that Anarkali took Rangwalla to was familiar to him in name only. Known locally as the Red Fort, the ramshackle three-storey tower in Marol had long ago been condemned by the municipal authorities. In another place this would have meant demolition and gentrification; in Mumbai it merely paved the way for a clandestine deal. An enterprising eunuch chieftain had offered an undisclosed sum to stay the demolition order. The offer had been accepted, and a tacit understanding arrived at, codified in no official document, yet one that had stood the test of time.

Each year the 'invisible lease' was extended by an annual payment that grew in direct proportion to the decrepitude of the premises it paid for. But the eunuchs handed over the gratuity without complaint.

Rangwalla understood why.

Though the eunuchs of India laid claim to a history that stretched back almost four thousand years, and had, at times, been valued, even feted, as harem guards, manservants, trusted messengers, and even privy counsellors, the simple fact was that for the most part their existence had been marked by hatred, prejudice, mistrust, and abuse.

Many years earlier he had investigated a case where one of the victims had been a eunuch. He had seen for himself how, in the modern world, they had been increasingly marginalised, forced into the shadows, both of society and of the cities they inhabited. In Mumbai, the eunuchs lived in communities known as 'deras', dotted around the city, usually in slums. Landlords in better areas would not offer rooms to eunuchs; where they managed to get rooms, they were often hounded from them by their neighbours.

In this ocean of hostility, the Red Fort served as a welcome bastion, home to at least one hundred eunuchs, a clan that prospered, instilling in its members a sense of self-worth and self-determination.

The Fort was run by a eunuch who had become a legend in the city: the Queen of Mysore.

As Anarkali led him through the Red Fort's wooden entrance doors he was struck by a twinge of unease. He had never been particularly comfortable around eunuchs – though he had to admit Anarkali was a useful informant – and had never met the Queen; but he had heard the stories.

The Queen had been linked to organised crime for years. She ran her coven with an iron fist, a tyrant whose past was shrouded in mystery. Some said she hailed from the state of Punjab in the north, others from the south. It was said that she had murdered three men as a teenager and that a warrant was still out for her in Mysore. For this reason she had been christened the Queen of Mysore.

Myths and legends surrounded her – there was no way of knowing which contained a grain of truth. In the city of Mumbai, she reigned as the queen of the eunuchs, lording it over her vassals from her seat of power.

Anarkali led Rangwalla through an anteroom smelling powerfully of jaggery and incense in which a number of eunuchs in saris sat in cane chairs, chatting and drinking tea, and into another room where eunuchs were hunched behind foot-treadle sewing machines stitching clothing.

Anarkali ordered Rangwalla to wait, and then ducked through a bead curtain.

Raised voices from an adjoining room tempted him to crane his neck around the doorframe – he saw eunuchs sitting at desks, writing in notebooks. A female teacher – a non-eunuch – translated a Hindi sentence scrawled on the blackboard into English. Some of the eunuchs wore jeans and trousers, he couldn't help but notice.

Anarkali returned. 'The Queen will see you now. Remember, do not offend her. And call her Maharani Bibi.'

They ducked through the bead curtain and entered a large room, red lit, with the curtains drawn. Rangwalla smelled incense and hashish, mingled with the scent of lotus blossom. A Bollywood song played on a CD player. He recognised it as the soulful lament from *Pakeezah*, a sorrowful tale of a doomed courtesan's trials and tribulations. The film was reputed to be the Queen's favourite.

The Queen of Mysore sat on a raised divan, smoking from an ornate jade hookah inlaid with lapis lazuli. He saw that she was even larger in person than her reputation had given her credit for – even larger than Anarkali – with a substantial heft about the shoulders, and a girth to match. Her skin was darkly lustrous, even in the gloom. Her face was broad, with a heavy chin and sloping brow. But the eyes . . . the eyes were beautiful, full of intelligence and light, as if twin genii had become trapped inside them and were now looking out at the world from within.

The Queen was wearing a sequinned mustard-coloured gaghra-choli – the tight-fitting choli bodice was filigreed with gold thread, and the gaghra, the long pleated skirt beneath, was bunched up around her. Heavy jewellery completed her ensemble: nose rings and earrings; bangles and anklets; signet rings, and a cascade of gold and silver necklaces.

Beside the Queen sat a young eunuch, cross-legged, with a red ledger open on her lap. She wore a staid white kurta pajama, and had a modern bobbed haircut.

'Welcome,' said the Queen.

Rangwalla licked his lips, wishing, once again, that his boss were here in his stead. 'Anarkali said that you wished to see Chopra,' he said, and then, recalling his instructions, added, 'Maharani Bibi.'

This courtesy seemed to please the Queen and she smiled broadly. 'Indeed, I did. But he has not seen fit to grace my court.'

The tone was more amused than angry, Rangwalla decided. 'He is tied up with another case. Perhaps I can help. What is the problem?'

'The problem?' The Queen toked on her hookah. 'The problem, Rangwalla Sahib, is all around you. People say we live in the modern age, but the minds of men are locked in the past. All over this country of ours my sisters and daughters are cast out from their homes, stripped of dignity, forced into lives we would not wish upon our worst enemies. And why? Because they were born different. But we are all creations of the Almighty, are we not? For us too, He must have had a purpose.'

'Times are changing,' said Rangwalla, defensively.

The Queen laughed, a hollow sound that bounced off the walls. 'Yes, this is true. The High Court now rules that a third gender exists. And then the Supreme Court decrees that our natural urges are "against the order of nature". You give with one hand and take with the other. Let me ask you, Rangwalla Sahib, how many eunuch teachers are there? How many doctors? How many politicians? Last week one of my girls was hounded from a train, the week before another was denied entry to a mall. "Dogs and eunuchs not allowed", the security stooge told her. We are more untouchable than the untouchables.' The Queen shifted her bulk on the dais. 'But let us talk about problems that we can do something about. I require assistance, the type of assistance that Anarkali informs me your agency may be able to provide.'

'We will help if we can.'

'A few weeks ago a limousine arrived outside the Red Fort. This was nothing new, you understand. We are accustomed to wealthy clientele. Not all of my girls choose to offer their charms, but those that do are much in demand. The driver said that his master wished to contract a number of eunuchs for a visit to his mansion. He would not say where – indeed, it was a condition that we would not be told the location of his master's home. He was willing to pay cash in advance and assured me that they would be treated well. I allowed the girls to consider the offer, though I was hesitant – these are troubled times and one must be wary of clients who come without recommendation. At any rate, my girls agreed to the deal. The driver took them to the mansion and for three days they were fed, watered, and looked after. And then they were returned.'

'So, what is the problem?'

'The problem is that *nothing happened.*'

'What do you mean "nothing happened"?'

'My girls spent three days there without meeting either the master of the property or any guests. Instead, they were asked to participate in meaningless games – poetry recitals, dance competitions, singing performances. And then the driver brought them back. The same farce has been repeated three weekends in succession. Each time a different set of girls has been requested.'

'Were you paid each time?'

'Yes.'

'I still don't see the problem. It seems to me a very good deal. Payment for services not rendered.' Rangwalla permitted himself a small smile.

'This is no laughing matter,' scowled the Queen. 'I do not like unexplained situations. Human nature is predictable in its unpredictability. I am afraid that sooner or later this client's true motives will surface and the whole farce will end in tears.'

'Perhaps he is just eccentric,' speculated Rangwalla. 'Perhaps he is one of those men who merely like to watch?'

'My girls say there is more to it than this. They cannot put their finger on it, but something is not right.'

'Then simply do not send him any more girls.'

'I told you I do not force my girls into anything. Don't believe everything you hear, Rangwalla. I am not quite the tyrant I am made out to be. Besides, I could not stop them if I tried. The money is extravagant. This man is clearly wealthy. The girls earn in three days of doing nothing what would take them weeks to earn doing many things, not all to their tastes. They will not say no.'

'So how can I help?'

'If he sticks to his routine, the driver will be back tomorrow evening for the next batch of girls. I want you to go with them. I want you to uncover the identity of this man and his reasons.'

'But I have not been invited!' protested Rangwalla. 'Besides, the driver will want eunuchs. He will not take me.'

The Queen waved a dismissive hand. 'I leave it to you to decide how to conduct the investigation. All I want are the answers.'

'I cannot agree to such a thing without talking to Chopra.'

'I will pay what you ask.'

'I will still have to talk to him.'

The Queen toked on her hookah, bubbling the water in the base as she drew smoke through it. 'Then go. And be sure to return tomorrow. The car will arrive precisely at seven.'

HIMALAYAN STUDIOS

P.K. Das's Himalayan Studios were located in the eastern Mumbai suburb of Chembur, just a stone's throw from the city's most famous production house, namely, the legendary R.K. Studio.

The latter had been inaugurated a year after Independence, the brainchild of the man many called the godfather of the Indian film industry, Shree Raj Kapoor, and thus enjoyed a unique place in the annals of Bollywood, having churned out hits for half a century. Many of these seminal works embodied a healthy dose of social commentary, as was Kapoor's wont. For this reason Chopra had always harboured a secret admiration for the larger-than-life maestro.

As a young man P.K. Das had worked closely with the great Kapoor, before eventually charting his own course. For a while the two men had been rivals, but the rivalry had been a friendly one, with each studio pushing the other to better its own efforts.

Das's Himalayan Studios sprawled over a magnificent estate that backed on to the fairways of the Bombay Presidency Golf Club, the oldest and most prestigious sanctum of the city's golfing elite.

It was rumoured that P.K. himself had one of the lowest handicaps on the circuit.

Having identified himself to the security guards Chopra trundled his van through the studio's wrought-iron gates, and followed a gravel path past the lavish seven-storey studio building to an equally opulent bungalow set to one side of the compound, the private residence of the studio's owner.

P.K. Das was in his home gymnasium, wheezing on a treadmill beneath the gimlet eye of his personal trainer, a burly man with a kabaddi wrestler's physique, a boulder-like gut bulging inside a tight-fitting vest. An impressive mat of fur clung to the wrestler-trainer's shoulders, and he snarled at P.K., 'Five more minutes, you sonofabitch!'

Ganesha, trotting behind Chopra, looked on, startled. As Das stepped off the treadmill, he quickly scampered on, only to be scooted straight off into an undignified heap beside the dumbbell rack. He immediately sprang to his feet, curled his trunk around a dumbbell, and attempted to lift it. It proved too heavy. He moved along the rack, testing each dumbbell, until finally finding one he could flourish above his head. He turned to Chopra with a look of triumph, but found that his guardian was occupied.

Das, sagging with relief at having his ordeal cut short, wiped his neck with a towel and led them to his office, where he fell heavily into a chair behind his desk.

An assistant delivered a glass of watermelon juice, which revived the great producer until finally he could focus on his visitor.

If a man's temperament was written on his features then P.K. Das was born to the role of village elder. He reminded Chopra of Indian cartoonist Laxman's Common Man, with an avuncular face, white wings of hair on either side of a bald dome, a bristling white moustache, and round spectacles perched on a round nose.

He considered again the words of Poonam Panipat.

There had to be a mistake. How could this man be a thug?

'Mr Das—' he began.

'Call me P.K.,' said Das. 'You say "Mr Das" and I look over my shoulder for my dear departed father. Now . . . tell me what this is about. You informed my PA you were here representing some wealthy clients interested in financing a movie.'

'P.K.,' nodded Chopra, savouring the secret thrill of addressing one of his heroes in such a familiar manner. He elaborated on the ruse he had concocted to gain a meeting with the producer at such short notice. He did not wish to reveal that he was here on behalf of Bijli Verma. Panipat's words, though hard to believe, were enough to encourage him to beware of trusting Das. 'The people I represent wish to remain anonymous at present but rest assured they are serious about entering the movie business.'

Das nodded as if he had heard it all before. 'Yes. It is all the rage these days. As soon as one of our new economy tycoons makes it big, the first thing they wish to do is dip a toe into the glamour of Bollywood. Little do they realise that there are crocodiles lying in wait for those who do not know what they are doing.'

'Precisely,' said Chopra. 'Which is why they have employed me to find out more.'

'Are you in the movie business?'

'No,' said Chopra. 'I am a private detective.' He handed Das his card.

'The Baby Ganesh Detective Agency. Ah. That would explain your little elephant,' said Das, glancing at Ganesha who was inspecting a poster of a Bollywood hero catching bullets in his teeth, a feat which seemed to greatly impress the elephant calf.

'My clients wish to follow in the footsteps of your current movie, *The Mote in the Third Eye of Shiva*, by employing your studio to make a film and casting Vicky Verma as the lead. I believe he is under contract to you. But they have heard some disturbing things about Vicky, and so I'm afraid I must start by asking you some difficult questions about him.'

Das seemed to deflate into his chair. 'I must admit, the boy has been a challenge to work with.'

'Is it true that you insisted the director hire him for the lead in *The Mote in the Third Eye of Shiva*?'

'That is correct. I saw – see – great potential in Vicky.'

'But you knew that he was not Agarwal's first choice?'

'Directors like to think they know best. But they are not always right.'

'Surely a more established actor would have better suited such a project? After all, it is the biggest production in the history of Bollywood.'

Das sighed again. 'Look, I will tell you something, Chopra, strictly off the record. I *did* approach some very big names for this picture. But as soon as they heard that it was a quadruple role that would tie them up every day for over a year, and that our budget was limitless, they thought they could hold me to ransom. Why, if I told you some of the demands these prima donnas made, you would fall off your seat! Do you know one of them actually asked me to purchase him Mike Tyson's tiger, the one they used in that Hollywood movie? And this was before we even discussed salary!' Das shook his head. 'It was simply not practical. The established stars these days are used to doing three or four movies at once, with myriad advertising commercials, celebrity TV shows, concerts, and foreign marketing trips in between. It is a miracle if I can get one shoot a month out of them. But young stars like Vicky are hungry.'

'And yet my understanding is that he has not lived up to the trust you placed in him.'

Das frowned. 'It is bad form to listen to on-set gossip, Chopra. And worse form to spread it. What goes on in a movie production should stay behind closed doors. We are a family and like any family we have our disagreements, our vagaries of personality and mood.'

'Forgive me, sir, but is it true that you recently had cause to, ah, *discipline* Vicky?'

'Whatever do you mean?'

'I mean, did you have him beaten?'

Das looked astonished. 'Have you lost your mind? Why would I do that? It's simply unthinkable. I am a pacifist by nature. I don't believe I have ever struck anyone in my whole life. Except Raj Kapoor once, but that was at his request. He asked me to punch him as hard as I could, just so he could prove to Nargis how tough he was. He was quite smitten with her, you see. Sadly, I underestimated my own strength and knocked out one of his teeth. He had to have it replaced, but it was a rush job as we were shooting the next morning. If you look closely you can see it in some scenes towards the end of *Shree 420*. It's the crooked one on the right side of his mouth when he smiles.'

Chopra was momentarily silent. Why would Poonam Panipat have lied? Or was it Das who was lying? Yet he seemed genuinely mystified.

'Tell me, Chopra,' said Das, 'what are you really doing here? I am no fool. Bijli called me this morning to tell me Vicky was indefinitely indisposed. I was most disappointed as we are already greatly behind schedule. Now you come here asking questions about the boy. Who are you *really* representing?'

Chopra shifted in his seat.

He had known, of course, that by questioning the veteran producer, he might ultimately be forced into revealing his motives. It had been a risk to come here, and one that Bijli Verma would not have approved of. But Chopra had long ago decided that his role as a private investigator would be based on the same foundations upon which he had built a successful career in the police service, namely his own judgement and the weight of his accumulated experience.

He had followed his instincts for longer than he cared to remember and they had rarely let him down.

'As I said, I am merely here on behalf of certain parties interested in working with your studio and with Vicky.'

Das stared at Chopra long and hard, forcing the detective to strike out in another direction. 'I took the liberty of visiting the set of *Mote*. Just to get a feel for your production, you understand. There was a man on set, tall, burly, wears sunglasses all the time, it seems. A Mr Pyarelal. I was told he works for you. Can you tell me what he does?'

Das's face stiffened. 'I am afraid I have no idea who you are talking about. But then, this production has literally hundreds of staff members. I couldn't possibly keep account of them all.'

'Is there someone I can talk to, to find out who he is?'

'Personnel records are confidential,' said Das, rising stiffly to his feet. 'And now I really must go. Raju will see you out.'

As Chopra left the compound, he reflected on the abrupt end to the meeting.

He had not learned a great deal about Vicky from Das that he did not already know. In truth, he had not expected to. But, after Poonam Panipat's testimony, he had wanted to get the measure of the producer, and he needed to discover more about the shadowy Pyarelal, a topic that was seemingly off-limits. Why? Who was this man that everyone seemed so afraid of?

Afraid. That was the right word.

And where there was fear, Chopra knew, intrigue was rarely far behind.

THE MAD WOMAN

In the kitchen of Poppy's Bar & Restaurant, preparations for Holi were proceeding apace. Azeem Lucknowwallah, the restaurant's head chef, had prepared a special eight-course menu for the occasion, one that would capture the essence of the festival of colours: a celebration of the arrival of spring, a time to forgive debts and forget past indiscretions, and a marker of the ultimate victory of good over evil.

Lucknowwallah, once renowned in the city's premier restaurant circles, had emerged from retirement to work at Poppy's, driven by the fact that his own father had been a policeman, killed in the line of duty. Lucknowwallah's arrival was a notable coup for the restaurant, yet sometimes Chopra couldn't help but wish that he was a less highly strung personality. The man was in constant need of reassurance.

Take today for instance.

Chopra had returned to the restaurant to catch up with Rangwalla. It was then that he had learned of the strange request made by the Queen of Mysore, a request that gave him pause for thought.

He had always treated the eunuch community with respect, but the thought of working for the Queen bothered him – he had no wish to align himself to a small-time king-pin. And yet, considering the matter, he wondered how he would feel if the Queen's suspicions ultimately proved correct – what if her girls came to harm? In a society so strongly prejudiced against them, the eunuchs needed some-one to look out for them. Chopra had always endeavoured to do so, and found that he could not abandon them now.

Setting aside his personal misgivings he agreed that the agency should take the case. He asked Rangwalla to handle the matter.

'But what do I do?' protested Rangwalla, aghast at the possibilities.

'I leave that to you,' said Chopra firmly. 'My hands are full with this Verma business.'

After the meeting Chopra had been summoned to the kitchen for a tasting.

Chopra had resigned himself to the trial ahead. The chef rarely did anything by halves, and his angst over a new dish could lead a perfectly sane man to drink. But such were the sensibilities of the artiste, Chopra reflected. In all good conscience, he could not complain. The man was a miracle worker and his efforts on behalf of the restaurant had afforded Chopra the time to devote to his detective agency. He did not wish to lose Lucknowwallah, and so he did his best to accommodate the chef's occasional bouts of crea-tive neurosis.

Now, as he stood at the kitchen counter, flanked on either side by the assistant chefs, Ramesh Goel and Rosie Pinto, with Irfan and little Ganesha looking on, he found himself sweating with nervousness. He knew, from past experience, that the chef took rejection very personally.

He picked up the spoon of umber-coloured pickle from its bowl, placed it inside his mouth, and swallowed. A few moments of nothing . . . and then, without warning, a grenade exploded between his cheeks.

Chopra yelped and ran to the sink. Thrusting his face under the tap, he allowed the water to roar into his mouth.

Behind him Ganesha dipped his trunk into the bowl of pickle and scooped some into his mouth, Irfan watching him carefully. Ganesha's eyes widened, and then he bugled a shrill note of alarm, trotted to the sink, butted Chopra out of the way, and stuck his trunk under the tap, before shooting water into his mouth.

Finally, man and elephant turned back to their waiting audience, Chopra's face scarlet, Ganesha's ears flapping in agitation.

'Well?' asked Lucknowwallah, practically swaying.

'What was that called again?' Chopra wheezed.

'That is my special Rocket Fuel pickle,' said the chef. 'Guaranteed hottest pickle in the city!'

'It's certainly hot,' coughed Chopra, wondering what further punishments the pickle would inflict on him as it corroded its way through his system.

The chef looked pleased. 'By the way, Poppy called. Irfan, she wants you to go to the bazaar and buy some Holi powder. And Chopra, she said to remind you that she expects you home for dinner with the Malhotras.'

Chopra scrunched his brow. He had completely forgotten.

Poppy had invited over a colleague from the St Xavier Catholic School for Boys, where she had recently begun teaching classical dance and drama. She had been reminding him for weeks, but he had paid little attention. Social engagements did not interest him; yet he did not wish to disappoint her and had, reluctantly, agreed to be there.

Cursing and grumbling, he headed home.

As Irfan and Ganesha swam along the Cigarette Factory Road in Chakala, breasting the foot traffic, they couldn't help but peer in at the row of hole-in-the-wall shops that lined the street on both sides. Streams of shoppers hurtled past, buzzing around each other as they flitted from vendor to vendor likes bees seeking the most fragrant flower. Negotiations were fierce – the voices of steely-eyed housewives could be heard above the din, beating down canny vendors who swore that if they reduced the price any further they would be put out of business and their children sold into slavery.

With Holi around the corner everyone – from vendors of coloured powder, water balloons, sparklers and windmills, to street-painters and rangoli artists – was enjoying a brisk trade.

Apu's Sweet Emporium, with its mouthwatering display of Indian sweets, was besieged.

Ganesha stared longingly at a steel tray piled high with yellow, ball-shaped ladoos, but Irfan, perhaps sensing that the little elephant was about to help himself again, tapped him admonishingly on the top of his head. They passed a fruit-seller with pyramids of melons and pomegranates; a bangle-seller whose neatly laid out boxes of bracelets and glass bangles reflected, in a million colours, the hanging festival lights criss-crossing the street; the spice merchant with sacks of chillies and powders and tar-like blocks of tamarind pulp; the idol-maker carving marble figurines of Lord Krishna; the boiled-egg-seller vying with the papaya vendor as they hollered for customers.

Ganesha paused outside a dimly lit pottery workshop, breathing in the great belches of hot air gusting from the entrance. A trio of potters in dirty vests were sitting cross-legged before their wheels, shaping red clay into tiny earthenware lamps for the upcoming festival. Irfan knew that the spinning wheels fascinated the elephant, and he would stop each time they passed this way.

The eldest potter looked up and grinned through blackened teeth. 'Ho. It is you again, Ganesha Sahib.' He beckoned the elephant forward. 'I think perhaps you were a potter in a former life, yes? Here,' he said, 'why don't you try?'

He sat back and waved a hand at the spinning wheel.

Ganesha glanced up at the smiling man, as if he couldn't quite believe his luck, then stepped forward and dipped his trunk into the ball of unshaped clay, watching in astonishment as it flared into a crude bowl shape.

The potter plucked off the misshapen artefact, and set it to one side. 'Not bad,' he said. 'It's better than half the things Ramu here produces. Come by and pick it up tomorrow when it is dried.'

At the mouth of a narrow alleyway that led off the Cigarette Factory Road, Irfan and Ganesha ran into the Mad Woman.

Two weeks ago the Mad Woman had taken up her station in between the public latrines and an enormous mound of rubbish. Together the two created a smell that no ordinary human could tolerate for more than a few seconds, yet the Mad Woman appeared to breathe it in as if it were the perfume of the legendary Valley of Flowers on Mount Nanda Devi.

To Irfan this was ultimate proof of her madness.

He had asked his friends about the Mad Woman.

'She is so mad, even the lepers shun her,' said one.

'If you go near her she spits on you and then you become just like her,' revealed another.

'They say she is a witch,' the postman Gopal had told him authoritatively. 'She was stoned out of her village for turning children into pye-dogs. Now she sits there all day eating cockroaches and sucking the blood from rats. Be careful she doesn't curse you. She cursed Nandu last week and he grew a boil on his backside so big he hasn't been able to sit down since.'

Irfan and Ganesha approached cautiously.

The old woman appeared to be dozing, sitting cross-legged against the baked brick wall of the toilet hut in her rags, her uncombed mass of grey hair ballooning about her head, her face caked in layers of dirt and grime. Even in the odiferous setting a strong stench emanated from her, though this did not seem to put off the trio of wild pigs rooting around in the rubbish nearby.

Suddenly, loud voices sounded from around the corner.

Irfan shrank back instinctively into the lee of a burnt-out bullock shed opposite the latrines, Ganesha following him automatically.

As they watched, three boys in school uniform emerged into the plot.

Irfan recognised the uniform – it belonged to the International Baccalaureate school that had just opened locally, attracting the children of the newly wealthy to its roster.

'What did I tell you?' said a tall boy who seemed to be leading the pack. 'There she is.'

'Is she really mad?' asked the pudgy specimen bringing up the rear.

'You bet she is. You know she's a witch, don't you?'

The pudgy boy gulped, and pushed his spectacles up his nose. 'Then shouldn't we leave her alone?'

'Grow a backbone, you mouse,' muttered the tall boy. He looked around and picked up a bamboo cane. Stepping forward, he poked the woman in the ribs. 'Hey, get up, you!'

The woman stirred to life, opening eyes encrusted with dirt and mucus. She blinked at the boys, but said nothing.

'What are you doing here, eh?' asked the tall boy.

'Wait! We should just leave her be,' protested a slim boy carrying a satchel. 'My dad said we should be kind to poor people.'

'Balls to your dad!' exploded the tall boy. 'And balls to poor people. They just clutter up the place, making the whole area look like a tip. What are they good for, anyway? Begging and stealing, that's what.' He turned back to the Mad Woman. 'We don't want you around here. Go on, get out.'

He punctuated his order by jabbing her again with the stick.

Without warning, her hand whipped out from beneath the rags, wrenched the stick from him, and flung it back. It clattered off the boy's shins with a satisfying crack, and he collapsed to the ground with a yelp of pain.

'Rahul!' cried his friends, racing to his aid.

The boy staggered to his feet, vigorously rubbing his shins. 'You saw her,' he ground out, 'she attacked me. She's insane.' He looked around, and picked up a rock.

'Rahul, wait!' said the slim boy in alarm. 'Let's just leave her here. She isn't harming anyone.'

'Speak for yourself,' said Rahul, and flung the rock. It struck the woman on the side of her skull. She cried out, her hand rising to her head.

'Oh!' gasped the pudgy boy, as if astonished that his friend had actually thrown the missile.

Rahul grinned, and bent down for another. 'I'll show you, you old witch.'

'Stop it!'

The trio looked around to see Irfan and Ganesha standing before them.

'Who the hell are you?' said Rahul, frowning, rock clutched in his hand.

'You'd better not throw that,' warned Irfan.

'Or what, pipsqueak?' glared Rahul.

'You'll be sorry.'

'I think it's you who'll be sorry,' the boy threatened, raising the rock.

Ganesha charged.

Rahul's eyes widened in astonishment. He threw the rock but it bounced harmlessly off Ganesha's hide as he steamed into the boy, knocking him backwards into the rubbish mound. His companions took one look and fled.

Eventually, Rahul extricated himself from the rubbish tip.

Gunk clung to him. Rotten mango pulp made his face glisten. At least, Irfan hoped it was mango pulp. The alternatives did not bear thinking about.

Rahul glared at the boy and the little elephant. 'I've seen you around,' he growled. 'I'll see you again, one day.'

'I'll be waiting,' said Irfan.

They watched as Rahul limped around the corner.

Irfan turned and looked at the Mad Woman.

Her eyes were wide open, staring straight ahead. Blood trickled from the wound on her skull, snaking down towards her chin, but she appeared not to notice. He realised that she no longer looked frightening. Just a sad old woman down on her luck. Irfan had slept on the streets himself, had known poverty and the pain of constant hunger, and the greater, more poignant pain of an irredeemably bleak future. He had suffered, and in that suffering had been tempered. But there had been times when he had prayed for help, prayed for a single ray of light in the darkness. His prayers had been answered in the shape of Chopra and Poppy, two good people whose kindness had shone in the empty desert of his former life.

He pulled a handkerchief from his pocket, and moved cautiously forward. 'I'm going to wipe off the blood,' he said.

Her eyes stared ahead.

Taking this as a sign of assent, he dabbed away at her skull as Ganesha looked on with concern in his dewy eyes. 'There,' he said finally. 'Good as new.'

The woman had still not looked at him.

'My name is Irfan. This is Ganesha. He's an elephant. We live in Poppy's Restaurant. It's not far from here. If you want I can get you something to eat.'

No answer.

'Why do you sit here all day? Next to the latrine? Isn't there somewhere else for you to go? Anywhere is better than here, surely.'

Silence.

'Those boys might come back. If I were you, I would find somewhere else to sit.'

Nothing.

'Well, we must leave now,' said Irfan. He looked thoughtfully at the woman. 'You know, a friend of mine told me that when people go into themselves they are searching for something. I hope you find whatever it is you are looking for.'

Finally, her head moved.

Her eyes wandered around his face, not settling, then she raised a hand and searched the air.

That was when Irfan realised that the Mad Woman was blind.

The realisation shook him, and he felt indescribably sad that he had thought of her as a crazy old witch. It taught him once again that one must never be too quick to judge.

He lowered his face and felt the woman's coarse fingers move over him. Then her hand dropped back to her lap. Suddenly, Ganesha moved forward. He raised his trunk and gently brushed the woman's face.

She sat still as he examined her.

When he had finished, tears glistened on her cheeks.

'Why are you crying?' asked Irfan. 'He was just being friendly.'

The woman said nothing, weeping silently, head bowed.

Finally, she hitched her shoulders.

'My name is Usha,' she said. 'Once upon a time I used to be a teacher.'

Chopra pulled the Tata Venture into the deserted car park of the Goldspot Cinema and checked his watch. He knew that Poppy would be annoyed, but there was one last errand he had to run before he could return home and sit down to dinner with the Malhotras.

He swung himself out of the van's front seat and stood staring up at the dilapidated façade of the cinema, a burst of nostalgia warming his heart.

The Goldspot had been a fixture of his youth. As a bachelor he had been inspired by his first action-packed Bachchan blockbusters here; later, as a married man, he and Poppy had come to the cinema – with its sooty exterior and tatty Rexine seats, its cracked plaster mouldings and velvet curtains, its odour of incense and bubblegum – to watch the screen come alive with the greatest romances of the age, Poppy squeezing his hand, held shyly in the dark . . . It had been their special place, and it pained him to see it humbled, brought low by the multiplexes that had spread like wildfire around the city. He knew that the Goldspot was locked in a long-standing dispute with the local authorities who wished to demolish it and raise a shopping centre on the site. But the owner, seventy-year-old Cyrus Dinshaw, had dug in his heels and refused to sell.

Chopra strolled past the ticket clerk asleep in his booth, and made his way into the darkened interior.

A black-and-white movie was showing: the Dev Anand classic *Guide*. Spidery lines jumped across the screen; the picture jerked fitfully between the moth-eaten curtains like a man caught in a nightmare.

Chopra made his way up a flight of narrow wooden steps, lined with old movie playbills from the sixties and seventies, to the projection room, where he found his friend Cyrus Dinshaw examining a section of old film stock under a magnifying glass. Beside him the ancient Leica two-reel projector whirred and clacked like a steam train.

Cyrus had steadfastly refused to bow to the new gods of digital technology, another reason his customer base had steadily dwindled. It was also the reason Chopra continued to frequent the cinema – he and Cyrus agreed on this at least.

'Take a look at this, Chopra,' grunted Cyrus without looking up.

Chopra bent over the old man's shoulder, looking past his balding dome to the strip of 35mm film, a series of black-and-white negatives of a scene involving two actresses that he recognised, screen legends both.

'Cellulose nitrate,' continued Cyrus. 'They stopped making this back in the fifties. The stock had a tendency to catch fire and explode. Very temperamental stuff, cellulose. I got this batch from an old collector. He died a couple of weeks ago and his wife wanted to clear out the junk. *Junk!* Hah!' He raised a hoary head and fixed Chopra with a bayonet glare. 'Now, what can I do for you?'

Chopra dragged over a wooden chair and sat before Cyrus, watching him work.

The old man was a rabid collector of knowledge about the movie industry. It was from Cyrus that he'd first learned how the Russians utterly adored the great Raj Kapoor. It was from Cyrus that he'd learned that kissing had been done away with in Indian cinema as part of the freedom struggle, a protest against the spread of British values. It was from Cyrus that he'd learned that the incomparable writing duo of Salim–Javed, despairing of the lack of recognition for scriptwriters in Bollywood, had once gone out in a rickshaw with a pot of red paint and painted their names on all the posters for their latest film. 'Of course, the rumour mill said they loathed each other. They used to salt each other's tea, and fight tooth and nail over every line they wrote.' He seemed to know every snippet of gossip going; given that he appeared never to leave the projection room of his beloved theatre, Chopra surmised he must be straining such information from the very air.

'I'm on a case—' Chopra began.

'How's that elephant of yours?' interrupted Cyrus. 'Discerning little fellow, as I recall.'

The last time Chopra had ventured to the Goldspot, Ganesha had accompanied him, and won Cyrus over by sitting glaze-eyed through the entire length of the old maverick's Guru Dutt collection.

The movie bug had bitten Ganesha deeply, to Chopra's mild annoyance.

'Still in love with the silver screen,' said Chopra. 'Which, as a matter of fact, is the reason I am here.'

Quickly, he explained the case that he was investigating. He knew that Cyrus could be trusted to be discreet – who would he tell, anyway? The old widower had almost no friends and rarely left his beloved cinema. 'I need to know more about P.K. Das. What can you tell me?'

Cyrus leaned back in his chair. 'One of our foremost producers – he's made some of the most successful films of the past forty years. He built Himalayan Studios up from nothing to one of the biggest production houses in the country. He's won just about every award imaginable. As far as anyone is aware he is a shining light of our cultural heritage, a grand old patron of the arts, an all-round good egg . . . Pah!'

'Pah?'

'It's the movie business, Chopra. Nothing is quite what it seems. There have been rumours for decades. Das is a notoriously ruthless character. He rules his productions with an iron fist and has been known to sink careers without a trace, to resort to blackmail and intimidation, anything to get his way. Over the years this has made him many enemies. But you know what they say: who needs friends when you have success? And Das has had a great deal of success. Frankly, just two short years ago, he was standing on top of the mountain. He had nothing left to prove and could happily have sailed off into retirement, rich and feted till his dying day.'

'But something happened.'

'*The Mote in the Third Eye of Shiva* happened. This movie has been Das's white whale for two decades. He could never get it off the ground because of the vast expense involved. It was only after the unprecedented success of his past three movies that he was able to get enough backers on board.' Cyrus scratched his chin. 'Das has sunk everything into this project. His studio is mortgaged up to the hilt. He's borrowed from every bank in the city. And it still wasn't enough. The rumour is that he has taken money from the underworld.' He shook his head sadly. 'We're back to the bad old days of the eighties. Do you remember that?'

Chopra did remember.

For decades the Indian government had refused to officially recognise the movie industry, effectively blocking producers from legitimate sources of funding. Inevitably, this let in the unscrupulous agents of the city's organised criminal gangs. The combination of glamour and a chance to launder dirty money via financially opaque movie productions was too tempting. In time, the underworld dons began to call the shots, and attacks on producers, directors, and actors who refused to toe the line became commonplace. Chopra himself had investigated more than one case of extortion and blackmail, and even a broad-daylight shooting of a well-known producer, which had blown the lid on the whole sorry affair.

Many believed those dark days were behind the industry, yet it seemed Das had so far overreached himself that he had had to go back to the poisoned well.

Chopra's thoughts fastened on Mr Pyarelal, the thug-like individual he had encountered at Film City. It seemed altogether probable that Pyarelal was representing whichever crime outfit Das had got into bed with, there to keep an eye on their investment.

'Let's assume you're correct,' said Chopra. 'Why would this outfit kidnap Vicky? Why would they jeopardise the production? If they've sunk money into it, then aiding its collapse will lose them everything. It makes no sense.'

A silence fell between them as they considered the matter, broken only by the chattering of the projector.

'I can tell you why they may have taken Vicky,' Cyrus announced at last. 'In one word: insurance. It's a relatively new practice, but as the costs of the big-budget productions have skyrocketed, producers have been investing to protect themselves against the vagaries of fate. After all, if you've just pumped one hundred million rupees into a film riding on the shoulders of Salman Khan, what chance have you got if something happens to him? My guess is that with costs racking up the way they are on Das's cursed project, his more unscrupulous backers have decided that the only way for them to recover their money is to bring the whole thing down on its head. I'm sure if you get hold of the insurance papers you'll see a kidnap-and-murder clause. It's standard practice these days. In the event of Vicky Verma's disappearance there'll be an enormous payout, you mark my words. And it wouldn't surprise me in the least if Das is in on the whole thing. He's a man gambling in the last-chance saloon.' He sighed. 'The terrible thing is that the whole scheme only works if Vicky never comes back.'

As Chopra settled down to dinner with the Malhotras this stark warning sat uneasily in his stomach. If his old friend was correct, then Vicky's life was in even greater danger than he had suspected.

'Something on your mind, Chopra?'

Chopra looked up from his contemplation of the Madras lamb curry before him.

Gulshan Malhotra, an amiable, middle-aged English literature teacher from Poppy's school, peered at him through round-framed spectacles.

'No, nothing in particular,' said Chopra, more gruffly than he intended. He realised that he was being an ungracious host. The Malhotras – Gulshan, and his wife, Sudha, who also worked at St Xavier – were perfectly pleasant people, good-natured and articulate. They had taken on the conversational load, deftly filling in the potholes left by Chopra's maudlin silences. Poppy, dressed in an eye-watering mustard-coloured sari, dark hair popped up in a topknot, cheeks flushed from the kitchen – or, possibly, Chopra suspected, from the high level of spice in the curry – had flashed him the odd look of mild irritation.

He felt a sudden sense of chagrin.

This was a special occasion for his wife. They rarely had dinner guests, and this was the first time Poppy had invited over colleagues from her workplace. Indeed, this was the first real job Poppy had ever had. For most of her life she had been content to manage her home while pursuing various social and charitable causes, but now, in thrall to her idol Sunita Shetty's vision of the Modern Indian Woman, Poppy had finally joined the rat race.

After twenty-four years of marriage, Chopra knew that his wife was an incurable romantic. She had a generous nature and a heart as wide as an ocean, yet she was quick to anger and could take offence at the slightest insult. It was one of the things he had grown to love about her.

He cleared his throat. 'Actually, you're right. I apologise for being preoccupied. It's a case I am currently investigating within the movie industry. I cannot reveal the details – and I must ask you to keep this in confidence – but I have been engaged by Bijli Verma.'

This pricked up everyone's ears. Malhotra leaned forward. 'Well, that's quite a coup for your agency, I'll bet.

You know, I've always loved the pictures. I came to Bombay as a young man determined to become an actor. I was a big fan of old Bollywood, especially Raj Kapoor. I still remember the first time I saw *Awaara*, when he unveiled his lovable Chaplinesque "little tramp". What a movie!' Stars shone in his eyes. 'So what's Bijli gotten herself into, then?'

'I'm afraid I can't say, but she's in genuine trouble.'

'Hmm. Well, she's always courted controversy. Do you remember after the 2008 terror attacks, she came out and made a big noise about right-wing fundamentalists operating in the city? There was one outfit, in particular, that swore to make her eat her words. Led by some rogue radical, if I remember, a scoundrel disowned by all the regular Muslim institutions in the city. A real fire-and-brimstone character. It's a pity he vanished into the woodwork before the police got to him.'

Later, as he helped Poppy load the dishes into their new dishwasher, Chopra dwelled on Malhotra's words. He recalled the furore in the papers at the time but, with the storm of news around the attacks, the death threat had quickly died its own death. It seemed hard to believe that the individual in question had resurfaced years later to carry out that threat, by kidnapping Bijli's son.

'You're overworking yourself again, aren't you?'

Chopra smiled at his wife. She stood, hands on hips, head tilted to one side, examining him with her dark, quick eyes. There was no one who knew him better, who cared for his welfare more fervently. And the same was true of his feelings for her, though he was decidedly more sober in his expression of those sentiments. His wife was a kingfisher, he had always felt, loud and iridescent; whereas Chopra thought of himself as more of a crow: dark, sombre, and willing to stay in the shadows.

'I'm trying not to,' he said. 'But—'

'But the weight of the world somehow keeps landing on your shoulders.' Poppy smiled ruefully. 'And here was I thinking after retirement I would see more of you, not less!'

Chopra hesitated. He wanted to tell Poppy that he missed her, that he wished his life – both their lives – were not so busy. But there was that nagging sense of responsibility that had always been his greatest asset and his greatest curse. 'I could always close the detective agency,' he mumbled.

Poppy stared at him, then tipped back her head to unleash a gale of tinkling laughter. 'You said that as if someone had told you to shave your moustache.' She leaned forward and hugged him. 'In all these years I have never asked you to be anyone other than yourself. And I never will. Just remember, *I* need you too. If the only way to spend time with you is to engage your services as a detective, then so be it. I shall have to find a suitable mystery for you to solve.'

Chopra smiled. 'How about the mysterious case of how to convince Irfan to accept your efforts to educate him?'

Poppy smiled. 'I know you don't think I should push him, but it's for his own good.'

'I wonder if *he* knows that? He's got along fine without it so far. It's going to take a lot for him to change his mind.'

'Well, *I'm* responsible for him now,' said Poppy firmly. 'And it just so happens that I'm very good at changing people's minds.'

'Okay, okay. I surrender!' Chopra grinned. 'Perhaps an easier problem for me to solve might be the mystery of the overspiced curry.'

Poppy frowned. 'You know, I thought it was a little hot today. It must be that jar of pickle you brought home with you.'

Chopra looked at her in alarm. 'You added that to the curry?'

'Shouldn't I have?'

Chopra paled. 'Didn't you tell me Malhotra has a delicate constitution? I hope the poor man knows a good doctor. Either that or a priest.'

THE RANSOM LETTER

At eleven o'clock the following morning, and for the second time in two days, Chopra parked the Tata van in front of the Antakshari Tower in Malabar Hill.

The lawyer Lal was waiting for him, pacing the courtyard beyond the gates in agitation. With his dark suit and grey widow's peak he looked like an impatient vampire awaiting his next victim.

Chopra let Ganesha out of the van, then followed Lal as he briskly led him up to the Verma apartment. The summons had been urgent, but once again the lawyer had remained infuriatingly tight-lipped.

They found Bijli Verma in Vicky's room, slumped in a cane rocking chair, staring at a poster of eighties starlet Rekha in her most famous role as Umrao Jaan, the luckless courtesan with the heart of gold.

Chopra waited as the chair creaked back and forth in the silence.

'You know, he only keeps that poster up to annoy me,'

said Bijli eventually. 'Everyone knows Rekha and I were bitter rivals.'

Chopra had indeed heard this, but forbore to comment.

Finally, Bijli pushed herself up from the chair and faced him.

He was momentarily taken aback. He saw that something had happened, something that had shaken the resolute woman. A tremor moved over her cheeks as she held out a letter.

He took it, his dark eyes quickly scanning the lines of aggressive text:

> WE HAVE YOUR SON. IF YOU WANT TO SEE HIM ALIVE AGAIN, DO NOT CONTACT THE POLICE. WE WANT TWO CRORES, IN CASH. GET THE MONEY BY THIS EVENING. WE WILL BE IN TOUCH. DO NOT TRY TO BE CLEVER OR WE WILL SEND HIM BACK TO YOU IN PIECES.
>
> THE PEOPLE'S JUDGE

Two crores! Twenty million rupees!

Chopra removed a bundle from his pocket – the threatening notes sent to Vicky over the past months. Comparing the handwriting, he saw that it was identical.

A photograph accompanied the letter.

It showed Vicky Verma slumped in a chair, holding up a copy of the *Times of India*. The date on the *Times* was today's. But what arrested Chopra was Vicky's face. It was obvious the young actor had been beaten: the right side of his face was swollen, the eye purpled and half closed. His lower lip, too, had swelled grotesquely, and a bruise was visible high on the left side of his forehead. Yet it was the eyes that shocked Chopra the most. A light seemed to have gone out of them – this wasn't the Vicky Verma he had seen cavorting onstage just days ago, confident, cool, and arrogant. This was Vicky stripped of all hubris, returned to the level of his fellow countrymen where bad things befell ordinary people, and being rich and famous was no protection against the iniquities of fate.

For the first time Chopra saw the real Vicky Verma: a boy, Bijli Verma's boy, no different to any other mother's son in the city of Mumbai. He felt a renewed strengthening of his resolve and vowed to himself that he would do everything in his power to return Vicky to his mother unharmed, or as unharmed as his captors permitted him to remain. For Chopra finally had to acknowledge that Vicky really had been kidnapped.

This was no stunt.

'How did you receive this letter?'

'It arrived by courier this morning,' replied Lal.

'Did you contact the courier?'

'If you mean to find out who sent it, then yes. But it was a dead end. The letter was handed in to their office, and paid for in cash. They are very busy. All they can recall is a man in leather and a motorcycle helmet. Useless.'

'How do they know it was a man?'

Lal frowned, but forbore from comment.

Chopra considered the letter again, his thoughts returning to his discussion with Cyrus Dinshaw the previous evening. On the face of it, the ransom letter did not tally with the hypothesis that Vicky had been abducted in order to derail the movie for an insurance claim. The sum was too paltry for any organised-crime outfit worth its salt, and the letter indicated at least a possibility Vicky would be returned.

But then again, perhaps this was all part of the scam.

Insurance companies were notoriously difficult. Perhaps Das's criminal financiers had orchestrated this elaborate charade to ensure that the kidnapping would be taken seriously.

Chopra knew from personal experience that it did not pay to underestimate the ingenuity of Mumbai's criminal overlords.

'What do you intend to do?' he asked eventually.

'Many years ago a famous producer tried to strong-arm me,' said Bijli, staring into space as she became lost in the past. 'He wanted me to do a movie which I had no interest in doing. This was at the height of my fame, you understand, and I was under contract to his studio. When he realised that this made no difference to me he tried another way. He said that if I didn't do the movie he would go public with the details of an affair I had been having with a very famous and respected actor. A married man with children. I had no fear for myself but I was in love with this man. I did not wish him any harm. But this producer wouldn't leave me alone. Finally, I had to take the matter in hand.

'One evening, I went to his apartment. I seduced him, even though it disgusted me to do so. And then, when he was sleeping, I tied him up and poured kerosene on him. When he awoke, in his sodden bedsheets, he saw me sitting at the bottom of the bed holding a lighter and smoking a cigarette. He screamed himself hoarse pleading for his life. In the end he agreed to release me from my contract. I don't think he ever told anyone about that night. I believe he genuinely thought I was insane.'

Chopra observed her face, the lines around the beautiful mouth, the shadows clouding her eyes, mesmerising still. He wondered if Bijli Verma had ever been able to separate herself from the *legend* of Bijli Verma. He wondered if the legend made demands upon the Bijli that was a mere mortal, demands that occasionally led her out beyond the realms of sanity.

'I don't like bullies, Chopra,' she continued, holding his gaze.

'Are you saying that you don't intend to pay?'

She drew in her chin. 'No. I will pay. This situation is different. They have discovered my Achilles heel. I would do anything for my son. He is my sole purpose for existing. I know that he has a reputation as a troublemaker, but he is my son nonetheless. He is all I have.'

'This is now a matter of life and death. I strongly advise you to bring in the authorities.'

'No!' Bijli's eyes blazed. 'The kidnappers have been clear. I cannot take the risk. And neither will you.'

'As you wish. Can you raise the money?'

'It will be done,' replied Lal.

'They will contact you at some point,' continued Chopra. 'To inform you of the details of the exchange. If they phone you, you must ask for proof of life. You must speak to Vicky directly and assure yourselves that he is alive. Do you understand?'

'Yes,' said Bijli.

'We wish *you* to deliver the ransom,' announced Lal.

Chopra hesitated. He had already realised that was why he was here. It was the only logical course of action. And yet the thought of becoming involved filled him with concern.

In his thirty years on the force he had dealt with only a handful of kidnappings, mostly low-key affairs. A boyfriend had kidnapped his former girlfriend after her parents had married her off to someone else. A father had kidnapped his son after his wife had divorced him. His last such case, the kidnapping of a widely disliked luxury car importer, had seen the family – for reasons of their own – refuse the ransom. In a bid to force their hand the kidnappers had tied the old man to the railway tracks at Kalyan Junction. The poor wretch had suffered a very messy end when, for the first time in living memory, the 09:15 to Khopoli had arrived on time.

'Very well,' said Chopra. 'I will help in any way that I can.'

'How could this happen?' asked Bijli. 'Who could have done this?'

'I'm not sure,' said Chopra, unwilling to speculate at this stage on the possible Das connection. Yet he felt Bijli needed something, something to cling on to in the sea of murk. 'Greta, Vicky's PA, says that she saw a strange man outside Vicky's changing room just before he vanished. A middle-aged Muslim man with a distinctive beard.'

Bijli's eyes sharpened. 'You think this has a link to my past? That fanatic who made threats after I spoke out against the terror attacks in 2008?'

Before Chopra could reply, the door swung back and a tall young man burst into the room.

Chopra had seen the boy before, but couldn't place him immediately. And then he had it: Robin Mistry. The youth was an actor, a contemporary of Vicky Vermas'. Indeed, if memory served him correctly, the pair had appeared together in a number of pictures.

The boy was good-looking with a head of shaggy brown hair streaked with blond stripes, and the V-shaped physique that most Bollywood actors sported these days – the age of cheerfully pudgy leading men had been consigned to the past by the influence of Hollywood.

'Aunty Bijli,' gasped the youth. 'I came as soon as I could.'

Chopra glanced at Bijli.

She blinked, then said, 'This is Chopra, Robin. He is helping us to resolve the situation.'

'But what do they want? These kidnappers? Surely, they can't mean to harm Vicky?' Mistry looked aghast.

'I take it that you have been apprised of the facts,' said Chopra, his brows knitting together in consternation.

'Robin is Vicky's childhood friend,' said Bijli defensively. 'They have practically grown up together. He was the first person I called when I discovered Vicky hadn't come home yesterday. He agreed with me that something had to be wrong. If Vicky had been anywhere else, Robin would have known.'

'The more people that know about this the greater the possibility it will come out and endanger Vicky.'

'I can keep a secret,' bristled Mistry.

Chopra turned back to Bijli. 'Until they contact you there is nothing we can do but wait. In the meantime I will continue my investigation.'

He turned and left.

Mistry caught up with Chopra as he was ushering a reluctant Ganesha back into the van. The little elephant had been enjoying the views of the Back Bay. A gentle breeze had leavened the afternoon heat, and the smell of jacaranda blossoms arose from the slopes that fell away below their feet.

'I can help,' said Mistry, planting himself in front of Chopra.

'No, thank you.'

'I know Vicky better than anyone,' he persisted.

Chopra evaluated the young man. 'Vicky has been receiving threatening letters for the past few months. To me they seem very personal. Is there anyone you can think of that Vicky has upset in this way?'

Mistry crunched his handsome forehead. 'Vicky isn't the most tactful guy, I'll admit. There are a few discarded girlfriends who'd love to get their claws into him. One – some bit-part actress – actually threatened to have him shot by her brothers when he dumped her last year. Apparently they're a real gang of ruffians. She has one of those one-name stage names – Apoorna, I think.'

Chopra nodded. This might prove to be an intriguing new lead. 'Thank you.'

'Does this mean I can help you look for Vicky?'

'If I need you, I will call you,' said Chopra, ducking into the van. As he drove away, in the rear-view mirror he saw Mistry staring after him, hands on hips, anger snarling his handsome features.

A VITAL CLUE

The hot-dog vendor had moved on.

As Chopra threaded his way through the bustling crowd towards the entrance to the Andheri Sports Stadium, Ganesha bundling along behind him, he found himself dwelling on the ransom note, and the motives of the kidnappers.

If, for one moment, Chopra put aside the possibility that P.K. Das was behind the abduction, then the tone of the letters indicated a genuine hatred of Vicky Verma.

What had the boy done to offend a potential kidnapper?

Robin Mistry had suggested that a former girlfriend may have held a grudge, had even threatened him. But, since leaving Bijli Verma's home, Chopra had called Babu Wadekar, Vicky's agent, and made enquiries. The upshot was that this Apoorna – whose real name was Jyoti Gupta – had moved out of the state months ago to pursue a career in the Telugu film industry, known as Tollywood. And the rumour about her having crazy brothers ready to shoot holes in Vicky at a moment's notice proved unfounded. She was an only child.

Which left Chopra back with the letters, and 'The People's Judge'.

Who *was* 'The People's Judge'? What was he judging Vicky for? And why send the letters at all? Why threaten a man you intended to kidnap? Why give him any warning? Unless . . . perhaps this too was part of Das's insurance scam, a means of creating a trail to later cement the notion that a demented kidnapper had done for Vicky, and thus allay the suspicions of the insurance agency's investigators.

The fact that Vicky appeared to have dismissed the threats out of hand was fortunate – for the kidnappers. But, of course, P.K. Das knew that Vicky Verma was an arrogant young man, convinced of his own invulnerability. Perhaps Das's associates had counted on this very weakness of character.

'On time as ever.'

Chopra turned to see Bunty Saigal bearing down on him.

'So,' said Saigal, 'what's this all about?'

Quickly, Chopra explained, asking for his friend's discretion.

'I suppose if you find him you'll want to crow about it to the whole world,' said Saigal. 'This'll be a real feather in your cap, eh?'

'Some might ask how Vicky was abducted under the noses of your staff here,' said Chopra mildly.

Saigal frowned. 'Hadn't thought of that,' he admitted, his bulletproof demeanour slipping somewhat. He straightened his shoulders. 'I stand by my team. They may not look like much, but they know what they're doing. Besides, security for us is about keeping the fans from tearing the stars' clothes off. If we'd had any intimation that Verma was receiving threats I'd have locked the place down.'

Chopra followed Saigal into the stadium and down into the dressing room below the stage.

The security chief waited as he carried out his examination.

The room was small and bare, bisected by a pair of load-bearing concrete pillars. Plain sandstone tiles on the floor and whitewash on the walls. A trio of tatty posters for concerts past drooped from the plaster. Twin tubelights threw shadows around the enclosed space. A fly buzzed about aimlessly.

Chopra stood beneath the trapdoor leading up onstage. A wooden ladder extended down from the trapdoor to a thick mat, the kind used in gymnasiums. The fall was only about seven feet.

How had the kidnappers extricated Vicky from here with no one seeing them? That was the real mystery.

He walked around the room, his mind whirling with possibilities. Ganesha followed in his footsteps until Chopra bumped into him, and scowled, encouraging his ward to go off and investigate on his own.

Suddenly, the little elephant froze, his bottom protruding from a large alcove to one side of the room. Something had caught his eye.

His trunk swept over the floor. Using the prehensile finger at the end of the trunk he picked up the glittering object.

'What have you got there, boy?'

Ganesha turned away, not yet ready to share his shiny treasure.

'Young man,' said Chopra sternly.

Reluctantly, Ganesha handed over his booty. Then he stomped off in a huff.

Chopra examined the find.

It was a chain bracelet, silver, with an ID plate. On the ID plate were scrawled the words: *To my dearest brother*. On the inner side of the plate were the jeweller's details: *Ghazalbhai Jewellers, Naya Nagar, Mira Rd.*

The plate was scraped, and the chain's clasp had broken.

He peered into the gloomy alcove.

A series of dark stains marked the rear wall about three feet up.

Chopra dropped to his knees and took a closer look, his fingertips brushing over the dried stains. A shiver passed through him as he realised that the stains were blood – he had seen enough such blood spatter to know that they had been deposited relatively recently. And yet the floor was devoid of similar stains. This was an anomaly, for if, as Chopra now surmised, Vicky Verma had been struck by a blunt object, rendering him unconscious and depositing the blood droplets, then some of those droplets should have fallen to the floor. The fact that they were not there indicated that something else had been.

Chopra had seen many such 'void patterns' at crime scenes, and had learned never to ignore the message they conveyed.

He took out his phone and dialled Greta Rodrigues, Vicky Verma's PA.

'Greta, I want you to think carefully back to the day of the kidnapping. Place yourself in the room below the stage. There is an alcove to the right of the trapdoor. There was something inside the alcove. Something large. What was it?'

A silence drifted down the line.

'You said that when Vicky dropped into the room he had to change costumes.'

'Yes.'

'Where were those costumes kept?'

'In a chest, of course . . . Oh, yes!' she exclaimed. 'You are right! That was where Vicky's costume chest was. The porters had brought it in earlier. It was a large wooden one, with brass fittings, very expensive.'

'Was it still there after Vicky went missing? Think carefully now.'

He could picture Greta biting her lip, and then she answered, hesitantly this time, 'No. I don't think it was. At least, I don't remember it. I simply assumed the porters had collected it.'

Chopra turned to Saigal. 'I must question the staff. Someone must have seen something.'

Chopra spent the next two hours individually quizzing everyone who had been on duty the night of Vicky's disappearance.

It took him until the seventh interviewee to make a breakthrough.

A guard named Madhav Holkar claimed that he had been coming out of a toilet in a backstage corridor – a corridor that led out to the delivery car park – when he had seen a man in a porter's uniform wheeling a large chest. The man had been tall, copper-skinned, wearing an Islamic prayer cap, and sporting a thin red beard, the kind that Hajjis wore – those returned from Mecca. The man smelled strongly of ittar – the alcohol-free perfume some Muslims favoured. Holkar had never seen the man before but had had no reason to stop him. Porters were constantly coming and going.

Chopra pulled out his notebook. Greta Rodrigues had seen a porter matching this description on the night of the disappearance.

'Do you have CCTV in the delivery car park?' he asked Saigal.

'Yes. We have a camera covering the rear door into the stadium.'

'I need to review the footage of the night Vicky disappeared.'

Half an hour later Chopra found what he was looking for: the red-bearded man wheeling out his loaded hand truck into the car park. Unfortunately, the CCTV didn't cover the car park itself so Chopra couldn't see the vehicle that he'd loaded the chest into.

Next Chopra went back through the footage until he found the kidnapper making his *entry* into the stadium, wheeling an empty hand truck. The timestamp on the video said 21:42. At that time Vicky had been onstage, fifteen minutes away from his abduction.

Chopra cycled between the two images of the man entering the stadium and leaving, trying to memorise his appearance. Something began to nag at him, but he couldn't quite put his finger on it. Something about the doorframe . . .

'Do you log in the deliveries?' he asked Saigal, eventually.

'Of course.'

In the car park he discovered that a veteran security guard named Pancholi had been on duty that evening. Pancholi was a large man with an unshaven chin and a pugnacious manner. He chewed betel nut incessantly and spat it in all directions. A tide of red stains lapped against his guard hut.

He immediately became defensive when he realised why Chopra was there. At first he refused to hand over his logbook. When Saigal ordered him to do so, he flung it over with bad grace.

Chopra ran a finger down the entries for that evening, trying to find a name that might match the description of the mysterious porter. There were quite a number of comings and goings that night, as might be expected for a major event. But none of the names felt right. He did not suppose that the kidnapper would have been foolish enough to give his real name but, in Chopra's experience, criminals lacked imagination when selecting aliases – they rarely moved far from the familiar.

'Do you note down every single visitor?'

Pancholi blinked, then spat another mouthful of betel nut on the ground. It splashed near Ganesha's foot, who shuffled hurriedly back. 'Every single one.'

Chopra turned to Pancholi's partner in the car park, a thin man who looked barely out of his teens. His uniform hung off him and his Adam's apple bobbed nervously.

'Do you note every single visitor?' Chopra repeated.

The boy, whose name was Khedekar, gulped, and looked at Pancholi.

'Answer the question!' roared Saigal suddenly.

'No, sir!' blurted Khedekar. 'Sometimes, Pancholi Sir just waves them through.'

'And why would he do that?' said Saigal menacingly.

'Sir, because we were watching the cricket.'

Chopra grimaced. Quickly, he described the red-bearded man. 'Do either of you remember this man? Do you remember him leaving? The vehicle he was in?'

'No.' Pancholi glared at Chopra. Khedekar hung his head.

Chopra turned away. So . . . an unknown delivery man had entered the stadium and later left with Vicky Verma's costume chest.

He was beginning to understand.

The kidnappers had kept things simple. A single kidnapper posing as a porter had snuck into the stadium, taking advantage of the chaos on concert night. He had entered the dressing room beneath the stage at about the time Vicky had dropped down to change costumes. He had overpowered the actor, striking him on the head with – presumably

– a blunt object as Vicky bent over his costume chest, and then bundled him into that same chest, which he had then calmly wheeled out of the stadium.

In order for this plan to work the kidnappers would have needed a combination of good fortune, a criminally lackadaisical approach to security around Vicky – but there was nothing unusual about that in India – and access to critical information, such as the exact time that Vicky was due to descend from the stage. He wondered what would have happened if Greta Rodrigues had not gone to use the washroom. Presumably she would have been incapacitated as well, possibly even kidnapped along with Vicky. Chopra did not doubt that the kidnapper had come prepared for such an eventuality.

A fleeting shadow passed across his features as he considered the possibility that Greta was involved. After all, she had access to the very information that such a plan required to succeed. And it was indeed convenient that she had chosen to step away at the exact time that the kidnapping had taken place . . . Was Greta Rodrigues the inside woman?

Chopra had no evidence to back up such a suspicion, but he felt this was an avenue he would need to investigate further. Then again, Greta's description of the red-bearded stranger she had seen that evening had now been corroborated by an independent witness, and by CCTV footage. If she had been involved in the crime, why would she have told Chopra about him?

Chopra reached into his pocket and took out the broken chain bracelet Ganesha had discovered in the alcove.

He thought he understood what had happened.

The costume chest had been inside the alcove. The kidnapper had been wearing the bracelet. When he had tried to move the chest he had scraped the bracelet against the wall, breaking the clasp. In the urgency of the kidnapping he had failed to notice that it had fallen from his wrist.

Chopra allowed himself a grim smile.

This was the vital clue, the breakthrough that he needed.

RANGWALLA DRESSES FOR THE OCCASION

Sub-Inspector Rangwalla (Retd) had been in many hairy scrapes during his time on the force. He had crawled, in turgid horror, through Mumbai's infernal sewers in pursuit of criminals; he had confronted a rampant leopard terrorising a hall full of pensioners from the Old is Gold Society, and concluded that he would rather tackle a herd of wild cats singlehandedly than ever again be harangued by the doyennes of that hallowed institution; he had been present at innumerable violent encounters with thugs and gangsters, surviving only by his steadfast commitment to the cause of his own self-preservation . . . yet he could not recall an occasion that had left him more petrified than this moment.

As he examined his reflection in the full-length mirror inside a tiny dressing room in the Red Fort, he couldn't help but think that he had fallen through a crack in reality, into some otherworldly realm where his worst nightmare had come to pass.

From the mirror a grisly apparition stared back at him.

He was dressed in a magnificent purple sari with a tasselled hem. A wig gave him a luxurious plaited pigtail that fell all the way to his waist. Bright lipstick adorned his lips, while earrings and a nose ring decorated his face. Kohl rimmed his eyes. But the icing on this heinous cake, the crowning insult to the Rangwalla ego, was his beard.

Or rather the absence of it.

As hirsute as many of the city's eunuchs were, a full-fledged beard would not have gone with the disguise Rangwalla had reluctantly adopted.

As he stared forlornly at his dark, pockmarked cheeks, he felt strangely denuded.

He wondered, once again, if he was mad.

The door opened behind him.

'Hmm,' said Anarkali, folding her arms and running her eyes up and down his costumed height. 'Truly, Rangwalla, you are a rare flower from the Ganges delta.'

'I suppose you think this is funny?' muttered Rangwalla.

Anarkali smiled. 'This was your idea, not mine. Come now, the Queen is waiting.'

In the Queen of Mysore's chamber Rangwalla waited as she regarded him at length.

'Well,' said the Queen finally, 'I am glad you are not one of my girls. I don't think I'd get a handful of mung lentils for your services.'

Rangwalla glowered as the Queen bubbled away on her hookah, a slow smile splitting her coarse features. 'The other girls will not know who you are. We cannot take the risk that they will give the game away.'

'I understand.'

'Do you?' said the Queen, her eyes narrowing. 'You have not lived this life. You have no idea what we must endure. But perhaps you will learn. They say that the path to true wisdom lies through a field of broken glass, Rangwalla. If so, you have a very large field ahead of you.'

A knock on the door interrupted them. A breathless eunuch entered. 'The limousine is here, Maharani Bibi!'

A group of eunuchs had gathered around the vehicle, talking animatedly and teasing the driver, a short potbellied man in a white uniform and peaked cap. They bombarded him with questions that he resolutely shrugged aside.

Then the door to the Red Fort swung back and the four ornately dressed eunuchs selected by the Queen to attend the mysterious summons sauntered out to catcalls and good-natured hoots of derision.

The eunuchs exchanged lewd jokes with their friends before disappearing one by one into the cavernous interior of the limousine.

Rangwalla felt a push in the back. 'Go on,' Anarkali hissed in his ear.

The former policeman's feet were encased in lead. A clammy sweat had broken out on his forehead. *What the hell was he doing?*

'The Queen is watching,' said Anarkali, her voice dropping several octaves.

Dragging his feet Rangwalla made his way to the vehicle.

Just before he ducked inside he took one last look at the world of common sense and reality that he was leaving. Then he slipped into the limousine, and the driver slammed the door shut behind him.

MIRA ROAD MYSTERY

The locality of Naya Nagar in Mira Road lay some fifteen kilometres north of Chopra's own home in Andheri East, a satellite suburb of the ever-growing metropolis, bounded on one side by the Sanjay Gandhi National Park and on the other by the relatively unpopulated Uttan coastal district.

An enclave of largely Muslim residents, Naya Nagar enjoyed a boisterous reputation, one that Chopra had yet to experience first hand. He had never come to this particular part of the city, and it took a while for him to find his bearings.

He finally located Ghazalbhai Jewellers on a short street named Pathli Gully.

The road was exceedingly narrow – indeed, as Chopra slid his van to a halt he could see a bullock-cart owner and a rickshaw-van driver engaged in a heated argument over right of way. The argument had been going on for some time, judging from the way local residents had pulled up chairs and were sipping glasses of tea as they commented on the merits of each combatant's position.

Chopra abandoned his van, extricated Ganesha from the rear, and set off on foot.

He paused at a barber's shop to ask directions. The shop was besieged, not by customers but by locals watching the cricket on the shop's tiny television set. Every time India's premier batsman Sachin Tendulkar hit another four everyone would cheer, and the barber, holding a strop razor, would swing his head around. His client, with a froth of shaving foam around his chin, would also swing about, risking slashing his own throat.

Ghazalbhai Jewellers was at the very end of the street.

This was the second time he had been inside a jewellery store in the past few weeks but the contrast could not be greater. The last occasion had been an emporium catering to the rich, a palace of glitz and glitter. This time he was in the type of hole-in-the-wall store found in every mercantile quarter in the country, a family-owned business run by craftsmen who had forgotten more about the art of jewellery making than any of the chain-store tycoons had ever known. In India, families became connected to their jeweller over generations. The jeweller was there for every major occasion: births, celebrations, marriages, even death. Jewellery was passed from mother to daughter, from father to son. Each piece had its own story to tell, and the jeweller sat at the very centre of this vast web of familial intrigue, a magnet for gossip and news.

In the store an old man with a white beard and a prayer cap was peering down at a glittering necklace on a velvet swatch spread over the counter. He looked up as Chopra entered, peering at him myopically through a loupe wedged into his right eye. Beside the man a youth in an astrakhan cap was staring raptly at a young girl trying on a succession of gold bracelets. The girl's mother, a leathery dragon, glared at the boy. 'Put your eyes back in your head,' she snapped. 'Just because you were friends in school doesn't mean you can get fresh with my daughter.'

The boy coloured.

'Mother,' said the girl, also blushing.

Her mother grabbed her by the arm and dragged her away. 'Come on! I don't want that *goonda* ogling us.'

Us? Chopra doubted that the boy had been ogling the mother.

'But what about the bracelet?' protested the boy.

'Hah, I wouldn't buy a bracelet from you if it was the last one on earth.'

'But she is still wearing it!' he cried desperately.

The woman appeared not to hear. She stormed from the shop, leaving the boy to look pleadingly at his father.

'Don't worry, son,' said the old man mildly. 'When she calms down she will be back. She is one of my oldest customers.' He turned back to Chopra. 'How may I help you, sir?'

Chopra reached into his pocket and brought forth the bracelet. 'Did you make this?'

The old man took the piece and examined it through his loupe. 'Why, yes,' he said. 'I made this for Aaliya, Aaliya Ghazi, old Mansoor's daughter. I believe she had it commissioned for her cousin. He recently arrived in the city, to offer support following the death of her mother.'

'Aaliya's mother is dead?'

'Yes. She passed away six months ago. She was a good woman.'

'What is this cousin's name?'

'I think she said his name was Ali, if I remember rightly.' He scratched his chin. 'Frankly, it was all a little puzzling. I've known that girl since she was an infant. She's never mentioned a cousin before. She told me that this Ali left the city when she was a child – before she and her mother moved into this area, together with that deadbeat father of hers – and has only now returned. He is the closest thing to a brother she has, hence the inscription.'

Chopra felt his pulse quicken. 'Where can I find this Ali?'

The jeweller stared at Chopra. 'How did you come by this? And what is your interest in Aaliya?'

Chopra hesitated, then decided to tell something akin to the truth. 'My name is Inspector Chopra, and I am following up a lead in a recent crime, the details of which I cannot reveal.'

'Aaliya involved in a crime?' The old man laughed, and handed the bracelet back. 'That girl has the sweetest disposition of anyone I've ever known. The day she's implicated in a crime is the day I'll lie down in my own grave. Of course, I've never met this Ali, so I cannot vouch for him. Aaliya lives close by. Why don't you talk to her?'

Chopra noted the address, and thanked the man.

The house was small, at the far end of a badly lit lane of similar homes, with thin plank-board walls, tin roofs, worm-eaten window frames, and plywood doors gnarled by sun and monsoon rain. A kerosene lantern lit the sagging porch. On the porch a broken water pot squatted beside a much-abused bicycle. A lizard scuttled away as Chopra approached.

'Hullo!' he shouted, announcing his presence.

Nothing.

He poked the door, and discovered that it was unlocked.

Chopra stepped inside, into a cramped living room set up with a small TV, a kitchen area, and a single battered sofa upon which a large man was splayed, his big belly rising up and down as snores emanated from his robust frame. A hairy-knuckled hand dangled on the floor. Beside it a bottle of unlabelled liquor rolled around, pushed back and forth by a trio of squabbling mice.

Chopra had seen many wasted lives over the years. Some were wasted through neglect, some through poverty, some through a simple lack of opportunity. But the most criminal waste, in his opinion, was that begat by the vice of alcohol. He had seen many men laid low by such demons of their own making, and it both saddened and infuriated him.

He looked around the room.

The walls were bare, with peeling whitewash. The only adornment was a single poster, framed in glass. It was for an old Bollywood movie *Queen of the Kohinoor Circus*, though the names of the actors were not mentioned. Various circus animals were ranged behind a woman in a scanty acrobat's leotard with a beehive hairstyle, clearly the star of the movie.

He'd never seen the film, but there was something familiar about the woman.

'What are you doing in here?'

Chopra turned to face what he assumed was a young woman, wearing a black burka, her face obscured behind a gauze veil.

'I'm sorry,' said Chopra. 'The door was open.' He held up the bracelet. 'I am looking for Aaliya Ghazi. Or rather I am looking for the man she gave this to.'

The woman's hands slid off her hips. Chopra could not be sure, but he sensed she was shocked.

Finally, she spoke. '*I* am Aaliya. But you are mistaken. That bracelet does not belong to me.'

'The jeweller told me that he fashioned it at your specific request.'

'He is mistaken,' she snapped. 'Now please leave before I fetch my neighbours.'

Chopra realised he would get no further by staying. Trying to strong-arm a Muslim girl here would not go down well. Besides, it was not his way of doing things. His intuition told him that something was not right.

That would have to be enough for now.

'Very well,' he said. 'I will leave. But I may be back. This is an important enquiry. A life is at stake. It will not simply go away.'

He walked past the woman and out into the night, where he found Ganesha investigating an old tyre with his trunk.

'Come on, boy,' he said loudly, knowing that the girl was watching. 'Let's get back to Andheri.'

Chopra walked back to the van, drove towards the house, and parked around the corner, before killing the engine.

He waited in the dark, hoping the girl would give herself away, or else that the elusive Ali might make an appearance. A thought suddenly occurred to him. When confronted by a stranger in her home, Aaliya had threatened to fetch her neighbours. Most people would have threatened to call the police. Was Aaliya afraid of the questions a policeman might ask?

His phone went off in his pocket.

Cursing, he extricated it from his trousers. 'Yes?'

'This is Lal,' said Lal. 'You must come to Antakshari right away.'

'Why? What has happened?'

'Something awful,' said Lal, and hung up.

Rangwalla looked around the spacious rear cabin of the limousine, taking stock of his travelling companions.

As the vehicle had made its way out of Marol, headed north, he had learned that the four eunuchs he was accompanying had been at the Red Fort for varying lengths of time, and had all been personally chosen by the Queen for the assignment. They were heady with excitement at the money they would make from a few days of relative idleness. Inevitably, speculation was rife as to the true motives of their mysterious benefactor.

'Well, if you ask me,' said Rupa, a slender eunuch in a purple sari and hooped earrings, 'he is probably one of those shy types working himself up to what he *really* wants.'

'As long as he doesn't try any funny business,' said Mamta, a large eunuch with a flat face like a shovel, broad and open. 'The last one who tried that with me got a pounding.'

Rangwalla could well believe it. Thick muscles corded Mamta's arms, the biceps stretching the short sleeves of her powder-green sari blouse.

'I never took you for a shrinking violet, Mamta,' said Parvati, a dumpy eunuch with a benign forehead and wide-winged nostrils. She was older than the others, Rangwalla felt, though it was hard to be sure under the layers of make-up.

'It wasn't that,' countered Mamta. 'I had gone there to collect a debt. He thought because I was a eunuch he could humiliate me in front of his friends.'

Rangwalla knew that the use of eunuchs as debt collectors was a recent innovation. After all, eunuchs spent much of their time collecting baksheesh from local businesses in return for their blessings. Sometimes the cash was handed over willingly, more often with great reluctance. But it was always handed over. When one thought about it logically, no one knew more about collecting money from those who didn't want to pay than the eunuchs.

'One day we will live in a world where no one will humiliate us.'

As one they turned to stare at the fifth member of the group, a eunuch who Rangwalla found disturbingly attractive – certainly she was the most feminine-looking and in her pale pink sari, in the right light, could have passed for any pretty young girl in the city.

Her name was Kavita and she was the youngest of the bunch.

And then, as one, the others burst out in cynical laughter.

'The poet speaks!' said Rupa.

'When that day comes, my dear,' said Parvati, 'you and I will be dust and bones.' She removed a flask from her undercarriage, and took a quick sip, winking.

'And what about you?' asked Mamta, peering at Rangwalla. 'Do you believe in paradise too?'

So far Rangwalla had successfully deflected attention from himself. At the beginning of their journey he had pre-empted his companions' questions by recounting the cover story Anarkali had provided him with, namely that he was an old acquaintance of the Queen – answering to the name of Sonali – who had been summoned to the Red Fort that very morning. The Queen had insisted he go on this trip. He knew that this perfunctory explanation did not satisfy the eunuchs, but so far they had resisted the urge to delve deeper. The Queen had made a decision. Who were they to question it?

Rangwalla was glad he could hide behind this shield of silence. The truth was that his discomfort had grown steadily. He had never been in such close proximity to a group of eunuchs before. His guts coiled each time he inadvertently brushed the eunuch beside him. In spite of his stern words in defence of Anarkali back at the restaurant, he felt that such chivalry was fine at a distance, but this close, he found his fragile principles wilting.

Before he could respond, the limousine ground to a halt.

The driver twisted in his seat, and passed a package through the screen. 'The Master wishes you to put these blindfolds on.'

'I told you,' said Rupa. 'Didn't I tell you? The kinky games have started, and we haven't even reached his mansion yet.'

'It is only because the Master does not wish to reveal the location of his residence,' explained the driver.

'And why not, eh?'

'It is the Master's wish,' said the driver calmly. 'I cannot continue until the blindfolds are on.'

Grumbling, the eunuchs pulled on the blindfolds.

What next? thought Rangwalla, as the limousine moved off.

THE BLOODY EAR

When Chopra entered the Verma home he had not known what to expect. What he did not foresee was Bijli Verma on the sofa, head back, a glass of whisky clutched tightly in her hand.

The former glamour queen looked terrible.

Her hair had been set loose and fell now in a river of onyx towards her shoulders. She had clearly been weeping – her make-up had run, smearing her handsome cheeks with garish swatches of colour. But it was her eyes that really shook him.

They were the eyes of a hunted animal.

Behind the sofa the lawyer Lal paced aggressively, smoking an unfiltered cigarette. Standing by the open balcony doors was Robin Mistry, Vicky's friend and fellow actor.

'What has happened?' asked Chopra.

Lal, who had been close-lipped on the phone, now strode to the sideboard and retrieved something from a silver platter. He walked towards Chopra, then, carefully shielding it from Bijli, showed him the small round tin he was holding.

'A tiffin box?' said Chopra. 'You called me here to show me your lunch?'

'What?' said Lal, in confusion. 'No! Of course not.' He unscrewed the box's lid, and tilted it towards Chopra.

Inside, lying on a bloodied white cloth, was the lobe of a right ear; an earring in the shape of a naked woman dangled from it.

'It's Vicky's,' Lal said, in a terse whisper.

Behind him Bijli Verma released a soft moan. Mistry sat down beside her, clasping her hand. 'It's okay, Aunty Bijli,' he soothed. 'We'll get him back.'

Lal reached into his pocket and took out a letter.

Chopra unfolded the paper and scanned it.

MIDNIGHT. MADH FORT. BRING THE CASH. COME ALONE. IF WE SEE ANYONE ELSE WE WILL LEAVE HIS BODY FOR YOU TO FIND. IN PIECES.

THE PEOPLE'S JUDGE

'This was delivered by courier?'

'Yes,' confirmed Lal. 'A different one to the first. Again they left no leads for us to pursue.'

'And there has been no phone contact?'

'No,' said Lal.

'So we have no way of knowing if Vicky is even still alive,' said Chopra, lowering his voice.

'No. But that is irrelevant,' said Lal. 'We must comply with their wishes.'

'Very well. Do you have the cash?'

Lal beckoned him to follow.

In the study, two black flight bags sat on a desk. Chopra flipped back the lid of one of them. Inside were bundles of five-hundred-rupee notes.

'Two crores, just as they asked,' said Lal.

Chopra buckled the lids on both bags. 'You know there's a good chance they've killed him already, don't you?' He stopped short of laying out his theory regarding P.K. Das and his organised-crime backers, and the insurance scam that would ultimately necessitate Vicky Verma's death.

'Just don't say that around Bijli. Do you know she got him those earrings for his twenty-first birthday?'

Chopra tried to imagine how he might feel if a kidnapper mailed him a part of someone he loved, Poppy, Irfan, or little Ganesha. No wonder Bijli Verma was in the state that she was.

'Mistry shouldn't be here,' he said eventually. 'The more people who know about this, the greater the danger.'

'It is not by my choice,' said Lal. 'Between you and me, I don't trust that boy.'

Chopra picked up on something in the lawyer's voice. 'Why not?'

Lal hesitated then plunged on. 'He and Vicky have been friends for a long time, that much is true. But they are also bitter rivals. Mistry was originally cast for the lead in *The Mote in the Third Eye of Shiva*. But at the last moment the producer changed his mind and insisted on Vicky instead. I think Bijli had something to do with that. At any rate, Vicky and Robin had an almighty fight about it. The matter went to fisticuffs. They made up afterwards, of course. Mistry claimed he had just had a bit too much to drink. Bijli asked P.K. Das to get him a part on another movie, some low-budget number. They're filming in Studio 16, next door to the main *Mote* set. Robin pretends to be happy for his friend, but I am certain he is secretly jealous. I don't trust his "Aunty Bijli" routine one iota.'

At that precise moment the door opened and Mistry entered. 'I want to go with you,' he said, looking at Chopra.

'No,' said Chopra firmly. 'The note was clear.'

'I'll hide in the back of your van. They won't even know I'm there.'

'I cannot take the chance. We cannot jeopardise Vicky's life.'

'Of course, it would work out well for you if Vicky didn't return at all,' said Lal.

'What?' said Mistry, frowning. 'What's that supposed to mean?'

'Nothing,' muttered Lal.

Chopra noticed that the old man's eyes were bloodshot and his usually immaculate widow's peak had become ruffled. For a lawyer Lal was taking all this very personally, he thought.

Chopra checked his watch. 'Madh Fort is a long way from here. If I am to make it on time, I must leave now.' He picked up the flight bags and went back into the living room.

Bijli Verma pushed herself to her feet as he entered.

Chopra saw that she was clutching a photograph in her fist. She held it out to him. It showed an adorable little boy, posing in a cowboy outfit. 'He has been my whole life. I cannot express what he means to me. Vicky himself wouldn't understand what he means to me. I would gladly give myself to them if it would save him.' She drew herself up. 'Bring my son back to me. *Please.*' The note of pleading struck Chopra deeply. He understood, once again, that in spite of her aloof and fiery public persona, Bijli Verma was a devoted mother, like any other.

'I will do everything in my power,' he vowed.

Then he turned and left.

THE MASTER'S HAVELI

Rangwalla and the eunuchs disembarked from the limousine, pulling off their blindfolds.

Then they stood and stared at the imposing mansion rising up into the moonlit darkness before them.

The manse was a haveli, a typically north Indian rural palace fashioned from yellow sandstone, with overhanging jharokha balconies, exquisite floral corbelling, and intricate frescos rolling over the upper elevations. Ropes of wisteria and hydrangeas climbed the walls. From various points brass lamps cast soft haloes of light.

To Rangwalla's eye, a sense of languid ruin enveloped the place.

As they waited, stunned into silence, surrounded by the noises of the night – the croaking of crickets and bullfrogs, the whisper of bat wings, the slither of snakes through the long grass that surrounded the haveli on all sides – they saw someone approaching through the mansion's entrance arch. The figure was stooped, emaciated, dressed in a white kurta and dhoti, a black Nehru jacket, leather sandals, and a black pillbox hat. Wire-framed spectacles sat on his nose above a peppery moustache. A smudge of crimson was prominent between his eyebrows, a red-bound ledger tucked under one arm. He swung a bamboo cane ahead of him as he limped along.

He stopped under the arch and scrutinised the new arrivals. 'Welcome,' he finally said, in a thin voice. 'My name is Premchand. I am the munshi of this estate. You will follow me. The driver and the watchman will bring up your suitcases.'

Rangwalla looked around and saw a shape melt from the shadows. A white-haired old man in a beige kurta and white dhoti shambled towards the limousine swinging a kerosene lamp: the watchman.

They followed the munshi – the estate's secretary – through the archway and into the first of two courtyards. The outer courtyard was dark and deserted. In the inner courtyard a number of rope charpoys were scattered around a covered well. A giant tonga wheel leaned against a crumbling brick wall, beside a water butt. A wooden swing-seat hung from the branches of a tamarind tree. Three peacocks, two colourful males and a drab female, milled about, pecking at invisible grains of rice on the tiled floor.

Premchand led them into a large, ornately decorated reception room, from which rose a double-spiralled marble staircase to the upper storey.

As they ascended the staircase, Mamta's voice cut through the silence. 'Who is this Master? We have a right to know.'

'The Master is the Master,' said Premchand cryptically. 'He has contracted your services for the next few days. *That* is all you need to know.'

'But why won't he show his face?' queried Rupa belligerently. 'And why doesn't he want anyone to know where he lives? Don't you think that's strange?'

Premchand stopped on the landing, and swivelled on his feet. He gazed down stone-faced at the eunuchs as they clustered on the steps below him. 'The Master is paying you handsomely for your time, not for your curiosity. If you wish to leave, the driver will take you back now.'

The eunuchs exchanged glances, but no further protests were forthcoming.

'Very well,' said the munshi, and turned away.

They were each shown to a separate bedroom.

Rangwalla looked around his lavish quarters, a more opulent place than he had ever slept in his whole life. A jack-arched ceiling soared above the chequerboard floor. The bed was fashioned from teak, with a carved headboard depicting a pivotal battle scene from the *Mahabharata*. In the corner a walnut wardrobe stood next to a clawfooted table inlaid with camel bone. Overhead, a mahogany-bladed ceiling fan swirled the warm air; fretworked shutters covered the room's single window.

Rangwalla threw open the shutters and looked out onto a vista of fields.

A warm breeze rippled the broomcorn and wheat. In the distance, moonlight reflected from a sinuously curving river and, beyond that, the lights of what was presumably a village.

Rangwalla locked the door, then sagged against it in relief. He lifted off his wig – which had been making him itch all evening – tore off his sari, kicked off his sandals, and showered in the en-suite bathroom. Then he changed into a pair of shorts and his habitual string vest before stretching out on the bed, sinking into the deep, feather-filled mattress.

Closing his eyes, he contemplated a very strange and disturbing day.

For the millionth time he questioned his own sanity.

What in the world had possessed him to take up this assignment? He wasn't Chopra. He loved his boss dearly but the man was an oddity. He had *ideals*. Rangwalla came from the streets and knew that ideals were a luxury that ordinary men could not afford. The best way to get your head shot off was to stick it above the parapet. As a consequence, he now possessed a lifetime's experience of knowing when to retreat while pretending to move forwards. Which made it all the more galling that he was now doing exactly the opposite.

Perhaps that was the difference between being a policeman and a private detective, he thought, sourly.

As the fan whirred lazily above him, he heard a gecko slither across the wall, and the rasp of a corncrake drifting in from the fields. Sleep stole over him, even as he wondered what the following day would bring.

RANSOM EXCHANGE AT THE MADH FORT

It took Chopra almost two hours to drive to the Madh Fort.

The fort was situated on the western flank of the city, on the southern tip of the coastal region known as Madh Island. To get there Chopra had to drive all the way up to Kandivali, circling around the Malad creek, and then back down again to the bottom of the promontory.

At this time of night the area was deserted, the fishing boats that trawled the Arabian Sea beneath the fort's sombre gaze beached, their pilots retired to the cluster of nearby villages.

In the rear of the van Ganesha peered out to the east where the lights of Juhu Beach – with its Ferris wheels, ice-candy stalls, horse-buggy rides, acrobats, and courting couples – shone brightly a few kilometres away across the open water.

Chopra parked beneath the fort's imposing stone walls, then let Ganesha out.

The little elephant stood in the darkness, craning his head up at the towering edifice. A stiff breeze blew in from the sea and ruffled the short hairs on the top of his skull.

Chopra checked his watch. It was 11:50 p.m.

Clutching the flight bags he strode briskly towards the nearest bastion. His instincts told him the kidnappers would be up on the fort's ramparts.

Worn stone steps led upwards.

Ganesha hesitated momentarily, one foot on the bottommost step, peering up into the darkness. Then he clumsily followed his guardian.

They emerged into a rectangular courtyard at the fort's northern tip.

Chopra squinted into the moonlit gloom, but could see nothing. The fort was laid out oddly, a seven-sided polygon with bastions at each corner, and a larger, circular bastion at the very centre. The walls were crumbling, broken at regular intervals, and threaded with vegetation.

He headed towards the fort's southern end.

They moved across the courtyard, skirting around a deep rectangular water tank and a row of eerie doorways leading into stone chambers in which, it was rumoured, the ghosts of ancient Portuguese soldiers still prowled.

They picked their way through the central bastion and emerged into a smaller courtyard at the southern tip.

As they entered the space, a dazzling beam of light erupted from the darkness ahead, blinding them.

'That's far enough.'

The voice was deep and rasping and instantly arrested Chopra in his tracks, Ganesha stumbling to a halt behind him. He narrowed his eyes and tried to make out the figure holding the high-powered torch. A man, tall, with a slight stoop, and wearing a Muslim skullcap. He could make out a beard, but the face was wreathed in shadow.

'I told Bijli Verma to come alone.'

'I *am* alone,' confirmed Chopra.

'Then what is that behind you? A ghost?'

'This is my elephant. He goes everywhere with me.'

The man hesitated, momentarily derailed from the script that he had prepared.

'Why do you have an elephant?' he asked, his voice tinged with incredulity.

'Is that relevant?'

The kidnapper shook himself back to the matter at hand. 'Is the money in the bags?'

'Yes.'

'Put them down and step back.'

'Where is Vicky?'

'I said put the bags down.'

'No Vicky, no money,' said Chopra firmly. 'That was the deal.'

'When I am safely away from here, I will call Bijli Verma and tell her where to find him.'

'No deal.'

'You're in no position to bargain,' said the man. His other hand rose up and Chopra saw that it held a gun. Fear brushed the walls of his heart, the heart that even now was thundering inside his chest. Once again he heard Poppy's voice, admonishing him for his recklessness. *How did a man with a heart condition keep ending up in these situations?* she was saying.

Chopra was beginning to wonder this himself.

He willed himself to calm, remembering that he had taken the precaution of bringing along his own revolver, tucked into the back of his trousers. He always carried it with him in the van, but hoped never to have to use it since becoming a private detective. Now he weighed the risk of going for his gun.

'I made Bijli Verma a promise,' he said finally. 'I cannot return without her son.'

The kidnapper did not reply, but instead moved forwards, lowering the torch and revealing himself fully. Chopra noted the man's grave, dark face, the expression of determination. So this was the man who had entered the Andheri Sports Stadium and nonchalantly walked out with Vicky Verma bundled inside a costume chest.

The elusive Ali.

'You are a stubborn man,' rasped Ali, finally.

'My name is Chopra. I used to be a policeman. Now I help people like Bijli Verma. She just wants her son back safe and sound. Is Vicky alive?'

A silence unspooled in the darkness. 'Yes,' said Ali finally. 'Though he is a great deal less arrogant these days.' He laughed grimly.

'Why did you cut off his ear?'

'It was only a *part* of his ear,' snapped Ali. 'Perhaps he'll listen better now.'

'Who are you working for?' asked Chopra. 'Is it P.K. Das?'

Ali's eyes narrowed. 'You ask too many questions, Chopra. Now . . . throw me the bags. I won't ask again.'

'How do I know you'll return Vicky once you have the money?'

'How do you know I won't shoot you where you stand!' exploded Ali.

Chopra made a decision.

He stepped forward and dropped the bags. Then he backed away, allowing his hands to drop to his sides, his thoughts leaping ahead. In order to lift the bags Ali would have to lower his gun. As soon as he did this Chopra would go for his own revolver. Then the tables would be turned and he would be the one demanding answers. He could not simply allow Ali to walk away with the ransom, not without proof that Vicky was alive.

A lifetime of policing had taught him that the word of a criminal was worth nothing.

Ali moved towards the bags.

He knelt down, put the torch on the floor and, with one hand, undid the buckle on one of the bags, while keeping his gun trained on Chopra. He glanced down at the bundles of cash. A grim smile compressed his lips.

He closed the bag, then straightened.

The night breeze whistled around the ramparts.

Chopra suspected that Ali was finally confronting the problem that he had foreseen: how to lift both bags and still handle a gun.

The awkward silence was shattered by the sound of raised voices and booted feet clattering through the darkness.

'You broke the rules!' hissed Ali, his dark features twisting into a snarl.

Chopra turned and peered in confusion behind him.

As he watched, a pair of police constables came bounding out into the courtyard. The first man ran straight into Ganesha, tumbling head over heels over the little elephant, his flailing feet catching the man behind. The second constable tripped and stumbled to the ground, accidentally discharging the rifle that he had been carrying. The gunshot exploded into the night, ringing out over the fort's ramparts.

'Who's firing? Who ordered you to fire? I want him alive, I tell you!'

That voice! Chopra froze.

And in that instant another figure tumbled into the courtyard, the last person on earth that Chopra expected to see . . . Assistant Commissioner of Police Suresh Rao, Chopra's former commanding officer and long-time nemesis.

For a surreal moment the ground swayed beneath Chopra's feet . . . What the hell was Rao doing here?

And then Rao was barking again. 'Get up, you dolts! Arrest him!'

Chopra looked behind him, but Ali had vanished, taking the bags with him. He assumed he had fled down the southern bastion. 'He's gone down the steps,' he said urgently, moving towards the bastion.

'Freeze right there, Chopra! You're not going anywhere.'

It finally dawned on Chopra that Rao intended to arrest *him*.

'Have you lost your mind, Rao? The kidnapper is getting away!'

'What kidnapper? The only person up here is you.'

Chopra gaped at the two constables training their rifles on him. 'I always knew you were an egomaniac, Rao,' he finally ground out. 'But this time you've gone too far. A man's life is at stake, goddammit!'

Rao moved forward and pushed his round, moustachioed face up towards Chopra's. 'We received a tip-off. Kidnapper at Madh Fort. And look who I find when I get here! As far as I'm concerned, I have the right man. This is the end of the line for you, my friend.'

'Even *you* can't possibly think you could get away with something this preposterous.'

'You have no idea what I can get away with,' Rao hissed under his breath. 'Take him away!'

He stormed back through the entranceway.

The two constables exchanged looks. 'What about the elephant?' said one. 'Do we arrest it too?'

His partner scanned the courtyard. But there was no sign of Ganesha. 'What elephant? There was no elephant. Don't ever mention that elephant again.' He advanced on Chopra with his rifle and jabbed him in the back. 'Come on. Get moving.'

Chopra glanced back over the courtyard. Where had Ganesha gone? Wherever it was, he hoped the little elephant was safe. As for Vicky Verma . . . there was nothing he could do for him now. Vicky's fate was out of his hands.

It was his own fate that had begun to worry him.

He knew, from long experience, that ACP Rao was a vindictive man. They had clashed too often in the past, most recently on the Koh-i-noor diamond case, where Rao had blamed Chopra for humiliating him.

It seemed that the ACP had finally stumbled across the opportunity to take his revenge.

Chopra could only pray that the man would come to his senses soon.

But he doubted it.

DANCING FOR THE MASTER

Rangwalla woke to the sound of a cockerel crowing.

For a moment he lay there, listening for the soft noises of his wife. He was a light sleeper and usually awoke before her, savouring the predawn hours before his children would begin their day in a clatter of unseemly energy. And then memory snapped back and he recalled where he was.

Stifling his incipient panic, he arose, washed, then wrapped himself in the detestable sari.

He stared at his reflection in the mirror, and once again shook his bewigged head. 'Insane,' he muttered.

He found the other eunuchs gathered together in a large, brightly lit room that looked out onto ornate gardens. The watchman, Shantaram, was wandering among the shrubbery with a steel watering can. A refectory table had been set up in the centre of the room and a magnificent breakfast had been laid out on silver swan platters.

Rangwalla fell into a seat and poured himself a glass of pomegranate juice.

'I'll say this much for the Master,' mumbled Parvati to his right, 'he knows how to put on a good spread.'

'You tell him that when he's throttling the life out of you in one of his kinky games,' muttered Rupa.

'I'll bet he's a virgin,' rumbled Mamta, chewing on a freshly baked parotta liberally smeared with ghee. 'I knew a man once. Fifty years old and never so much as looked at a woman. But once I coaxed him out of his cage he was like a tiger with its tail on fire.'

'What if he's not a man?' said Rangwalla.

The conversation stopped, and they all looked at him. 'Here, you don't think . . . ?' said Rupa.

'I merely point out that we shouldn't jump to conclusions. A good investigator keeps an open mind,' said Rangwalla, quoting Chopra.

Parvati squinted at him curiously. 'Sonali dear, you sound like Byomkesh Bakshi.'

Rangwalla coloured at the reference to a popular fictional detective. He had almost given the game away. 'I read a lot,' he said gruffly.

At that moment Premchand materialised in the room.

'That man walks like a ghost,' muttered Rupa, under her breath.

'After breakfast it is the Master's pleasure that you dance for him,' announced the munshi.

'Well, at least that doesn't sound too taxing,' said Parvati. She picked up a slice of watermelon and sank her teeth into it with succulent relish.

Premchand led them out into the gardens.

Fruit trees filled the air with a melange of scents. Birdsong resonated from the branches. Occasionally, Parvati stopped to pick mangoes and lychees, wrapping them into a knot at the tip of her sari. 'For later,' she winked.

The sun felt strange on Rangwalla's raw cheeks. He noticed that peacocks strolled everywhere among the trees. The Master clearly had a penchant for the beautiful birds.

On a wide lawn backing up against the western face of the great haveli, a musical troupe had set up their instruments – tabla drums, a sitar, a double-reeded sundari, a harmonium, an alghoza double-flute.

Premchand clapped his hands. 'Whenever you are ready.'

'But where is the Master?' asked Mamta.

'The Master is watching,' said Premchand primly. He nodded up at the haveli.

Rangwalla panned his gaze around the façade. There were any number of openings through which the Master could peer down without being seen at the strange tableau he had commanded.

'I suppose it's up to me to show this Master what his money has purchased,' said Rupa, striding purposefully into the centre of the lawn. 'Out of the way, ladies.'

She peered haughtily at the musicians then bade them begin.

As the melody took hold, Rupa began to dance.

Rangwalla had to admit, the prickly eunuch was very good. She appeared to have been classically trained. As she whirled around, occasionally stamping a foot to the rhythm of the music, or snapping her wrists together, her belled anklets jingled and her sari whipped about in a riot of colour. The other eunuchs began to clap in time and yelled encouragement.

When the dance finished, Rupa strutted back to the others, a preening look on her gaunt features.

One by one the eunuchs danced.

Eventually, it was Rangwalla's turn. He blanched. 'Not me!' he protested. 'I can't dance.'

'What do you mean you can't dance?' said Mamta in astonishment.

'I mean that I *can not* dance,' repeated Rangwalla.

'But you are a eunuch. All eunuchs can dance. It is what we do.'

'Not this eunuch,' said Rangwalla, through gritted teeth.

'What is the delay?' came Premchand's voice.

'Look, I don't care if you don't know how to dance,' growled Mamta. 'You have no choice. Now get out there!' She gave Rangwalla a push.

Sweating with panic, Rangwalla stumbled out onto the lawn. He tried to recall the last time he had attempted anything so sordid as a dance. He would rather be charging into a warehouse full of armed gangsters than doing what he was doing now.

'Come on, you idiot!' hissed Rupa.

Rangwalla closed his eyes and began to move around in a circle. He kicked out a leg, then an arm. He clapped. He jiggled in a horrendous parody of something he had seen on television, stumbled, righted himself, and turned the movement into a farcical about-face with his arms stuck out for balance.

He continued in this vein for ten excruciating minutes before finally staggering back to the others.

'You're the worst dancer I have ever seen,' declared Rupa.

'Never mind,' said Kavita, giving his arm an encouraging squeeze. 'We all have different talents.'

Rangwalla noticed that Parvati was staring at him strangely. But before she had a chance to say anything Premchand spoke again. 'Now the Master wishes to hear you sing.'

Rangwalla groaned.

It seemed that his ordeal had only just begun.

WELCOME TO HELL

Chopra stared at the ceiling. Above him a fly staggered along a crack in the grey stone. Suddenly, a gecko darted in from the corner and snapped up the fly. Its head swivelled down to fix Chopra with two baleful eyes.

Chopra shivered.

He hated the creatures, had done since he'd been a boy.

He sat up, slid off his bunk, and began pacing the cold flagstones of his cell. On the cell's other bunk the second occupant of the room snored on, occasionally mumbling incoherently under his breath.

Chopra resisted the urge to pinch himself.

He knew only too well that he was not dreaming.

The events of the previous night tumbled around his mind, but no matter how many times he reviewed them, he could still make no sense of his predicament.

After Rao had arrested him he had been bundled into the back of a police truck and taken to a police station where, having confiscated his phone, Rao left him locked in the truck while he had disappeared for over an hour. Chopra's constitutional rights were irrelevant. This was India and he was neither famous nor wealthy. His rights as a prisoner were exactly those his captors deemed them to be.

Eventually, Rao had returned.

He gazed at Chopra through the bars of the truck. 'I told you one day you would pay for your arrogance,' he finally said. 'I have made arrangements for you, Chopra. You have troubled me for the last time. Goodbye.'

He turned and stalked away.

Chopra could only sit helplessly as he was driven out of the city.

Four hours later, the lights of Mumbai long vanished in the darkness behind them, the truck pulled into the lee of a forbidding stone building surrounded by dusty fields. Chopra recognised the bleak fortress instantly.

He had been here twice before, both times escorting a prisoner.

For this was Gouripur Jail, a rural prison where hardened criminals were sent to serve lengthy sentences under the eyes of prison guards whose brutality had become legend. Gouripur Jail was where the scum of the earth ended up; the gutter into which the worst inmates of the Indian penal system were eventually swept, far away from the civilisation whose rules they had chosen to forsake.

And now Chopra was here too.

As dawn was breaking he had been hauled out of the truck and dragged, still protesting, through the jail's arched entranceway. Behind him the fifteen-feet-high cast-iron gates had ground shut with an ominous clang. To the ululations of a dawn call to prayer, he had been marched through stone corridors to the warden's office.

The warden, a small man with a perfectly round, lacquered head, had smiled at him from behind a bare desk. 'Welcome, Chopra,' he said, gesturing towards a chair. 'My name is Mukherjee. May I offer you some tea? Fresh from Darjeeling.'

Chopra sat down awkwardly, his hands cuffed before him. 'There has been a mistake,' he said.

'Ah!' smiled the warden, tapping his small white teeth with a spoon. 'If only I had a rupee for every time I have heard that particular refrain. Why, I would be as rich as Tata himself.'

'I am a former policeman,' said Chopra, reining in his temper. 'I have an identity card in my pocket. You will see that I am a special advisor to the Chief Minister.'

'Of course you are,' said Mukherjee. 'Of course you are.'

He did not bother to ask for the card. Instead, he slurped at his tea, which he drank from a delicate porcelain cup. He pointed at a shadow on the wall. 'Do you know what used to be there? It was a clock. I removed it on the day of my fifth anniversary here. You see, the very worst thing about running a prison such as this is ennui. The death of the soul by a thousand cuts. I was not born to this life, Chopra. I am a poet at heart. I have even had a modest volume of my work published. Nothing to send the literary giants of this world scurrying for cover, but I take a quiet pleasure in my endeavours. One must bow before one's muse, yes?' Slurp, slurp. 'Do you know how many years I have been here? In this graveyard of the mind? Ten years. Ten long years in the middle of nowhere, surrounded by murderers and rapists, arsonists and whoremongers. At first I thought it would be the ideal place to hone my talent. A haven away from the hustle and bustle of city life. But now it is all I can do not to smash my brains out against these very walls.' Slurp, slurp. 'And then fate drops the star of fortune into my lap.'

He set down the cup. 'Last night I received a call. From a, let us say, political heavyweight. He tells me that a prisoner will shortly be arriving at my little fortress, a man by the name of Chopra. This Chopra, I am told, is a special case. He is to be held at Gouripur at the High Court's discretion, pending trial. Indefinitely held, incognito. No phone calls, no contact of any kind. I do not know what you have done, Chopra, or perhaps I should say, I do not know *who* you have upset, but it does not pay to make the gods angry.' The warden drummed his fingers on the desk. 'I find myself facing a moral dilemma. The poet in me shrieks at the injustice of it all. And yet, one man's misfortune is another's silver lining, yes? I suppose there is a subtle poetry in this, too . . . What do I long for? A princedom by the sea, a quiet place where I might break a lance with like-minded souls. If I follow my instructions, if I simply do what is requested of me, then I will be set free. I will escape the ignoble irony of being a prisoner in my own prison. I will be *transferred*. To another post, perhaps even out to Kolkata, the cultural capital of our great nation. Instead of child murderers and bandits, I will spend my days in the company of lyricists and wordsmiths. I must say that I find the prospect . . . soothing.'

'And what happens to me?' asked Chopra.

'You have a choice before you. Settle in and do your time quietly. Or kick up a fuss. If you should choose the latter, then I am afraid your stay here could be most unpleasant. After all, how do you think your fellow inmates would react should they discover a policeman has taken up residence in their midst?'

Chopra bristled at the implied threat. 'I am innocent,' he growled.

Mukherjee smiled. 'I knew a man who once tried to prove to me, a priori, that he was immortal. In the midst of his soliloquy he was struck down by a heart attack that froze him stone dead in his chair.'

He picked up a bell and rang it.

Two warders entered and lifted Chopra briskly to his feet.

'This is wrong and you know it,' said Chopra, through gritted teeth.

Mukherjee grimaced. 'The world is an imperfect place. I wish that it were not. I urge you to consider Tagore's words: "If you cry because the sun has gone out of your life, your tears will prevent you from seeing the stars." '

That had been a few short hours ago.

Since then, Chopra had been stripped, given a white prison uniform stamped with black chevrons, and dumped into a cold cell on the second tier of one of the prison's ten inmate blocks.

His cellmate had slept through his arrival, which was just as well. As the guards had walked away Chopra had held in the urge to protest his innocence. In one thing Mukherjee had been correct – Chopra could not let his fellow inmates discover that he had once been a policeman.

He had paced the cell in silent fury, before flinging himself onto the bunk, his mind aflame with bitterness, and the first intimations of a genuine terror. But, try as he might, he could not think of his next move. Eventually, he felt his eyelids drooping as sheer mental exhaustion took its toll.

Half an hour later a banging sounded along the corridors, waking him from a fitful sleep.

The prisoners were assembled outside their cells, then marched out into the courtyard. Chopra was ordered to stand with a group of other new arrivals.

A fierce sun burned off the last tendrils of morning fog.

An enormous man emerged from a whitewashed stucco barrack set apart at one end of the courtyard, and swaggered over to the new arrivals. Chopra regarded the colossal bulk, the thick, shaven head, the lantern jaw. One eye was white with disease. His scarred knuckles were like walnuts, and his biceps strained the sleeves of his black uniform, which marked him out as a prisoner who had been conferred the privilege of supervising his peers.

The huge man washed the gathered inmates with a baleful look.

'My name is Buta Bheem Singh. When I was twelve years old I shot my father through the eye with a crossbow and strangled my mother. I once killed a man with a kettle because he spilled my tea. When they finally caught up with me they sentenced me to death. But the gallows collapsed when they tried to hang me. They called it an act of God and gave me a life sentence instead. I have been here seventeen years and I have killed seventeen men in that time. They can't do anything to me. In here I am God and the Devil. When I tell you to do something you will do it. If you don't, I will kill you.'

Chopra heard one of the new men whimper behind him.

Having delivered his welcome speech Singh wandered away.

They returned to their block groups, where they were split into work gangs and bundled into labour trucks. The gates of the prison creaked open, and the trucks roared out from the compound, swirling dust in their wake.

An hour later they were deposited at a sandstone quarry.

Here, the prisoners were handed pickaxes and rock hammers, and ordered to begin hacking away at the quarry face or breaking down hewn rocks. Others piled the broken rock into rusted wheelbarrows and dumped the contents into industrial trucks, which roared out of the quarry at regular intervals, bound, no doubt, for the insatiable construction sites of the big city.

Chopra stood in the sun, looking around him at the dust and noise. He was reminded of the workers who reshaped Mumbai's profile on a daily basis, faces bleached by dust as they broke cinder blocks into rubble, an army of ants that never stopped. He glanced down at the manacles that shackled his ankles together. The sheer implausibility of his predicament froze him.

'You!' growled a voice. 'Those rocks won't break themselves.'

Chopra turned to see the brute Buta Singh glaring at him. Singh was wielding a bullwhip, which he flicked menacingly.

A movement from above made him look up.

Perched on the lip of the quarry, high above the toiling prisoners, a man with a rifle across his knees sat and smoked. Behind him, in the cloudless sky, vultures circled, riding the thermal currents that rose off the baked earth below.

'I would do as he says,' muttered a voice to Chopra's right. 'His patience is as limited as his intelligence.'

Chopra hefted his pickaxe and struck the wall with all his might.

Chips flew in all directions, one slashing his cheek. A droplet of blood welled up, fell, and was instantly soaked up by the dust at his feet.

'Not like that!' admonished the voice. 'What are you trying to do? Bring down the cliff? Don't exert yourself. Work when he is looking. The rest of the time, *pretend* to work. Here, watch me.'

Chopra looked around at his neighbour, a diminutive, elderly man with a goatish grey beard and a white skullcap. He recognised the man – it was his cellmate.

He watched as the man tapped at the rock face with a practised rhythm. 'My name is Iqbal Yusuf,' he added eventually.

'Chopra,' said Chopra.

'You have the look about you.'

'What look?' Chopra began tapping the wall, copying Yusuf's metronomic movement.

'As if you don't belong. As if you can't quite believe that you are here. You must lose this look. This look sends a signal to the others. It is like a wounded deer in a field of lions.'

'What do I do?'

'Act like a hardened criminal.'

'I am not a criminal at all,' said Chopra.

Yusuf sighed. 'Only God knows what we truly are, my friend. But for now, you must decide whether you will be a deer or a lion. Proclaiming that you are not a criminal will not help your cause, of that much I can assure you.'

A ruckus behind them made Chopra turn.

He saw another of the new arrivals standing motionless by a rock, weeping. The man was tall, but there was a babyish quality to his bespectacled features, a softness to his frame that spoke of years of good living.

'A political prisoner,' observed Yusuf dryly. 'These days if you upset the wrong people you end up here. That is not to say he is not a criminal. Whatever he has done, he made a bad mistake.'

A sense of nervous dread stole over Chopra as Buta Singh approached the man, crunching over the stony ground in his black sandals. 'Why have you stopped working?' he growled.

The quarry fell silent as, one by one, the inmates turned to watch the hapless newcomer.

'I shouldn't be here,' sniffled the man. 'I'm not a criminal like you. I merely moved some numbers around. What's wrong with that? Everyone does it. It was *my* cream!' he yelled suddenly. The man had worked himself up, as if he had forgotten where he was, and who he was speaking to.

'You have been badly treated?' said Singh sweetly. 'You shouldn't be here with scum like us, yes? You should be somewhere nice, where they give you an oil massage before bed, and allow you to watch TV all day?'

'Yes! Yes!' nodded the prisoner eagerly. 'I knew you would understand!'

'Let me see what I can do,' said Singh. He turned around, tapping his lip thoughtfully with a meaty finger.

Then, in one fluid movement, he spun back and lashed the bullwhip at the hopeful prisoner, catching him across the cheek.

The man shrieked in pain, his spectacles flying off to crack on a nearby rock, blood spilling on to his uniform. He fell to the floor writhing as Buta Singh continued to lash at him.

Finally, he lay still, whimpering pitiably.

'It is your first day,' growled Singh, wiping a sleeve across his brow. 'So I will be lenient. The next time . . .'

He turned, and stalked away.

The prisoners resumed work with redoubled vigour.

'He is insane,' whispered Chopra, the metallic taste of fear settling at the back of his throat.

'Of course,' said Yusuf. 'What did you expect? Welcome to hell, my friend.'

A TUTOR FOR IRFAN

Poppy, balanced precariously on the cane stool, hooked the last of the marigold garlands to the nail on the wall, then stepped down to examine her handiwork.

Criss-crossed by garlands of flowers and paper rosettes, the office was a profusion of colour.

From the sofa Poppy's mother, Poornima Devi, sniffed disapprovingly. 'I suppose you intend to turn the rest of the restaurant into a brothel too,' she carped.

Poppy sighed. 'It *is* the festival of colour, Mother.'

'Then why don't you decorate *me* while you're at it? A widow in her white widow's sari painted every colour under the sun like some streetwalking strumpet. I am sure your father would approve.'

'My father loved Holi,' said Poppy.

'That's because he was a bigger fool than you!'

Poppy was too tired to argue. The thought irritated her and she pushed it to one side. She was not used to being tired. She had always considered herself possessed of an exceptional level of energy, but lately she had been finding herself overcome by sudden bouts of fatigue, and in the middle of the day too! Ever since she had begun her job at the St Xavier Catholic School for Boys, in fact. Between that, managing her home, spending her spare time at the restaurant, and looking after Irfan, Ganesha, and her husband, she had more than enough to do, consuming every hour God threw her way. She did not resent any of these duties – they filled out her life, and gave her a happiness that she could not have imagined just a short year ago.

And yet, there was that matter of finding her eyes closing when she least expected it, and sleep stealing over her at the most inopportune times.

Being the Modern Indian Woman wasn't easy, she reflected, no matter what Sunita Shetty said on her show . . . Am I getting old? she wondered briefly.

She dismissed the heretical thought immediately. A woman in her early forties, old? Nonsense. Her mother was old. Chef Lucknowwallah was old. Her boss at St Xavier, Principal Augustus Lobo, was old. But Poppy . . . Poppy was as young as the day she had married Chopra.

Talking of her husband, where in the world was he?

When she had awoken that morning, there had been no sign of him. Of course, ever since he had started the detective agency it had necessitated him sneaking off at odd times of the day or night to pursue some unwary suspect. It was a compromise she had learned to live with, the price of her husband being able to continue doing what he loved since retiring from the force. But they had agreed he would always notify her in advance. She would prepare a tiffin, and lecture him on the need to take his angina tablets. He would roll his eyes, but take the tiffin anyway. And it was always empty the next morning when he stumbled in bleary-eyed, having wasted another night playing Mr Big Shot Private Detective, when he should have been tucked up in bed beside her.

At least he had promised to take things easy. She hadn't forgotten about his ailing heart even if he had, gallivanting around like the star of his own action movie.

But this time it was different. He had told her nothing.

He had not come home, and she had been surprised to discover that he had not even phoned her. She had tried calling him, but he hadn't picked up. Then it had been time for her to go to work, forcing her to put the matter to one side.

It had been an exceptionally busy day at St Xavier – a sports day for the students – and she had barely had time to sit down. Yet she had called him again and again, to no avail. With each call her anxiety grew.

When she had finally arrived at the restaurant it was to discover a very agitated Ganesha pacing the compound. The fact that Ganesha had returned but her husband had not convinced her that something was deeply amiss. According to the staff the little elephant had refused his feed. He had trotted over to Poppy and immediately wrapped his trunk around her arm, tugging at her in a gesture she knew signified his anxiety.

There was a knock on the door, and one of the waiters entered with Poornima's supper.

The old woman inspected the contents. 'I swear that oaf's cooking gets worse by the day. Can't he see that I am an ailing woman?'

Poppy sighed again.

Earlier that week her mother had twisted an ankle. Rather than stay at home she had chosen to continue attending the restaurant. 'You don't expect me to leave that dolt in charge of the place, do you?' Poornima had said, meaning Chef Lucknowwallah. 'The man can barely cook and remember to breathe at the same time. You'll be bankrupted in a week.'

The long-simmering feud between the chef and Poornima had been a source of much consternation to both Poppy and Chopra. Both were combative types, and proprietorial about the restaurant, neither willing to concede an inch. They existed in a state of uneasy alliance, which fractured all too frequently.

A second knock sounded on the door. 'There is a woman here to see you, madam,' said the waiter.

Leaving her cantankerous mother to take a rickshaw home with her supper, Poppy walked through the kitchen and out on to the rear veranda.

The woman waiting for her on the planed boards of the veranda was tall, broad-shouldered, and dressed in a staid navy blue sari with a white trim. Her thick grey hair was pulled into a severe bun, and her dark face was flat and sombre. She clutched a bamboo cane in her right hand. The hand had been badly burned; the scars were old but vivid.

There was something about the woman's forthright gaze that bothered Poppy.

'I have three conditions,' the woman said. 'They are non-negotiable.'

'Excuse me?'

'Firstly, my salary. I require five thousand rupees per month, not a paisa less.'

Poppy's mouth fell open, but nothing emerged.

'Secondly,' said the woman, without waiting for a reply, 'two meals per day will be provided by you.'

'But—' Poppy began.

'Lastly, and most critically, I will do things my way. There will be no interference from anyone. That goes for you, too. Do you agree to these conditions?'

Poppy was not often at a loss for words, but this was one of those rare occasions. The woman's manner had disconcerted her, but now she found herself rallying. 'Madam, I don't know who you are, but you are clearly either insane or labouring under some gross misapprehension.'

'This is Poppy's Restaurant, is it not?'

'Yes.'

'You are Poppy, are you not?'

'Yes.'

'There is a boy called Irfan who lives here, yes?'

Poppy hesitated. Sudden alarm shot through her. 'Who are you?' she asked, her tone now wary.

'I am his new tutor,' asserted the woman.

Poppy gaped at the woman. 'Tutor? But-but . . . who *hired* you?'

'*I* hired me,' said the woman. 'My name is Usha Umrigar. I would provide you with references but they will not be necessary. I have been teaching for over thirty years; that is all you need to know.'

And then Poppy realised what had been bothering her. 'But you are blind!' she gasped.

'And clearly you are not. Now, where is the boy?'

Poppy felt as if she had walked into a surreal plot twist. Of course, it was common knowledge that Poppy harboured dreams of educating young Irfan. But the boy himself had made a mockery of her well-intentioned efforts. Irfan had grown up on the streets, surviving on his wits. He simply did not see the benefits of an education. And the harder she tried, the greater his resistance.

Over the past weeks a succession of tutors had arrived and left the restaurant.

Some had simply proven unsuitable to the task, such as Baba Peshwa, an indolent Brahmin who snorted snuff from a lacquered snuffbox, until Irfan had replaced it with chilli powder. And Poppy herself had discovered old Master Madhurao – who was eighty-three and suffered from chronic piles – fast asleep on the veranda where Irfan's lessons took place. Finally, there had been Haribhai Khot, a pinched-faced man from the south, who, unbeknown to Poppy, had been suffering from marital problems and would pause in the middle of his lessons to launch a furious invective against 'woomankind', much to the delight of Irfan. It was the only time he paid attention.

'Are you really a teacher?' asked Poppy.

The woman reached out a hand and found her face. Poppy submitted to the gentle examination. 'You seem like a sensible woman,' said Usha eventually. 'My understanding is that the boy is not keen on being taught. Let me try. I think he will let me teach him.'

Poppy heard the sincerity in the woman's voice. It carried a reassurance that filled her with hope. 'I'll fetch him,' she said.

When Irfan arrived – clad in his shocking-pink restaurant uniform – he stopped in front of the woman and peered at her curiously.

'Good morning, Irfan,' said Usha. 'I am your new tutor.'

Irfan's face crunched into a frown. Something about the woman's voice . . . 'Who are you?' he asked.

'Don't you remember me?'

Irfan continued to stare at her in puzzlement . . . and then it dawned on him. 'You're the Mad Woman!'

'Irfan!' admonished Poppy.

'Rumours of my madness have been greatly exaggerated,' smiled Usha.

'But where did you get those clothes?' persisted Irfan. 'And your hair! It's so clean!'

'Some very kind people at the local Destitute Women's Centre helped me. I could have gone there long ago but I wasn't ready. Now I am. The question is: are you ready for *my* help?' She lowered her blind gaze towards the boy. 'Now, we will study each day for two hours. You will work very hard and there will be no more nonsense. Are we agreed?'

Irfan looked up at the imposing woman. Then he looked at Poppy. Something passed over his walnut-brown features. Finally, he mumbled, 'Yes, madam.'

'You have a good heart, Irfan, and this is fine. But in this world if you do not have an education you are at the mercy of others. Do you wish to be at the mercy of others?'

'No, madam!'

'Then it is settled. Now, why don't we have a little chat first? Perhaps over supper?' Usha tilted her head towards Poppy.

'Yes, of course,' said Poppy happily. 'I will see to it right away.'

She walked off, leaving Irfan and the old woman to seat themselves on the veranda and begin their first lesson.

Her smile lasted only until she reached her office, where she discovered Bijli Verma, accompanied by an ashen-faced Lal.

Poppy's instinctive delight at seeing the famed actress – of whom she had long been a fan – evaporated as Bijli said, angrily: 'I asked for Chopra. Who are you?'

'I am his wife,' replied Poppy stiffly, taken aback. 'And he is not here.'

This seemed to incense Bijli, and the actress began pacing the room, her sari swishing around her ankles. 'Where is he? Where is that rogue? What has he done with the money? *Where is my son!*'

Overcoming her shock, Poppy drew herself up. No one shouted at her in her own restaurant, not even a legendary screen goddess. 'My husband informed me that he was working for you. But that is *all* he told me. I have no idea what money you're talking about, or where your son is. And if you don't lower your voice, I'll have you thrown out,' she added hotly.

The two women glowered at each other, the air crackling between them, Lal careful to stay out of the way lest he be inadvertently incinerated.

'Yesterday, your husband left my home with a considerable sum of money,' Bijli eventually ground out. 'He was supposed to deliver it to the men who have kidnapped my son. But he never called back, and Vicky has not been returned. I want to know where Chopra is. I want to know where my son is.'

Poppy felt the bottom drop out of her stomach. Her knees trembled, but she refused to buckle before this woman, despite her worst fears being realised . . . So this was the mysterious case her husband had been working on! What, in God's name, had he got himself into?

She examined Bijli's face, looking behind the anger, sensing the worry that consumed the former actress. A mother's worry. Poppy sighed. 'I don't know where he is. He didn't come home last night. He won't answer his phone.'

From her expression, Poppy saw that it was Bijli's turn to feel the earth tremble below her feet. 'But – but he *promised* me,' she said hoarsely. 'He promised to bring back my son.'

They stared at each other, the mutual anger leaking away, until Poppy guided her to the sofa. She ordered tea, and listened as the whole sorry tale spilled from the distraught Bijli, her sense of alarm growing by the second. The words of her colleague Malhotra came back to her now: the notion that a raging fanatic had targeted Bijli, and might have crossed paths with her husband, was almost too much to bear.

'Don't you think we should involve the police now?' asked Poppy. 'I mean, your son is still missing, and now so is my husband. You say he took a ransom to exchange for your son. If he hasn't returned, and hasn't contacted you – or me – then something has gone badly wrong. I know my husband. He is the most honourable person I have ever met. If he had accomplished his mission he would have brought Vicky back to you, safe and sound.'

Bijli stared at her, perhaps weighing the sincerity in her eyes. 'I believe you,' she said eventually. 'But what am I to think? Your husband has vanished. I sincerely hope that no harm has befallen him, but I *cannot* risk involving the police. The kidnappers have expressly forbidden it. All I can do is hope that somehow there is a reasonable explanation for what has happened. But I am afraid, deathly afraid. I can't move forwards and I can't move back. Not until I know Vicky is safe.' She hovered on the edge of tears.

Poppy, who was being eaten alive by her own worry for Chopra, squeezed her hand. 'We must be patient. We must be brave.' Her insides trembled as she willed herself to believe these words.

A clamouring sounded outside the door to the office, and then, suddenly, it swung back, and Chef Lucknowwallah backpedalled into the room, waving a ladle around and yelling, 'Ho! Ho! You can't just barge in here! Who do you think you are?' He was followed in by a gang of thickset, unsavoury-looking men.

The largest of these – wearing a dark Nehru jacket and sunglasses – spotted Bijli Verma, and brought his palms together in greeting. 'Ram ram, Bijli. How are you today?'

'Pyarelal?' said Bijli, rising to her feet. 'What are *you* doing here?'

'I must ask you the same question. Should you not be tending to your son? Ensuring that he rises from his sickbed and returns to the set as soon as possible?'

Bijli's eyes narrowed. 'Did Das send you to threaten me? Have you been following me around?'

'Not at all. We are merely concerned friends of Vicky.' His mouth slithered into a smile. He turned to Poppy. 'And how is Mr Chopra?'

It was Poppy's turn to glare. She had instantly sensed the menace emanating from the big man. 'What concern is that of yours?'

Pyarelal's smile widened. 'My concern applies to all matters pertaining to Vicky. And my understanding is that your husband is now, shall we say, an *involved* party?'

'I don't know what you're talking about. And my husband isn't here.'

'That is a shame,' said Pyarelal. He tapped a heavy hand against the side of his leg.

'Look, if you don't get out of here right now I'll call the authorities,' interrupted Lucknowwallah.

'No!' said Bijli.

'No!' echoed Poppy.

'We were just leaving,' said Pyarelal, flashing another menacing smile. His men backed out of the room. Pyarelal turned as he reached the door. 'Isn't it strange how easily people seem to disappear in this city of ours? Ram ram.' He left these final words hanging threateningly in the air.

'Who was that?' asked Poppy, once the door had closed.

'A man I don't trust, who works for a man I don't like,'

replied Bijli. She turned to face Poppy. 'If your husband contacts you, will you call me?'

'Of course,' said Poppy. 'And if he contacts you first, *you* must call *me*.'

'And if he contacts neither of us, then what shall we do?'

The two women stared at each other. 'One thing is for sure,' said Poppy, forcing out a grim smile. 'Neither of us is the type of woman to stand by and do *nothing*.'

Bijli nodded tightly. 'In that you are right. If anything happens to my son, I will tear this city apart.'

'And if anything happens to my husband, I will be right there by your side.' Poppy led Bijli to the door. 'In the meantime, I will pray for both his and Vicky's safe return.'

'I don't believe in prayer,' said Bijli. 'But I thank you anyway. Let us hope God listens to you, because he surely stopped listening to me a long time ago.'

A VIOLENT ENCOUNTER WITH THE PAST

If Chopra had thought that his trials for the day were over once they had returned from the quarry he was mistaken. After a meal of thin lentil soup and stale chapatti, he was informed by his cellmate Iqbal Yusuf that they were now required to spend the evening assisting in the quartermaster's storeroom. 'My previous cellmate used to assist there too,' explained Yusuf. 'You will take his place.'

'What happened to him?'

'I'll tell you another time,' said Yusuf, not meeting Chopra's eyes.

The storeroom was located at one end of the enormous compound, together with a cluster of whitewashed administrative buildings.

Working with a dozen other prisoners Chopra helped unload sacks of grain and lentils from the incoming delivery trucks under the gimlet eyes of the quartermaster, a broad, flatfooted prisoner with greasy hair and double chins wearing another of the black uniforms denoting rank within the dubious prison hierarchy. He couldn't help but notice that baskets of vegetables and fruit were among the provisions, and yet such fare had been noticeable by its absence in the prison canteen at lunch.

His stomach growled.

'When do we get those?' he asked.

'Never,' said Yusuf. 'The quartermaster sells the good produce on. We get the refuse that's left over.'

An hour later Chopra found himself stacking shelves inside a dimly lit storeroom. Cockroaches skittered across the cool stone. After the dust and heat of the quarry it was almost pleasant in here. For the first time in hours his churning thoughts settled, spiralling inevitably towards his predicament.

But before he could dwell on the matter he heard the door creak open behind him.

He turned to find a big man with a stubbled jaw hulking in the doorway. His eyes dropped to the knife clutched in the man's fist. A spear of alarm embedded itself in Chopra's chest. 'I have no feud with you, friend,' he said, his heart pounding.

'That's where you're wrong, *friend*,' said the man, stepping forward. 'You don't recognise me, do you? Well, I recognise *you*, Chopra. I knew you the moment I set eyes on you in the quarry. If I hadn't been chained up I would have finished you there and then.'

Chopra squinted at the man. The beery face was beginning to look familiar. 'Rastogi,' he said eventually.

'It is good that you remember me. It is important to know who is about to end your life.'

Chopra ransacked his memory.

He had arrested Rustom Rastogi ten years earlier. Rastogi had been an enforcer for a local gang. Back then he was rumoured to have killed half-a-dozen men. But it was for the murder of his young wife that he'd finally been convicted. Rastogi had stumbled home drunk one evening and his wife had refused his advances.

That was all it had taken.

Clearly, Rastogi held a grudge.

The former gangster advanced. Chopra backed away.

Rastogi charged. Chopra plucked a tin from the shelf beside him, and flung it at the demented prisoner before leaping sideways. The can ricocheted off Rastogi's skull, eliciting a howl of rage. Chopra crashed into a shelf, taking it down with him, tins raining down on him as he fell to the floor.

He thrashed about, struggling to regain his feet, but his efforts were cut short by a heavy foot that lashed into his ribs, then his stomach.

The air went out of him.

Coughing and wheezing, Chopra fell back, spots flashing before his eyes. A shadow blurred in and out of focus above him.

'I am going to enjoy this,' hissed Rastogi.

Chopra heard the shuffle of bare feet across concrete, and then a shriek. He saw Rastogi fall back, clawing at his eyes. The knife clattered to the floor.

'Come on,' hissed a voice in Chopra's ear, as he was hauled upright.

Iqbal Yusuf placed Chopra's arm around his shoulders, then limped him out from the storeroom.

Behind them Rastogi continued to thrash around on the floor, weeping pitiably.

'What did you . . . do to . . . him?' Chopra gasped.

'Chilli powder,' said Yusuf. 'You'd be surprised how many uses one can find for the stuff.'

That night Chopra lay on his bunk replaying the events of the day. His muscles fluttered with fatigue. The back-breaking labour of quarrying rocks had exhausted him. The punishment inflicted by Rustom Rastogi added a secondary chorus of pain – his body registered its protest with each trembling breath.

Iqbal Yusuf, having brought Chopra back to his cell and palpated his ribs with his fingers, had assured him that no bones were broken. Fetching a coconut shell wrapped in old newspaper from beneath his bunk, the old man had smeared a thick paste over Chopra's bruises, making his nose twitch violently at the smell of turmeric.

In the hours since the attack Chopra had learned a great deal more about prison life from his cellmate, none of it good. The only note of optimism had been Yusuf's reassurance that Rastogi would not tell anyone else that he had recognised Chopra.

'How can you be sure of that?' Chopra had asked.

'Because he wants to kill you himself,' replied Yusuf, matter-of-factly.

Chopra wondered just how long the old man had been at Gouripur. Yusuf's brow crinkled with the effort of recollection.

'I don't know,' he said. 'I gave up counting years ago. I remember, a month after I was sentenced, they shot Indira.'

Chopra was aghast. 'But that was thirty years ago! Surely you have served your sentence?'

Yusuf shrugged. 'One year, thirty years. What does it matter to me now? What would I do even if they released me? I have nowhere to go.'

Chopra realised that the old man had become so thoroughly institutionalised that he would be unable to function in the real world, a world that had changed beyond recognition since he had entered the penal system. 'What did you do?' he asked at last. It was the question he had been putting off.

He was not sure that he wanted to know the answer.

Yusuf fell silent. When he finally spoke his voice was weighted with a deep sadness. 'I was a younger man, then. They called it a crime of passion, but that wasn't true, not really. It was a crime of revenge.

'I murdered a man. In cold blood. He was the son of a district collector, a boy, no more than twenty. He attended the same college as my daughter. She was my only child. When we had her something went wrong and we were told we could have no more children. She meant everything to me. So what if I didn't have a boy? She was as good as any boy in my eyes. Clever, beautiful, and the sweetest nature imaginable. I always used to say to her, God must have been in a good mood the day he made you. She told me she was going to become a politician. She was going to *change* things. Help run this country right.' Yusuf paused as the eye of memory took him deep into the past. 'He was a very charismatic boy, the collector's son. My daughter was not impressionable, but he made an impression. He convinced her of many things. That her cause was his cause; that he too wished for change. I discovered afterwards that it was all lies. He was well known for it. It was a game to him.' Yusuf sighed. 'And after he had taken what he wanted, he abandoned her. He had promised marriage and my daughter believed him. When she realised he had betrayed her – that she was left with nothing but the mark of her shame – she confronted him.

'He did not expect this, I suppose. He thought she would simply vanish, like so many others before her. But not *my* daughter.' A note of pride entered the old man's voice. 'The confrontation turned ugly. He ended up strangling her.' Chopra was astounded at the flatness with which the revelation was delivered. 'But he was the collector's son. I knew long before the verdict came down that the court would clear him. The judge said he had acted in self-defence. The boy walked free with his blessings, grinning from ear to ear.' Yusuf stared at the wall. 'Two days later I caught up with him. I stabbed him forty-five times as he sat in his car. And then I walked into a police station, and told them what I had done. I was at peace.'

Chopra was stunned by the terrible tale.

Morality was a spectrum, and the judgements human beings raised against one another could never be explained or understood unless viewed through the prism of context. Chopra had always been a scrupulously moral man. He believed in the ideal of justice while recognising that it was often unattainable, particularly in India with its ineffectual judicial system.

And yet he could not bring himself to condone Yusuf's actions.

Murder was murder. Besides, had Yusuf's terrible revenge solved anything? He had spent his whole life inside these barren walls with the ghost of his murdered daughter. What had happened to his wife in that time? Revenge had its consequences, not just on those it was exacted upon.

Yusuf asked about Chopra, then. The former policeman explained the circumstances that had brought him to Gouripur Jail.

Yusuf scratched his grizzled beard, evaluating Chopra with a thoughtful expression. 'I have had more cellmates than I can remember,' he said eventually. 'Most have claimed to be innocent in one way or another. Yours is the first story I might actually believe.' His brow furrowed. 'If what the warden said to you is true then you are in big trouble. It is easy for a man to disappear in our prisons. Even if Rastogi, or someone else, doesn't kill you, they may simply transfer you elsewhere. They'll keep moving you around until you become another statistic. They have the power. In here we are corn before their sickle.'

'I have a wife. I have friends. They will look for me. A man cannot simply vanish.'

Yusuf burst out in cynical laughter. 'I am living proof, my friend, that when the forces of wealth and power are ranged against you, anything can happen in this great country of ours.'

Chopra considered his words. 'In that case the only option I have is to escape.'

'No one escapes from Gouripur.'

'Are you telling me no one has ever tried?'

'Many have tried. Most have died. That brute Singh is merciless. But he is not the one you must fear. Do you recall the guard above the quarry, with the rifle?'

Chopra nodded.

'His name is Tiwari. He is a former sharpshooter from the army. They discharged him years ago. I believe they thought he was mentally unstable. Hah! Imagine that. Too unstable for the army! They sent him back to his village. A few weeks later he climbed the water tower and started shooting people. He killed five of his neighbours before the tower collapsed on him. He had spent years on the Line of Control up in Kashmir and I suppose he couldn't stop seeing enemies each time he opened his eyes.

'Because he was a soldier they wouldn't give him the death penalty. They didn't want to execute a man who had worn the uniform. And so they gave him to us instead, one more madman for the asylum. And then they put a rifle in his hands.

'He has shot dead twelve men since he arrived. Every once in a while someone thinks they can make a run for it.

But Tiwari never misses. That murderer could shoot the wings off a fly. He sits up there all day, smoking, waiting. You think he's half asleep, and some poor idiot sees a flash of freedom. But it's an illusion. You know, if he wanted to, he could probably escape himself. But he never will. He likes being up there, waiting, like a hawk, for the next man foolish enough to run.'

A mouse crawled out from under Yusuf's bunk. Chopra watched as the old man allowed it to climb up into his palm and nibble on a piece of stale chapatti.

He leaned back against the wall and closed his eyes.

It was becoming clear that his predicament was worse than he had imagined. In his heart, he had believed that Rao's outrageous duplicity would swiftly be discovered and that he would be returned to Mumbai. But now he remembered what Rao had said to him when Chopra had bested him in the Koh-i-noor diamond case. The investigation had discomfited many high-ranking parties in the city. Rao had warned him, through a face suffused with rage, 'You have made enemies of some of the most powerful men in the country. Worse, you have made them look foolish. They will not forget. And they will never forgive.'

The words seemed prophetic now.

Chopra thought about Poppy, about what must be going through her mind. He had promised to stay out of trouble, and yet fate seemed determined to undermine his good intentions. And to vanish without so much as a goodbye! He cringed at the thought of what she would do to him if she ever got hold of him again.

Perhaps he was safest in here, he thought, ruefully, far from her wrath.

His thoughts lingered on the life he had so recently left behind. Already it seemed unreal, a shimmering veil beyond which lay another man's cosseted existence. Mornings at the restaurant, the smell of Chef's carrot-and-onion bhajis, Rangwalla arriving in a breathless rush, Irfan slipping into the office to give him a hug, Ganesha rooting with his trunk in Chopra's pocket for the bar of Cadbury's Dairy Milk chocolate he always brought along for the little elephant.

Karma, he thought. Once again, it all boiled down to fate.

To wrest his mind from his seemingly hopeless situation he turned his thoughts to the Verma case, reviewing what he had learned before his investigations had been so unceremoniously cut short.

Chopra had long been a devotee of Sherlock Holmes – particularly as played by Basil Rathbone in the forties – and wished that he had his calabash pipe with him. He did not smoke, but he liked to chew on the pipe while he pondered.

He cast his mind back to the ransom drop at the Madh Fort.

Firstly, he considered how Rao might have found out about the exchange. Who had informed him? Why? Who gained by sabotaging the safe recovery of Vicky Verma?

He had too few facts to attempt an answer.

Meanwhile, Ali had slipped away from the fort and vanished into the night while Rao had been engaged in arresting Chopra. The ransom had vanished with him . . . But what had happened next? Had Ali released Vicky? Or had Chopra's worst fears been realised? Was Bijli Verma even now being summoned to the morgue to identify the body of her son? It depressed him bitterly to realise that she would blame Chopra for such a turn of events. He hated the thought of letting Bijli down.

Meanwhile, the kidnapper was still out there, somewhere.

Ali.

But how was Ali connected to P.K. Das? It made sense to Chopra that Das's organised-crime backers would use low-rung operatives to carry out the actual kidnapping. It was their usual modus operandi. After all, it was well documented that Mumbai's ganglords routinely employed impressionable villagers to carry out assassinations, paying what was to them a king's ransom to enter the city, commit their ghastly crime, then vanish once again into the vast hinterlands. It was almost impossible for the authorities to locate such 'day-rate' killers.

Had something similar happened here?

Was Ali a hired gun, a low-level cog in the insurance scam orchestrated by Das and those he had inadvisably got into bed with?

Or did Ali have absolutely nothing to do with Das?

An earlier thought now resurfaced in Chopra's mind. Something Poppy's colleague Malhotra had said at dinner, about Bijli receiving death threats after she had decried right-wing groups in the city following the 2008 terror attacks that had shocked the world. The rogue radical who had made the threats had vanished – could he have returned to make good on his dire promises by kidnapping Vicky? Was Ali that same man?

It seemed a far-fetched scenario, Chopra thought, though he was not yet ready to dismiss it entirely.

At least he had one lead. The girl from Mira Road, Aaliya Ghazi, Ali's cousin.

If he could have found a way to make a phone call he would have asked Rangwalla to follow the girl. Perhaps she would lead them to Ali. And if Chopra could find *him*, then he was certain he could uncover the truth.

A couple of other things were bothering him too.

Two insignificant details that circled his brain like a pair of troublesome mosquitoes.

Firstly, the CCTV images of Ali entering and leaving the stadium on the night of the kidnapping. Something had nagged at him at the time, but he couldn't quite grasp what it was, or why it should be important. Secondly, his thoughts kept returning to the faded film poster he had seen in Aaliya Ghazi's home. There had been a woman in the poster, an actress from yesteryear whose face had seemed familiar. For the life of him, he couldn't work out why this memory troubled him. What possible bearing could it have on the case? And yet it was like an itch he could not scratch. There was something incongruous about the poster itself. In a house where the paint was peeling from the walls, where there were no other photographs, paintings, or posters, why had this one been put up? Why *this* movie, and not another?

And then it came to him.

There was something intensely personal about the poster. Which meant that the actress was important to Aaliya

Ghazi. If Chopra could discover who she was, he might learn more about Aaliya, which would bring him one step closer to Ali.

Perhaps, when he returned to the land of the living, he would find the answers he needed . . . *If* he returned.

POPPY AND SHOOT-'EM-UP SHERIWAL GO HEAD TO HEAD

Poppy was worried; more worried than she had been in a long time. Throughout his career in the police service her husband had placed himself in harm's way on numerous occasions. And yet she had always maintained a quiet belief that he would return home each evening unscathed. This belief had settled like a core of iron at the very centre of her being. She had fashioned it from Chopra's own self-confidence, his calm demeanour, his resolute determination. It was as if his innate goodness served to throw a cloak of invulnerability about him, one that, as the years passed, only grew more impregnable.

And then had come the heart attack.

Ever since Chopra's diagnosis – as a sufferer of something called 'unstable angina', two loathsome words that continued to fill Poppy with dread each time she heard them – she had become overly anxious for his safety.

The doctors had been unequivocal in their advice.

No stress. No excitement.

And yet her duffer of a husband continued to race around town, neck deep in conspiracy. He was like a boy playing with fire who simply would not listen to common sense.

Now, having learned of his bid to procure Vicky Verma's release – a bid that appeared to have gone terribly wrong – fear petrified her.

Ever since the events of the previous summer she had believed implicitly that little Ganesha was more than he seemed. She believed, too, that he shared a special bond with her husband, a bond that went beyond affection or explanation. And she knew that Ganesha would not have returned to the compound alone unless something awful had happened.

Panic had settled like a dragon around her heart.

That evening Poppy called everyone she knew, but no one had seen or heard from her husband.

Finally, she did the only other thing she could think of.

She went to the police station.

The Sahar station lay a short rickshaw ride away from the restaurant.

As Poppy entered the tiled courtyard with its terracotta bricks and steel gate, she reflected on just how few times she had visited in the twenty-odd years her husband had been posted here. Chopra had always been stuffy about procedure and had made it clear that he didn't appreciate 'personal visits' while on duty. At first she had bristled at his attitude and then she realised that this too was a part of who he was, as integral to him as his magnificent moustache and his aversion to ginger.

She stepped through the saloon-style front doors, and found herself confronting a scene of quiet efficiency.

Four desks were laid out in the reception area, each with its own stack of files. At two of the desks officers were taking down statements. At a third an officer drank tea from a glass while talking earnestly into the phone tucked under his chin. Behind him a garlanded portrait of Lord Ganesh looked down benignly.

At the fourth desk Poppy found a familiar face.

Young Sub-Inspector Surat was stamping an official document. Having applied the rubber seal, he picked up a pen and painstakingly inscribed his name across the bottom. He admired his handiwork, and then noticed the visitor. 'Poppy Madam!' he exclaimed in obvious delight. 'How lovely to see you!'

'Lovely to see you too, Udhay,' said Poppy. 'How handsome you look in your new uniform.'

Surat blushed.

He had recently been promoted to sub-inspector, and with rank had come the long-dreamed-of privilege of wearing full trousers.

Quickly, Poppy explained her errand, omitting any mention of Vicky Verma's kidnapping. She said simply that her husband, last known to have been on his way to Madh Fort, had vanished. Bijli had impressed on her the need to keep further details a secret – both Chopra and Vicky's lives could depend on it. There was no telling how the kidnappers would react if the kidnapping became public, particularly if the police got involved.

Yet Poppy couldn't simply sit around and do nothing.

In the end she had decided to approach the new chief at Chopra's old station, someone who might help without requiring too much in the way of detail.

Alarm fluttered over Surat's plump features. Poppy knew that Surat idolised her husband, and would be genuinely fearful for his safety.

He led her briskly to Chopra's old office, and rapped on the door.

'Come in.'

Poppy entered to find a tall dusky woman in a khaki police inspector's uniform standing behind Chopra's old desk scrutinising a map on the wall. Poppy saw that she was a handsome woman. Not exactly pretty, but regal in a tough-looking sort of way.

She had, of course, heard from her husband that a woman had taken over at Sahar. The news had delighted her. Poppy held strong views about women being in charge. And when she had learned that the woman was none other than Malini Sheriwal – better known in the media as Shoot-'em-Up Sheriwal, notorious Encounter Squad specialist and pre-eminent dispatcher of underworld gangsters – she had been thrilled. She had been meaning to visit the celebrity police officer, although not under the circumstances that had brought her here today.

'Yes?' said Sheriwal. She seemed annoyed to have been disturbed from her contemplation of the map.

Breathlessly, Surat explained the situation. Sheriwal listened, then examined Poppy with a critical eye. 'Leave us, Surat.'

Surat looked from Poppy to his boss, then saluted, and left the office.

'What makes you think your husband is in trouble?' asked Sheriwal. She did not offer Poppy a seat.

'He hasn't called. No one has seen or heard from him since yesterday evening.'

'What does that prove? Perhaps he is busy.'

'He would have called me.'

'You seem very sure of yourself.'

'I know my husband.'

Sheriwal raised an eyebrow. 'He is a man. They are not known for their consideration.'

'You don't know my husband.'

'You are wrong. Since I have been working here I have heard a great deal about him.'

She said nothing more, leaving Poppy to decide whether this was intended as a compliment or otherwise.

'Well, *I* am certain he is missing.'

'What if he has simply decided to take off?'

Poppy's brow furrowed. 'What do you mean . . . *take off*? He is not an aeroplane.'

'I am sure you understand what I mean. How long have you been married? What if he has decided to move to where the grass is greener?'

Poppy coloured. She drew herself up angrily. 'Now you listen here,' she said, 'I don't know what you're implying—'

'You know exactly what I'm implying,' interrupted

Sheriwal calmly. 'He wouldn't be the first husband to run out on his wife.'

Poppy was aghast.

She had come to the station fully expecting to find a sympathetic ear, that a female officer would surely appreciate her predicament. Instead, here she was, listening to garbage about a man she had trusted for twenty-four years. 'My husband has not run out on me,' she hissed. 'He has vanished. I am requesting police assistance. Now, either you will provide it or you will not. If not, then you can go to hell.'

It was Sheriwal's turn to frown.

Clearly, she was not used to being spoken to in this way. 'There's no point in becoming hysterical. Your husband has been missing for barely twenty-four hours. If you've still had no contact from him in the morning I suggest you return and file an FIR. Then we will see what we can do.'

But Poppy had stopped listening.

'Hysterical? *Hysterical!*' Her face had darkened, and her slender frame quivered with rage. 'I have no idea what sort of man you are married to, but I know my husband. He is worth a dozen of you. I will find him on my own. And if anything happens to him in the meantime, *then* I will show you the meaning of hysterical!'

Poppy turned to storm from the office. She stopped at the door, and turned back. 'And there *is* no greener grass!'

She slammed the door on her way out.

Malini Sheriwal sat down heavily in her chair.

She knew she should have handled the encounter differently. But she had been in a bad mood. Lately, she seemed always to be in a bad mood.

She hated the political kowtowing that had necessitated her transfer from the Encounter Squad to this backwater station where literally nothing seemed to happen. In the Encounter Squad she had lived on adrenalin. Each day brought fresh challenges and the very real threat of injury to life and limb – invariably someone else's life and limb, but that was beside the point. But here, in the middle of nowhere, she was confronted by matters of such sublime unimportance she felt her brains would turn to slush and dribble out from her ears.

She wondered how Chopra had put up with it.

She had heard enough to know that the man had been a very capable officer, honest and well respected. But just because he had disappeared for a day it didn't mean the world had stopped turning. His wife seemed a highly strung type.

Sheriwal had meant what she had said. Men were notoriously fickle. It wasn't entirely beyond the bounds of possibility that Chopra had simply walked out for pastures new. Perhaps, even now, he was setting up shop with another woman. This thought brought a pang of unwelcome distress. She had enough self-awareness to know that her view of men had been incurably coloured by her own experiences.

As a younger woman she had married a man her parents had believed would be a good match.

They had been wrong.

After two years of emotional turmoil she had finally admitted to herself that he was an incorrigible cheat. To her horror she had discovered that the wretch had been keeping not just a mistress, but a second wife, too. He even had a child by this supernumerary spouse!

Sheriwal had confronted the scoundrel with her service revolver, listened to him claim innocence, then, as it dawned on him that she was to be made a fool of no longer, plead for mercy. The grovelling wretch had even dared to claim that she had driven him to it, that in the matter of marital passion he found her to be a cold fish.

That was when she had shot him in the foot.

Fortunately, her husband had refused to press charges, suspecting that his deranged wife would return to finish the job if he did.

They divorced a month later, and Sheriwal had joined the Encounter Squad, where she had found an outlet for her rage against the dominion of men.

She was sick of men getting away with it. Perhaps they could with Malini Sheriwal, but Shoot-'em-Up Sheriwal was a different matter.

Shoot-'em-Up Sheriwal would not allow any man to get away with getting away with it.

And yet . . . She knew that sometimes her prejudices clouded her judgement.

She tapped her desk with the butt of her revolver, and considered the troubled woman who had come to her for help.

Sighing deeply, Inspector Sheriwal picked up the phone.

A SINGING GHOST

Rangwalla's eyes opened into a flickering gloom. A candle beside his bed guttered in the breeze from his bedroom window. For a moment he was disoriented . . . and then he snapped back to the present.

Something had woken him.

He slipped from the bed, rudely disturbing a mosquito that had been feasting on his throat.

He put on his sari and wig, and poked his feet into his worn leather sandals.

In the corridor he stood for a moment, frozen in a shaft of moonlight falling in from an open balcony.

He strained his ears, listening for the noise that had roused him.

There! It sounded like singing. A woman's voice. Not the voice of one of his eunuch companions, but a softer, higher-pitched melody. He shuddered momentarily, recalling the travesty of his attempt to carry a tune earlier, the cries of the music maestro: 'Hai! Hai! Is a donkey being castrated?

Has a train derailed?'

This Master was a strange beast. Paying a king's ransom just so he could hide in the shadows and watch a bunch of eunuchs – and one pseudo-eunuch – dance and sing. What the devil was he up to?

Rangwalla believed in simplicity. If a man murdered another man it was usually because of money, a woman, or drunken bravado. This Master was a deviant. That was the simplest explanation, regardless of the suspicions of the Queen of Mysore. He was a voyeur who took his pleasure from watching eunuchs perform.

As deviants went, Rangwalla had seen worse.

And, so far, the only person harmed by the whole sordid business was Rangwalla himself. And if his wife ever found out! Allah forfend!

The haunting voice broke into his thoughts again.

He followed it to the rear wing of the mansion. Here the haveli scattered into a maze of corridors lined with rooms, many of them padlocked shut. The walls of the corridors, Rangwalla noted, were painted in rolling murals of peacocks' tails. As he padded past the colourful blue-green frescos, dotted with iridescent eyes, he couldn't help but feel that other eyes, human eyes, were following him. Was the Master behind those walls? Was this how he operated, spying on his guests through secret passages in the labyrinth of his mansion?

Rangwalla turned a corner just in time to glimpse the hem of a sari flicking around another corner further ahead; he heard the padding of feet, the jangle of ankle bracelets. He quickened his pace as the voice receded.

He turned the corner, and braked to a halt.

He had come to a dead end.

He was standing in an alcove. Before him, two marble leopards – with rubies for eyes and inlaid with lapis lazuli – flanked a brass-mounted, teak chair decorated in low relief with squares and a foliate frieze. Behind the chair, hanging from a whitewashed wall, was an enormous gilt-framed painting covered by a cloth.

He looked around in mystification.

Where had the singing woman gone? Had she vanished into thin air? Or had he made a mistake? Had the singing been in his mind?

He pinched himself, and felt his eyes water. He was definitely awake.

He reached up and pulled back the cloth covering the painting.

The portrait was of a late-middle-aged woman, dressed in a heavy, brocaded maroon-and-gold Rajputi sari. The woman exuded a regal bearing and looked down on Rangwalla with an expression of supreme haughtiness. Her greying hair was pulled severely back. Behind her Rangwalla could see the haveli rising into darkness.

He found himself arrested by the expression in the woman's eyes. Cold, dark, and utterly devoid of empathy.

Even though it was a warm night, former sub-inspector Rangwalla shivered.

He considered something that had been bothering him. Since arriving at the haveli this was the first picture he had encountered. Usually such mansions paraded their dynastic heritage with endless galleries of self-aggrandising images, but here there was a complete absence. Who had lived here through the generations? Why was this woman's portrait covered? And why did this one painting remain when all others had been excised from the walls? Why would the Master himself not show his face?

Still consumed by this puzzle Rangwalla turned away and immediately bumped into a figure that had ghosted around the corner. A howl of alarm escaped him before he realised that he was looking at the watchman, Shantaram, holding up his kerosene lantern, the light throwing a ghostly radiance over his careworn features.

'What's wrong with you?' hissed Rangwalla. 'Sneaking up on people in the middle of the night!'

The watchman said nothing. He had a hangdog face, Rangwalla saw, deep canyons of age carved into the thin grizzle of grey clinging to his cheeks.

Rangwalla turned to the painting. 'Who is this woman?'

The watchman craned his neck to look at the portrait. For a long time he seemed to examine it with his sorrowful gaze. Then he shuffled forward and pulled the cloth back over the woman's menacing presence.

Rangwalla watched the old man shamble away, his lamp throwing moving shadows ahead of him as he went.

ACP RAO FACES THE MUSIC

Assistant Commissioner of Police Suresh Rao squinted at his reflection in the mirror, then reached up with a pair of scissors to snip at his prim moustache. Satisfied with the result, he slipped the scissors back into his pocket and retreated to his desk.

It had been a busy morning at the Central Bureau of Investigation headquarters in Nariman Point.

Rao had closed out one long-standing bribery case, and received a number of intriguing new leads, including allegations that a senior member of the State Cabinet had been fraternising with a junior colleague of the same sex.

Such information, in the right hands, would be of considerable value.

The CBI was tasked to investigate complaints against public officials – including the police force – as well as any major crimes of a sensitive or sensational nature that might be sent their way. As a consequence those in the bureau commanded a great deal of power, power that was routinely employed to the benefit of those exercising it.

Rao thought of himself as the spider at the centre of a vast web.

Flies continually fell into the web. Sometimes the spider would eat the fly straight away – after all, the bureau needed to demonstrate its bona fides to those who held the purse strings in New Delhi. But at other times it was more judicious to wrap the fly up and save it for a rainy day. And the fly would be so pleased with this illusionary reprieve that it would offer the spider a token of its gratitude, a token Rao and his colleagues gratefully accepted.

That was how the game was played, and Rao was a past master at it.

ACP Rao had navigated the courtly intrigues of the Brihanmumbai Police for over thirty years. He had seen a great many things, and the one lesson he had learned early in his career was this: honesty was a virtue that only saints and madmen could afford.

A knock on the door interrupted his breakfast, a plate of deep-fried spinach pakoras. 'Sir,' said the peon, 'there is a Mrs Chopra here to see you. She says it is about her husband.'

Rao almost choked.

Poppy Chopra? What the devil was she doing here?

A shadow passed over his moon-faced features.

Before joining the CBI Rao had commanded Chopra for many years at the Sahar station. The man had long been a thorn in his side, continually embarrassing Rao in front of his seniors with his unholy dedication to his job. It was despicable the way he made a virtue of his honesty! A man slaved his whole life to attain rank. What was the point of having it if you didn't benefit from it? But Chopra sat there like a modern-day Gandhi, presiding over the rest of them with his stomach-turning integrity.

And now, even after the insufferable man had retired, he continued to clash with Rao, culminating in the recent humiliation when Rao, tasked to recover the Koh-i-noor diamond, had been undermined by Chopra's own private investigation.

And then two days ago, a gift-wrapped opportunity for revenge had dropped into Rao's lap: an anonymous call to the CBI unit accusing Chopra of involvement in a sensational crime – the kidnapping of Bollywood film star Vicky Verma. One of Rao's colleagues had fielded the call. Knowing of the ACP's animosity, the man had passed the information to him, lodging a favour that he would, no doubt, call in at a later time.

Rao had been sceptical about the tip-off. Kidnapping? A man like Chopra? Impossible.

Nevertheless . . . the caller had said that Chopra would be found at midnight at the Madh Fort with his accomplices.

Rao had raced to the fort where, to his astonishment, he had indeed discovered Chopra, albeit without the ransom, accomplices, or any sign of Vicky Verma.

Having arrested his nemesis, Rao had paused to think the matter through.

He finally had Chopra where he wanted him. The former policeman had made many enemies during the Koh-i-noor investigation, enemies with long memories and even longer reaches. Rao now had the opportunity to deliver Chopra's head on a platter. In one fell swoop he could earn the gratitude of those who truly ran the city of Mumbai. The issue of Chopra's guilt, when viewed in such a balance, was immaterial. Rao was not one to allow a man's innocence to get in the way of justice. This was what Chopra had never understood. Justice in India was not a finely tuned instrument. It operated on the general rather than the specific level.

In the ACP's opinion this made it no less effective.

Swiftly – while Chopra stewed in the back of the police truck – Rao had formulated a plan.

Then he had made some calls.

Two hours later he had dispatched Chopra to the Gouripur Jail, confident that he had finally seen the last of his nemesis.

But now, here was his wife. How had she found out?

Rao had no wish for his actions to come to light, and so had told as few people as possible what had happened. The only ones who needed to know, in good time, were Chopra's enemies, the city mavens who might ultimately reward Rao for discreetly taking revenge on their behalf. In the meantime, what did Rao care if Vicky Verma had been kidnapped – if, indeed, that was true?

He had half a mind to turn Poppy away, but he was intrigued.

He wiped a napkin over his mouth. 'Show her in.'

Poppy entered the office and looked around hesitantly.

She had had a difficult morning. Her meeting with Malini Sheriwal the previous evening had left her frustrated and afraid. But then, to her surprise, later that same evening, Sheriwal had called her back.

There had been no apology.

The bellicose policewoman had, ultimately, decided to help. She had made some calls and discovered that an ACP Rao at CBI headquarters *might* have arrested a man named Ashwin Chopra at Madh Fort the night before. She could uncover no further details. Instead, she advised Poppy to visit Rao first thing the following morning.

At the CBI HQ Poppy had stared up at the run-down old building and felt the first tremors of anxiety. She was a woman not easily cowed, but the building seemed to loom over her with the full extent of the monolithic and immoveable bureaucracy that had crushed the souls of millions of Indians over the years, ever since the first Indian had filed the first chit back before the dawn of time.

Now, as she looked at Rao's round face and fish-like eyes, fear constricted her throat.

She knew from her husband that ACP Rao was not an honourable man. This thought sat in her mind like a glistening black rock as she took a seat. She knew that she would have to rein in her desire to rail at Rao. She understood that emotional restraint was not her strongest suit, and there was no subject that gripped her emotions more fiercely than that of her husband and his welfare.

Yet today she would need to exercise restraint if she wished to find a path through the forest before her. Yes,

Poppy promised herself, if this was what was required, then she would be the very definition of patience and tact.

'Mrs Chopra, isn't it?' said Rao. 'How can I help—?'

'Where the devil is my husband?' exploded Poppy.

'Mrs Chopr—'

'I demand to know this very instant!' Poppy thumped the desk, causing Rao's plate of pakoras to leap several inches into the air.

'But this is quite unaccept—' Rao spluttered.

'You have arrested my husband!' bayed Poppy. 'Take me to him right now or I will tear this place apart around your ears!'

Rao squirmed on his seat, waiting for the furious harridan to calm down. Was she possessed? He studiously avoided Poppy's basilisk glare. Finally, he spoke: 'Who told you that I arrested him?'

'A police officer,' said Poppy.

'But this is confidential information!' whined Rao.

'How can it be confidential?' shouted Poppy. 'You have arrested my husband. I have a right to know where he is.'

'I am afraid I cannot help you, Mrs Chopra,' said Rao primly. 'There are proper channels for these things. This is CBI business, after all. We can't just go around giving out details to any old person.'

'Any old person!' exclaimed Poppy, rising to her feet in agitation. 'I am his wife! I demand to know where he is!'

Rao pushed back his chair. 'My hands are tied, Mrs Chopra,' he said, keeping his expression wooden. How delicious! he thought, privately. Chopra in prison, and his wife grovelling for his life! How long had he waited for such a moment?

A loud rapping sounded on the door.

Without waiting for an answer, a woman entered the room. A policewoman in khaki. She looked vaguely familiar. From the stars on her shoulders he saw that he outranked her.

'Who are you?' he brayed angrily. 'Can't you see I am in a meeting?'

'My name is Malini Sheriwal,' said Sheriwal. 'I am here with Mrs Chopra.'

Rao continued to glare at the woman. Sheriwal? Why did that name seem so familiar? . . . And then his eyes dropped to the ivory-tooled grip of the handgun at her side.

The colour drained from his face.

Malini Sheriwal.

Shoot-'em-Up Sheriwal.

A cold sweat broke out on Rao's forehead. What the hell was the Encounter Squad's most lethal killer doing in his office? If the rumours were true the woman was completely insane. She had probably killed two men before breakfast that very morning.

Rao licked his lips. 'Ah, how can I help you, Inspector?' he said carefully.

'You can help me by telling Mrs Chopra exactly where her husband is.'

Rao gaped. 'But – but that is a CBI matter,' he asserted lamely. 'It is no business of yours.'

'I am making it my business,' said Sheriwal calmly.

Rao gulped. 'Well, I can't just reveal CBI business to anyone who walks through the door. If you wish to know then there is paperwork to be completed, forms to be filled . . .' His voice tailed off as Sheriwal slid out her automatic weapon, and pointed it at a potted plant in the corner of the room.

'You know,' she said conversationally, 'someone once asked me to fill out forms. I shot him in both knees.'

Rao grinned maniacally. 'Ha ha,' he squeaked. He stifled his panic, and endeavoured to reassert a stern expression. 'Look here, Inspector, you can't just expect me to—'

The plant holder exploded in a shower of terracotta chips.

Seconds later the peon came rushing in. 'Sir!' he exclaimed. 'Are you all right?'

Rao's head emerged from behind his desk. He coughed. 'Of course I am, you idiot. Get out.'

After the peon had left, Sheriwal, still nonchalantly swinging her weapon around, said, 'Where is Chopra?'

Rao's eyes were mesmerised by the gun. 'Gouripur Jail.'

'What is he doing there?'

'He is accused of a kidnapping.'

'Kidnapping!' exclaimed Poppy. 'But that is preposterous! *He* is not the kidnapper.'

'He was caught red-handed.'

'Who caught him?'

Rao gulped. 'I did.'

Sheriwal brought the gun to bear on him. Rao felt his bowels perform a complicated somersault.

'Get him out.'

'I cannot.'

'You put him there, you can get him out.'

'You don't understand. I had to enlist certain parties to organise Chopra's transfer to Gouripur. It was highly . . . irregular.'

'Then enlist those parties again.'

'It would do no good,' quavered Rao. 'Chopra has made powerful enemies. Now that they have him where they want him, they will not release him.'

'You will have to convince them.'

'They won't listen to me!' wailed Rao. 'I am nothing!'

Sheriwal pointed the weapon at Rao's head.

'I'm telling you I can't do anything. It's out of my hands!'

Sheriwal pulled the trigger. Rao gurgled as the chamber clicked empty.

She lowered the gun as he slumped back in his executive chair, bathed in a lather of perspiration.

'You will keep trying,' pronounced Sheriwal. 'I will be back tomorrow, and the next day, and each day until Chopra is released. Do you understand?'

Rao nodded dumbly. The woman was a raving lunatic. Why the hell had they let her on to the force?

Sheriwal followed Poppy out of the office. 'Your master needs a new pair of trousers,' she informed the peon. Then, turning to Poppy, she said, 'Despite my threats this is going to take time. It has gone beyond my reach.'

Poppy was crestfallen. 'How can this happen? What kind of country are we living in? My husband is the most honest man I know.'

'I believe you,' said Sheriwal. 'Sadly, in our country honesty is like the scent of blood in shark-infested waters.' She glanced at her watch. 'I have to go. Don't lose heart, Mrs Chopra. I am sure your husband will return. One way or the other,' she added under her breath as she strode away.

THE SECRET OF THE MYSTERIOUS PORTRAIT

The breakfast room was abuzz with conversation when Rangwalla arrived.

For a moment he hovered in the doorway, listening to the eunuchs as they laughed and quarrelled good-naturedly. He found himself dipping in and out of their talk, their concerns and hopes, their dreams and fears. In his short time with them he had learned a great deal about them. For instance, that they were absurdly fond of storytelling, engaging in competitions in the evenings as they ate dinner. 'We are fabulists at heart,' Parvati would say pompously. 'We like nothing better than to sit around a fire, regaling each other with the most wonderfully tall tales.'

But not everything they recounted was untrue. The day before Mamta had shared a story about how as a young woman she had gone to the temple to pray for an ailing friend. Here she had been prevented from entering by a gang of local youths, pelted with coconuts, and harried away. Rangwalla recalled, with a sense of shame, that he had seen something similar just a month earlier, ruffians harassing a pair of eunuchs who had tried to join the queue for a posh new multiplex cinema where he had taken his children. The ruffians had been aided and abetted by the security guards, who had chased the eunuchs away with lathi sticks. Rangwalla recalled now that those eunuchs had been dressed in their finest clothes, had come along, like any other visitor, to experience the new cinema and enjoy the movie. They had been chased away like dogs, and Rangwalla had done nothing to stop that from happening. Worse, his children had looked on as he had stood by, not sparing a second thought for the distressed eunuchs. Why should they, when their own father, a policeman, did not care?

This thought now filled him with self-recrimination.

Rangwalla finally understood what the eunuchs meant when they talked of their ultimate goal, that of being treated as any other citizens of their country, with the ability to have families and jobs, to visit a cinema or a shopping mall and not be stared at or abused.

It seemed to him strange that he had never considered them in this light before. If he had ever thought of them at all it had been as simply another of the many factions that made Mumbai such a melting pot of intrigue and anarchy. He had known Anarkali for years, but only as a somewhat intimidating presence who occasionally frequented the station, one of many eyes and ears that he cultivated on the streets of the city. He had never dwelled upon what lay beneath her swarthy exterior.

He slipped into a chair beside Mamta, who was crunching loudly on a piece of toast smeared with mango pickle. The big eunuch eyed Rangwalla's careworn features. 'You look like you've just entertained a team of kabaddi wrestlers.'

The others guffawed loudly, as Rangwalla scowled. 'I didn't sleep well.'

'If I danced and sang like you, sister, I wouldn't sleep at all,' said Rupa icily.

'Oh, leave her alone,' said Parvati good-naturedly. 'She just needs a little training, that's all. Why don't you show her a few steps?'

'Hah!' said Rupa. 'Do you think one can fashion the Taj Mahal from a pile of dung? No offence, sister.'

'None taken,' muttered Rangwalla, brushing away a persistent fly from his plate.

'What is troubling you, dear?' asked Parvati. She suddenly belched and covered her mouth. 'So sorry! This food seems to disagree with me.'

'Are you sure?' said Mamta. 'The way you've been eating, I assumed you were getting on like a house on fire.'

Parvati patted her belly. 'Well, I wouldn't want to offend our host. But you are right. If I keep eating like this my clients won't want me when I return.'

'They don't want you now,' sniped Rupa.

'I am a tree whose fruit is always ripe,' responded Parvati, smiling broadly.

'Talking of our host,' said Mamta. 'Am I the only one who finds those peacocks' eyes everywhere unsettling? I think our host is watching us quite closely – from behind the walls.'

A momentary silence fell on them as they looked around at the carved wainscoting and peacocks' tails mural.

'I saw something last night,' said Rangwalla, putting down his spoon. 'A woman, singing. I followed her but she disappeared.'

'What do you mean "she disappeared"?' said Rupa.

'Did anyone else hear her?' asked Rangwalla, ignoring Rupa.

'I'm afraid I slept like a baby,' said Parvati. 'All that singing and dancing was very taxing.'

'I listen to music when I sleep,' declared Rupa. 'And if this woman's singing was anything like yours, sister, I'm very glad I couldn't hear her.'

'I heard nothing,' declared Mamta. 'But I'm a heavy sleeper.'

'You're heavy full stop,' muttered Rupa. She turned to her left. 'What about you, Kavita? Did you hear anything?'

Rangwalla focused his attention on the youngest eunuch. Kavita seemed withdrawn. The day before, she had complied with the requests to sing and dance – and indeed had excelled at both – but had done so as if distracted. He wondered if she, too, was succumbing to the unsettling atmosphere that lay over the haveli. Rangwalla found himself beginning to worry for the girl. And then he began to worry that he kept thinking of her as a girl, rather than a eunuch. The lines were beginning to blur for the former sub-inspector and this too made him deeply uncomfortable.

'No,' said Kavita. 'I heard nothing.'

At that moment Premchand materialised in the room.

The munshi's appearance was, as ever, immaculate. His white kurta and dhoti gleamed, his Nehru jacket was faultless, and his black pillbox hat formed the perfect apex to the fine figure he cut. A fresh tilak had been applied to his forehead, as if he had just returned from the temple.

'Why don't we ask *him*?' said Mamta, rising to her feet. She folded her arms and fixed the munshi with a stern look. 'We want some answers.'

'I have already told you: the Master is not paying for the privilege of answering your questions.'

'It's not the Master we want to know about. Sister Sonali here saw something strange last night. A woman wandering around the haveli. Singing.'

Premchand's face was an impenetrable mask. 'Impossible,' he said eventually. 'There are no women in the haveli.'

'Does the Master have a wife?' asked Parvati.

'The Master is not married.'

'You, then?'

'Certainly not! I would not dream of soiling myself with a woman.'

'Is that so?' said Mamta, narrowing her eyes.

'I am a Brahmin and a brahmacharya. I have taken a vow of celibacy.'

'That's a shame,' said Rupa sarcastically. 'I could have shown you a thing or two.'

'The woman was singing an old love song,' said Rangwalla.

'Love songs are dangerous,' remarked Parvati. 'Why don't you sing us a few bars, dear?'

'Heaven help us!' muttered Rupa.

Rangwalla realised that he had talked himself into a corner. But he had begun this; he could not back out now. He cleared his throat and began to sing.

'Stop!' said Premchand. A look of alarm had leapt onto his placid features.

'Didn't I warn you?' said Rupa. 'That voice could send the dead running for cover.'

'Do you recognise the song?' asked Mamta, her eyes focused on Premchand. 'Does it mean something to you?'

'It – it is a song from the Master's childhood.' The munshi seemed shaken.

'Could Rangwalla's mystery woman have been the Master's mother, then?' asked Parvati.

Premchand shook his head. 'No. The Mistress – Thakurani Jaya Rathore – has been dead for many years.'

'What did she look like? This Mistress?' asked Rangwalla, thinking suddenly of the mysterious portrait he had discovered the night before.

'What does that matter?' said Premchand sharply.

Rangwalla hesitated, then said, 'Follow me.'

He led the eunuchs and the protesting munshi upstairs, and through the maze of corridors along which he had pursued the mysterious woman the previous night. Arriving in the alcove at last, he paused below the covered painting. Then he swept aside the curtain.

The eunuchs shrank back.

'By Shiva, she is hideous,' exclaimed Rupa.

'Let us not be uncharitable,' said Parvati. 'She has a certain charm. In the right light.'

'Yes,' said Rupa. 'Pitch black would be best.'

'There's something evil about her,' declared Mamta, echoing Rangwalla's own thoughts.

'It's the eyes. They follow you around,' said Rupa with a shiver.

Rangwalla glanced at Premchand. The old martinet seemed transfixed. 'Is this the Master's mother?' Rangwalla asked.

Finally, Premchand revived. 'Yes,' he answered.

'What about the Master's father?' asked Mamta.

'The old Thakur? He died when the Master was young. The Mistress raised him herself.'

'She ran this estate on her own?' asked Rangwalla, intrigued. Widows in rural India held little status, even the widow of a landowner. The tides of prejudice and precedent would have been set against her from the very beginning.

'She was a formidable person.' The munshi strode forward and covered the painting. 'We have a busy schedule.'

'But what about the woman?' persisted Mamta.

'There was no woman. Your colleague is mistaken.'

'No,' said Rangwalla. 'I know what I saw. I know what I heard.'

'Perhaps it was a ghost,' said Kavita quietly.

'A ghost?' shivered Rupa. 'Do you really think so?

'Nonsense,' said Premchand dismissively.

'There was a ghost in my village once,' mused Parvati. 'He used to put coconut oil in people's hair and massage their scalps.'

'That doesn't sound so bad,' said Rupa.

'Their scalps were no longer attached to their skulls.'

Rupa shrieked dramatically. 'I want to go home,' she wailed.

'You cannot go home,' said Premchand firmly. 'You have made an agreement. You will honour it.' He turned and walked away.

'There's something not right about that man,' muttered Rupa, as the munshi disappeared around a corner.

'There's something not right about all of this, sister,' said Parvati. 'There are old secrets here and they are beginning to smell. But . . . he is right. We have made an agreement. Come, let us see what surprises the Master has in store for us today.'

THE GREAT ESCAPE

The covered wagon juddered along the rural road as it meandered towards a row of low-slung hills. Beyond the hills, the sky was illuminated by the blood orange of a late-afternoon sun. Ahead, the winding path crested a shallow ridge. And below the ridge lay the sandstone quarry, the quarry in which, Poppy Chopra knew, her husband was toiling under God-only-knew what duress, surrounded by human ghouls.

Since returning from the meeting with ACP Rao, Poppy had alternated between fits of despair, terror, and rage. Not only had her husband been arrested, laid low by powerful forces whose influence she could only guess at, but to top it all off he had been whisked away to a prison renowned for its brutality and excess.

Gouripur Jail.

Last waystation on the road to hell.

How could God have allowed this to happen to a man like her husband? The most honest person she had ever known, a man whose goodness had illuminated each and every day of their union.

She had paced the office at the restaurant, her mother watching from the sofa. 'Wearing a hole in the floor isn't going to help anyone,' observed Poornima Devi.

'Then what do you propose I do?' snapped Poppy.

'Call the Chief Minister,' advised Poornima primly. 'That's what I would do.'

'And what makes you think the Chief Minister will listen to me?'

'Well, if you ask me, your husband has brought this on himself. Who asked him to go meddling in other people's business? I told you no good would come of it.'

'Oh, Mother!' wailed Poppy. She stormed from the office, and walked out through the kitchen to the rear courtyard.

She found Ganesha hunkered under his mango tree, staring forlornly into the mud between his feet. The little elephant remained thoroughly disheartened.

On the veranda, Irfan was being tutored by Usha Umrigar. Both sat cross-legged on the polished planks, Irfan with a rectangular black slate on his lap, his malformed left hand hooked under it. As Poppy watched, Irfan crunched his brow and pressed a piece of chalk to the slate. Then he lifted the slate to Usha.

The old woman raised an eyebrow. Irfan coloured. He kept forgetting that the woman was blind.

'I'm sure it is fine,' said Usha. 'Now kindly recite what you have written.'

Irfan broke into a toothy beam of satisfaction, and then he began to read from his slate.

The scene brought a lump to Poppy's throat.

If there was a living example of her husband's generosity and good nature then it was Irfan. How many others would have taken in an urchin from Mumbai's unforgiving streets, given him a job, and invited him into their life? The fact that Irfan chose to live at the restaurant rather than at their home was neither here nor there. The boy wished to be close to his best friend, little Ganesha, and Chopra had respected his wish.

Poppy knew that her husband sometimes thought of her as overwrought, even flighty.

Perhaps, at times, she was.

But she lived by her emotions and she saw nothing wrong in this. Every couple needed a balance. Chopra was her balance, and she his.

'Why don't you tell me what's troubling you, dear?'

Poppy turned to see Chef Lucknowwallah leaning against the wooden fence that bounded the courtyard. He had just strolled in from the street via the alley that ran out onto the bustling Guru Rabindranath Tagore Road. Her nose crinkled as a fragrant cloud wafted from the thick cheroot sticking out of his mouth.

Poppy examined the chef's avuncular features, his rosy cheeks, his gleaming pate, partially hidden beneath the cricket umpire's cap that he wore to disguise his encroaching baldness.

She had grown fond of the man.

Lucknowwallah was excitable, temperamental, and inordinately precious about his kitchen; in many ways he was similar in disposition to herself. And yet he was also an intelligent and generous man, a happy widower who had travelled widely, with a store of worldly wisdom that was available to anyone who asked for it.

Quickly, she explained the situation.

Lucknowwallah's face creased with alarm. He drew deeply on his cheroot, then threw it to the ground, crushing it beneath his heel. 'It seems to me you have only two choices,' he said. 'One: butt your head against our monolithic bureaucracy to try and secure Chopra's release, or, two: do something about it yourself.'

'What can *I* possibly do?' said Poppy miserably.

'That I don't know. But I would be happy to sit with you and throw some ideas around. Chopra is a good man. I like to think that we have become friends. And Azeem Lucknowwallah never leaves his friends in the lurch.'

Poppy gave a watery smile. 'I could use all the help I can get.'

The wagon bounced out of another pothole, jerking Poppy back to the present.

'Hyah!' cried Lucknowwallah, wrestling with the reins.

The chef, seated on the wagon's box seat beside Poppy, planted his feet on the buckboard, lifted his crop, and tapped the plodding bullock across its expansive behind. The beast responded by snorting breathily, lifting its tail, and relieving itself. A cloud of pungent steam washed back over him. He cursed loudly, and smothered his nose with his hand.

As the wagon laboured up the ridge the quarry came into view.

Poppy took out the binoculars she had rescued from her husband's study and examined the open mine's layout. The quarry had carved out a bowl-shaped depression in the earth: on one side it ended in sheer cliffs of naked sandstone while on the other it formed a shallow slope dotted with scrub, stunted trees, and clumps of brackish grass. High up on the far ridge, above the sandstone rock face, Poppy could make out the shape of a man sitting with his back against a boulder. A rifle lolled between his knees as he smoked.

She swung her binoculars back down to the quarry floor where approximately one hundred white-suited prisoners toiled in the heat. A handful of khaki and black uniforms moved between the ragged company. One of them, an enormous brute, occasionally lashed a prisoner across the back with what looked like a bullwhip.

Poppy swept the binoculars over the panorama searching for . . . *there*!

Her heart leapt as she caught sight of her husband. He was chipping slowly away at the sandstone rock face on the far side of the quarry, dressed in prison uniform, turned away from her. But she would have recognised him from any angle. The set of his shoulders, the grey at his sideburns.

Tears blurred her eyes and she forced herself to look away. She could not afford to smudge her make-up. Her disguise was integral to the plan.

Poppy was dressed as a traditional Kathak dancer. She wore a fuchsia pink blouse overlain with a dark mirror-worked waistcoat, and tight-fitting churidar trousers, above which she wore a pink lehenga – a loose, ankle-length skirt with gold and silver bands radiating from waist to hem. The skirt was cut on the round to enhance the flare of the lower half during spins. A peaked cap and heavy bangles completed the ensemble. Beside her Chef Lucknowwallah wore a shimmering beige silk kurta above white trousers. Seated on the wagon's tailboard, Irfan was dressed in a similar fashion with the addition of a colourful turban. And trotting behind the wagon came little Ganesha, his forehead painted in an intricate floral design of red and gold.

A tremor of anxiety ran through Poppy once again as she considered the plan that she and the chef had hastily thrown together earlier, after Lucknowwallah had made discreet enquiries and determined that new prisoners at Gouripur were routinely assigned to work gangs at the local quarry.

It seemed impossible that their makeshift scheme could work. But what choice had they?

The thought of doing nothing while her husband was left to rot in Gouripur Jail was unbearable. Time was of the essence. If Chopra's fellow inmates discovered that he was a former policeman, his prospects of a safe return from this nightmare would plummet. Perhaps they already knew, and even now were plotting against hi—

She shook away such thoughts. *Concentrate on the task at hand!*

The wagon rolled to a halt at the top of the slope leading down into the quarry. Fifty yards along the path a crude spit had been staked together beside a parked prison truck. A trio of badly plucked chickens were roasting, droplets of fat sizzling into the fire, an occasional singed feather erupting into flame.

'Hah,' muttered the chef. 'Call that roast chicken?'

A guard emerged from behind the truck, zipping up his trousers. He spotted the wagon and immediately called down into the quarry.

Moments later the big man Poppy had seen beating the other prisoners swaggered up from the quarry floor.

'Ram ram, sahib!' grinned Lucknowwallah ingratiatingly. 'We are a troupe of travelling musicians. May we offer you some entertainment?'

The brute furrowed his brow. 'This is a prison work gang. What are you doing here?'

'We are travelling through the region, sahib. We perform, and gratefully accept whatever kindness our patrons can offer. I assure you our performances are renowned throughout the state.'

The brute swung his crop at the toiling figures below. 'Do they look like they need entertainment?'

'Then perhaps for you and the other guards, sahib? Important men like you should be permitted a break, yes?'

The guard scowled, but his imminent rebuke was forestalled by Poppy slipping down from the wagon's box seat and sashaying towards him. Abruptly, she stopped, bowed at the waist, then launched into a series of spins, sending her brocaded skirt whirling around her.

His eyes glittered.

It had clearly been a long time since he had last been in the presence of a woman as attractive as Poppy Chopra.

As Poppy danced, another of the guards trudged up the rise, then another. Soon she had attracted an audience. Suddenly, she ground to a halt.

The brute frowned. 'Why have you stopped?'

'We are humble travellers, sahib,' explained the chef. 'We dance to fill our bellies, nothing more. Let us entertain you with our performance. And, in return, perhaps you will reward us with a few rupees for our efforts?' He reached into a straw basket between his feet. 'Perhaps we can offer something to accompany your food?' The bottle of cheap whisky glinted in the dying rays of the sun.

A trembling coursed through the guards. They looked at one another.

'Very well,' the brute said.

The sun continued to slip below the cliffs, emblazoning the ridge with colour, and throwing shadows across the quarry. Against the burning umber disc, vultures wheeled and cawed endlessly.

On the path above the quarry the guards had settled themselves around the fire. Those left down with the prisoners looked up enviously, drooling, wishing they too could join the impromptu festivities. Tiwari, the solitary guard stationed above the quarry on the cliffs, watched the scene with the eyes of a hawk, and the patience of a monk.

Standing before the fire, Poppy prepared to dance.

She willed herself to calm. She was a trained dancer – indeed, at the St Xavier Catholic School for Boys she taught classical Bharatanatyam and Kathak dance. But never had so much ridden on her talent as it did now. She bit her lip and looked over at the chef who was sitting on a rock with a double-headed dhol drum balanced across his knees. He gave her an encouraging nod. She glanced behind her to Irfan who jangled his tambourine brightly. The boy's face split into a grin and once again Poppy berated herself for bringing him along. Why had she allowed the chef to convince her? What kind of mother would put her child into danger? For Poppy did think of little Irfan as her child, regardless of what anyone said. A mother was, first and foremost, one who loved, and she loved the boy, and little Ganesha too. Her eyes moved to the young elephant, who gripped his own tambourine in his trunk and bashed it against the ground. The sound seemed to delight him and he bashed it again.

A round of raucous laughter lifted from the guards.

The chef had been right, Poppy reflected. Ganesha and Irfan made good additions to the troupe, a humorous and welcome distraction adding authenticity to their charade. In an ideal world, she would not have placed them in harm's way. Well, there was nothing to be done about it now . . .

She took a deep breath, then flung herself into the dance, Lucknowwallah beating out an accompanying rhythm on his drum. The guards began to wolf-whistle and clap, waving the greasy chicken legs in their fists.

Poppy concentrated on the dance, whirling around the fire, teasing with gestures of her hands, and occasionally striking a dramatic pose.

The classical Kathak dance told a story, and the story Poppy told now was one of hope and despair, of darkness and light, of love and betrayal. She poured every ounce of her lifelong affinity with the art form into her performance. As she whirled ever faster, the cheering grew, until even the prisoners down in the quarry paused and squinted up in the dying light to the pirouetting figure high above them. There was a timeless quality to the moment as if past and present had been brought together for one brief instant, and through Poppy something ancient and primal had been reignited in the world.

After a while Irfan laid down his tambourine, picked up the bottle of whisky and a cluster of steel cups, and began to move around the fire, pouring out a generous measure for each guard. Out of the corner of his eye Lucknowwallah watched as each man smacked his lips and drained his glass before demanding a refill.

Irfan cheerfully obliged.

Within minutes the cheering voices began to slur and eyelids began to droop.

The chef smiled inwardly. Evidently his special additive was beginning to take effect. It was time to begin phase two of the operation.

'Perhaps we can offer some water to your prisoners?' he said, with an oleaginous grin. 'It must be thirsty work, breaking rocks in the hot sun.'

Singh flung his cup at the fire, sending up a burst of flames. 'Pah! What do they need water for? They are lucky I don't . . . I don't . . . don't . . .' He lost his train of thought, and stared drunkenly at the chicken leg in his massive fist.

Poppy danced closer. 'Surely a great man like you would not begrudge water to such pitiful creatures?' she said, directing a winsome smile at the brute.

Singh looked blearily up at her, then lunged for the hem of her skirt. He missed and fell flat on his face, to the slurred laughter of his colleagues.

As he lay there Ganesha trotted over towards him and banged the tambourine on Singh's upturned bottom, eliciting another round of inebriated laughter. The little elephant dropped the tambourine and pretended to fumble for it. Quick as a flash, he plucked the set of manacle keys from Singh's belt and put them into his mouth. Then he picked up the tambourine and jogged over to Poppy who pretended to pet him. Deftly she took the keys and transferred them to a pocket sewn into her skirt.

Meanwhile, Singh had flopped his great body over.

He lay flat on his back, belly heaving, staring up at the twilit sky above. Finally, he flapped a hand at Poppy. 'Very well. Water for the prisoners. But in return I will have a private dance.'

Poppy picked up a leather waterskin and raced down into the quarry.

She ran quickly from prisoner to prisoner, occasionally stopping to offer water in order to allay the suspicions of the few guards remaining on the quarry floor. She recoiled in horror at the marks of beatings, hunger, and something else, a weariness etched onto their souls. She understood now what her fellow Mumbaikers meant when they talked of the brutality of Gouripur Jail.

Finally, she reached Chopra.

He watched her approach; the only sign that he recognised her coming was the momentary widening of his eyes. 'Poppy!' he hissed in astonishment as she placed the steel cup in his hand and splashed water into it. 'What the hell are you doing here?'

'Did you think you could just vanish without so much as a by-your-leave and I wouldn't notice?' she hissed back.

'This is no time for humour, Poppy!'

'I am not laughing,' said Poppy evenly. 'We are here to help you escape.'

'Have you lost your mind? Helping a prisoner escape is a criminal offence! If they catch you, you will end up in chains, just like me!'

'Then so be it,' said Poppy her eyes flashing angrily. 'But you didn't expect me to leave you here to rot, did you? Besides, who says it is always Ram's job to save Sita?' Her mouth clamped into a rectangle of obstinacy.

Words failed Chopra. His astonishment was second only to the fierce pride that welled inside him. Each time he thought that his wife's magnificence could no longer surprise him, she found another way to prove him wrong. 'Poppy,' he whispered. 'I don't know what to say.'

'Don't say anything. You'll probably just give me a lecture. You need to get out of those chains. Here.' She surreptitiously handed him the keys.

'How did you get these?'

'It doesn't matter. Listen carefully. You must wait for my signal. Then you must unlock yourself and run. Get up that slope and on to the road.' She nodded at the slope on the far side of the quarry, covered by scrub and stunted trees.

'What then?' asked Chopra. 'The guards have guns. Do you plan to outrun bullets?'

'You will have to wait and see,' said Poppy, mysteriously. 'It's all in hand.'

'There is one more problem. Up there.' Chopra raised his eyebrows to the ridge above the quarry. 'There's a guard with a rifle. An expert marksman.'

'Don't worry. He will be taken care of,' assured Poppy. 'You just be ready to go on my signal.'

'What is the signal?'

'You will know it when you see it.'

Chopra nodded. 'Go now, before they become suspicious. And Poppy . . . please be careful.'

Above the ridge Irfan approached the solitary guard named Tiwari.

To his left he could see the quarry laid out below his feet, wreathed in shadow. He saw Poppy moving among the prisoners and wondered briefly which one Chopra was. He reflected on the stroke of good fortune by which he had overheard Poppy and Chef Lucknowwallah planning Chopra's escape. He had insisted on coming along, and although Poppy had been against it, the chef had finally convinced her.

Irfan would have done anything for Chopra.

After all, he owed the man much more than mere loyalty. Chopra was Irfan's hero and now his hero needed him.

Irfan would not be found wanting . . . And besides, what a first-class adventure!

Irfan padded stealthily towards the edge of the cliff, but even so the stationary man somehow heard him approach. He spun around from his boulder, the rifle between his knees instantly materialising in his hands. As he sighted down the weapon, it seemed to Irfan for one steep second that the man would shoot. Fear froze him to the spot, and he almost dropped the bottle of whisky that he was carrying.

Tiwari, a gaunt man with a drooping moustache and a hollow face, stared at the boy, unmoving, before finally lowering his rifle.

Gathering his courage Irfan moved forward and poured out a measure of whisky. With trembling hands he held the steel cup out to the guard.

Tiwari's eyes were ghostly in the dusk. There seemed something immeasurably wounded in those eyes, as if Tiwari had seen things that had changed him beyond all recognition. Whatever it was, it stirred up a sudden terror in the boy.

He placed the cup on the ground, then turned and raced back the way he had come.

Chef Lucknowwallah fumbled in his pocket for his watch.

It was almost time.

He stood up from behind his drum. 'And now, great sirs, let us present the climax to our entertainment!' He strode over to the wagon, clambered in the back, and emerged with a wooden crate. He hauled the crate to the fire, then opened it and removed coloured objects of all shapes and sizes.

Fireworks.

Around the fire the drunken guards watched with sleep-heavy eyes. Some dozed, snoring into the encroaching dusk.

The chef set up a ring of fireworks around the spit. Then he nodded at Poppy, Irfan, and Ganesha. 'I suggest you all move back.'

He waited as they clambered back into the wagon. Poppy pulled on the reins, awakening the dozing bullock, and steered the wagon back around the curve of the winding path, Ganesha following. Once out of sight of the guards, she headed for the spot where the road met the shallow slope leading up from the eastern side of the quarry.

The chef lifted a flaming branch from the fire, lit the ring of fireworks, then stepped backwards into the shadows.

As the first of the fireworks shrieked into the sky, Lucknowwallah glanced down into the quarry. In the dying light every face was turned upwards. The firework reached its zenith and exploded in an extravaganza of sparkling contrails. A ghostly residue of light illuminated the watching prisoners.

Satisfied, Lucknowwallah turned and jogged back along the road, following the wagon.

Down in the quarry Chopra bent towards his ankles. Using the key Poppy had given him he quickly released himself. Then he jogged to his neighbour, Iqbal Yusuf, and bent to his manacles. 'What are you doing?' protested Yusuf.

'I'm not leaving without you.'

Yusuf looked up at the coruscating sky. '*You* are responsible for this?' A rueful smile twisted his greying features. 'You are more resourceful than I gave you credit for, Chopra. Now go. Don't waste your advantage on me.'

'I told you I'm not leaving without you. You've served your time. You don't deserve to die in this godforsaken hole.'

'We all receive the death decreed for us, my son.'

'I won't leave you to the mercy of these brutes. Now, come on!' Chopra shook the manacles off Yusuf's feet. Grabbing the older man by the forearm he led him towards the scree-covered slope, moving around the edge of the quarry, sticking to the shadows. Around them prisoners and guards gazed up into the sky, transfixed by the fireworks.

From the path Poppy watched Chopra and the other prisoner scrabbling up the slope. Terror and anxiety fought inside her. Just a little further! Then surely they would have pulled it off!

Another fusillade of fireworks screamed into the sky.

Suddenly, silhouetted on the rim of the quarry's western ridge, Poppy saw the solitary guard, Tiwari, crouched beside his boulder, sighting along his rifle.

Horror froze her limbs.

Why was he still alert? She turned to Irfan. 'Irfan, did you give the guard on the cliff the whisky?'

'Yes,' said Irfan, his face sombre in the flashing darkness.

'Did you see him drink it?'

Irfan began to nod, then hesitated. 'No,' he said, miserably.

Poppy looked back down into the quarry. 'Dear Shiva,' she whispered, 'if I have ever pleased you with my devotion then let me ask one thing of you now and I will never ask for anything again. Bring him safely to me. Please!'

Down on the slope Chopra ducked low as they scrabbled towards a stunted khejri tree. He could hear Yusuf wheezing behind him. 'Not much further—'

Something whizzed past his ear and pocked into the soil before him, sending up a puff of dust.

Chopra froze. And then, without warning Yusuf charged into him, bearing him to the ground. What the—?

He felt the old man's body convulse. Once, then a second time. Another puff of dust erupted by Chopra's face, sending a pebble skimming past his nose.

And suddenly he knew what was happening.

Tiwari! The marksman was shooting at them.

Chopra scrabbled out from under Yusuf, grabbed the old man by the arms, and dragged him behind the tree. He cradled the old man's grizzled head.

'What did you do?' he whispered.

Yusuf coughed. Chopra could feel a wet warmth seeping from Yusuf's back onto his legs. 'Don't fret, Chopra,' he said hoarsely. 'I've been waiting for this day for more years than I care to remember. Finally, I will be with my daughter again. Now you must make it back to the ones you love.'

Chopra stared down at the wizened old face, the dying light in those rheumy eyes. 'You saved my life,' he said.

'Not once, but twice!' grinned Yusuf. The grin dissolved into a hacking cough. Droplets of blood fell from his mouth onto his grimy uniform. 'Now don't let . . . my efforts . . . go to waste. *Go!*'

His eyes closed, and his head lolled back.

Finally, his ragged breathing rasped to a halt.

A deep sadness yawned through Chopra, a sense that something sacrilegious had occurred. During his career he had witnessed many men expire. Most of those men had been criminals of one feather or another; some had been colleagues from the force. This was a rare occasion when he felt the loss of a criminal as deeply as if he had been a man in the uniform of the Brihanmumbai Police. Yusuf's death, murderer though he be, seemed to him a crime against the intrinsic harmony of the world.

He laid the old man gently down on the ground.

Then he peered out from behind the tree, squinting up at the ridge from which Tiwari was taking aim. Instantly, wood chips exploded above his head, showering over him.

He ducked back hurriedly.

He was trapped.

Chopra cursed, his mind whirling.

He had no doubt that should he make a dash for it, Tiwari would cut him down. He knew too that somewhere up there Poppy was waiting for him. He couldn't let her see him die like this. She didn't deserve that.

Sweating hard against the tree, Chopra wondered what the hell he did now.

Ganesha raced along in the dusk.

The sun was almost below the horizon, the path ahead illuminated by its dying rays and the fireworks blazing overhead. Ganesha knew that Chopra was in danger. He knew that if he did not act, Chopra would die. Pebbles bounced beneath the little elephant's feet, ricocheting over the edge of the cliff and down into the quarry.

He arrived at the top of the ridge.

A boulder loomed before him. Beside the boulder, he saw a man crouched in the dirt, sighting down a rifle. Ganesha lifted his trunk and smelled the high wind that had struck up across the quarry. He smelled the fine mist of sandstone particles; the sickly sweet odours of blood and sweat; the bitter aroma of human misery. And there, beneath everything, a distant scent, a scent as familiar to the little elephant as his own.

Chopra.

Ganesha put his head down and charged.

He steamed into the sniper's back just as Tiwari fired again.

The shot went wild as the guard tumbled forward and over the edge of the cliff. He rolled down the sheer slope, crying out, scrabbling at the rock face to slow his fall. He landed in a heap atop a pile of chipped sandstone, bellowing in agony as an ankle twisted under him.

The rifle clattered away.

Ganesha squinted across the yawning crater to where he had scented Chopra.

An elephant has poor eyesight, but he could just about make out the tree on the shallow slope on the quarry's far side, behind which Chopra was hidden.

He flapped his ears, and twirled his trunk.

Then he turned and raced back along the ridge.

Chopra knew that he had to move.

Taking his courage in his hands, he risked another peek . . . and saw Tiwari tumbling from his perch. And then he saw the elephant-shaped silhouette hovering on the edge of the cliff.

Ganesha!

Chopra leapt up from behind the tree and propelled himself up the slope, pebbles scattering under his feet.

He reached the top and found Poppy beckoning him towards a covered wagon. He could see Lucknowwallah on the wagon's box seat, the reins gripped in his hands, a sheen of anxious perspiration on his features. Beside the wagon Irfan was hopping from foot to foot.

At that moment Ganesha came trotting out of the darkness.

'Let's go,' said Chopra. He grabbed Poppy by the hand and headed towards the wagon.

'The only place you are going is hell.'

Chopra turned.

Staggering out of the dark behind Ganesha came Buta Singh.

The brute's face was twisted in rage; a knife glinted in his massive fist. Behind him Chopra saw three other guards lumbering groggily down the road, one of them clutching a rifle.

Singh stumbled to a halt before the wagon. 'Do you know what the punishment is for trying to escape?' he rasped.

Chopra felt the crawl of helplessness. His eyes measured up the brute, the muscles that strained Singh's uniform. Chopra had little doubt that Singh would make short work of him. And if that happened, what would be the fate of those he left behind?

His mind raced ahead. There had to be *something* he could do.

'No?' said Singh. 'Me neither. This is because no escaping prisoner has ever got back to the jail alive to be punished.' He stepped forward. 'Prepare to meet your maker.'

A distant buzzing erupted along the road like a swarm of bees.

As they stood, caught in bewilderment, the noise became a wall of sound, a thunderous rapture . . . and then, erupting from the darkness, cresting a rise in the road, there came a fury of noise and light.

Chopra raised his hands to ward off the stupendous onslaught. He squinted through his fingers into the blinding light, and saw . . . an armada of motorcycles, arriving in wave after pounding wave like the hosts of hell, the beams of their headlights banishing the darkness, the roar of their 500cc engines heralding an ear-splitting apocalypse.

The Bombay Bullet Club.

The Bisons were on the move.

The guards behind Singh looked at each other, then turned and fled.

A motorcycle skidded to a halt in front of Chopra. The rider pushed back the visor of his helmet. 'Need a lift?' said Gerry Fernandes.

Chopra was dumbfounded. But he had no time to wonder about the presence of the Bullet Club now. He clambered onto the back of the motorbike, even as Poppy, Irfan, and the chef did the same. He glanced at the wagon, unceremoniously abandoned along with its mystified bullock. Nothing to be done about that now, he thought. No doubt the bullock would eventually wend its way home. And then he remembered Ganesha. 'Wait!' he said. 'Ganesha!'

'It's all taken care of,' shouted Fernandes over his shoulder.

Chopra looked around and saw that Ganesha had clambered into a reinforced sidecar on one of the bikes.

'He's in good hands!' yelled Fernandes, and gunned the bike.

They roared away from the quarry leaving the enraged Buta Singh standing dumbfounded in a cloud of dust and fumes.

As they vanished around a curve in the road Chopra looked back, and thought once more of Iqbal Yusuf, a convicted murderer who had given his life for him. He remembered Gandhi's words: 'The best way to find yourself is to lose yourself in the service of others.' Perhaps, at the last, with his selfless act, Yusuf had rediscovered his true self, the man he had been before the black storms of fate had engulfed him.

RANGWALLA TRAILS A GHOST

Rangwalla could not sleep.

The hem of his sari swished over the floor as he made loops around his bedroom. He glanced at the clock on the wall.

Midnight.

Would the singing girl appear again tonight? In spite of Premchand's scepticism Rangwalla knew that the girl was real. There was a mystery here that he was certain would shed light on the Master's interest in the eunuchs of the Red For—

A bloodcurdling scream shattered the silence.

Rangwalla's heart leapt into his mouth.

In the corridor he found the other eunuchs spilling from their bedrooms in terror and bewilderment.

'What was that?' asked Mamta. 'It sounded like a banshee.'

'It sounded like someone was being murdered,' shuddered Kavita.

At that instant the door to Rupa's bedroom opened and she raced into their midst, clutching her pigtail, from which a trail of smoke arose.

'Help!' she shrieked. 'The ghost tried to kill me!'

'Calm down,' advised Mamta. 'Tell us what happened.'

'What's all the racket?' asked Parvati, emerging from her room, wiping sleep from her eyes.

Rangwalla shrank back in fright. 'Your face!' he gasped. 'It's hideous!'

Parvati crossed her arms. 'Well, that's a fine way to greet a friend,' she pouted.

'It's her face mask,' explained Mamta.

'This?' said Parvati. 'Just something my grandmother used to swear by. Papaya extract, flour, cement, and a dash of cow dung. Nothing beats the homemade recipes.' She turned to the sobbing Rupa. 'Come now, Rupa, get a hold of yourself. What happened?'

'I don't know!' wailed Rupa. 'One minute I was fast asleep, the next my hair was on fire! The ghost tried to burn me alive!'

Parvati and Mamta exchanged glances. 'Rupa, dear,' said Parvati delicately, 'were you by any chance smoking when you fell asleep?'

Rupa held up the end of her plait. A thin stream of smoke arose from the charred stump. 'Do you think a cigarette did this?' she snapped, before adding, 'What if it possesses me? My God, what if it makes me talk like a *man*?'

'You *do* talk like a man,' muttered Rangwalla.

Behind them Mamta slipped off into Rupa's bedroom, returning in short order. Pincered between her thumb and forefinger was a half-smoked cigarette. She wafted it under Rupa's nose. 'How many times have I told you not to smoke in bed? It's a wonder you didn't set the whole place alight!'

'I suggest we all return to our bedrooms,' said Parvati. 'We have another busy day ahead of us. Sonali, dear, may I have a word with you?'

When the others had left, Parvati fixed Rangwalla with a bird-bright eye. 'Forgive Rupa. She acts like a fighter, but, in truth, she is the frailest of us. Her family cast her out as a child. They did not wish to endanger the marital chances of her siblings. Ignorance, I'm afraid, has always been our greatest enemy. Many people don't even understand how eunuchs come to be, though they are happy to condemn us. Most eunuchs are not born; we willingly undergo the castration ritual – which for us is a defining moment in our lives, one of celebration – because we understand from a young age that we are *different*, and there is no place in normal society for us. Some day someone will do for us what Ambedkar did for the untouchables, and we will take our rightful place in this world. Until then the men of power think that acknowledging us will tip society into moral ruin. That is why we are loyal to the Queen. She fights for us; she teaches us to stand up for ourselves.' She sighed. 'And the Queen thinks there is something amiss here. I must say I agree with her.'

'Is that why she sent you?'

Parvati smiled. 'You did not think it was because of my looks, did you, sahib?'

Rangwalla coloured. 'Sahib?' he said weakly. 'You mean "sister", don't you?'

Parvati continued to smile.

Rangwalla sighed. 'How long have you known?'

'From the very beginning. You cannot become a eunuch merely by putting on a sari and a bad wig, I am afraid. But let us concentrate on the matter at hand. Let us try and work this out from first principles. The most important questions in life are those men ask of themselves. So . . . what is the question the Master is seeking to answer with this elaborate charade?'

Rangwalla realised that he had underestimated Parvati's keen mind. He supposed it was something that routinely happened to the eunuchs; it was a human failing to think less of those one looked down upon. 'I don't know,' he confessed.

'Whatever it is, it is rooted here, in this place. I can feel it. Perhaps it even has something to do with this mysterious singing girl of yours.' She grimaced. 'I, for one, will be relieved when the Master finally reveals his hand.'

After Parvati had returned to her bedroom Rangwalla headed back to his own room.

At the last instant an idea occurred to him.

He opened the door, shouted, 'Goodnight, sisters!' then slammed it shut, without entering. Instead, he tiptoed across the corridor and shrank down beside a large clay vase on the landing.

Then he settled down to wait.

Rangwalla was a veteran of countless stakeouts and had learned to vacate his mind, so that he might pass hours in a state of suspended animation before leaping into action at the opportune moment. He found his mind drifting back to his home, his wife, who'd stood by him through thick and thin – and there had been plenty of thin over the years. He'd had to tell her that Chopra had sent him out of town on a case: that was as close to the truth as he dared admit. And then there were his children, beloved and infuriating. Wasn't he supposed to meet his son's tutors this week? The boy was bright but refused to knuckle down and study. Unlike his sister, who was warning her father that she intended to go to university to study law. He tried to imagine his temperamental daughter as a lawyer. Heaven help the opposing counsel. Heaven help the judge! But how was Rangwalla going to afford the fees? And what university did she intend to go to, anyway? He would certainly have to put his foot down if she insisted on studying outside Mumbai. How would he keep an eye on her if she left the city?

He thought of Chopra, and wondered how he was getting on with the kidnapping case. What would he make of Rangwalla's present situation? Twenty years he'd followed Chopra's instruction, and never once found himself questioning the man. Honesty, of the incorruptible type, was so rare in the service that when they'd first met Rangwalla had been given pause. He would never admit it out loud but over time Chopra had become his hero. *This is what we must all aspire to*, he had said, without actually saying it. Rangwalla had thought he'd spend the rest of his days following where his senior officer led. But life has a way of springing nasty surprises, like a lizard down the back of the neck. Chopra's heart attack, for instance, and then Rangwalla's dismissal from the force on trumped-up charges – an act of petty revenge by ACP Rao – placing his home, his family, his very existence in jeopardy. And into this murk had come Chopra, riding to the rescue with his offer of employment at the agency.

In truth, Rangwalla knew that he was blessed. He had a loving family, a job he enjoyed, and people around him he liked and respected. All of this stood in stark contrast to the eunuchs, who had only each other.

He realised that he could hear singing. It was the same voice he had heard the previous night.

He waited, breathlessly, as the voice approached.

Peeking from behind the vase he saw a woman. She was dressed in a plain white sari, like a widow, the loose end of the sari pulled over her head so that it formed a cowl.

The woman stopped for a moment in the corridor, just yards from Rangwalla's room. He was certain the other eunuchs would hear her, but their doors remained closed.

Then the woman turned and glided away back down the corridor.

Rangwalla did not hesitate.

Ghost or no ghost, he had to get to the bottom of the mystery. Besides, he had always been too much of a cynic to place an excess of belief in the supernatural. India may have been a place of mystery and mysticism, but the truth was that behind most seemingly occult occurrences lay perfectly mundane explanations, impressive only to the gullible. And Abbas Rangwalla was nobody's fool.

Rangwalla followed the singing woman along the same circuitous path as the previous night. He watched as she turned into the alcove where the painting of the Master's mother hung.

The singing abruptly stopped.

He raced around the corner . . . but the woman had vanished.

This time Rangwalla was not content to leave without an explanation. He knew what he had seen. The woman could not have disappeared into thin air.

He began to examine every inch of the space, using the skills he had honed from countless crime scenes. He scrutinised the floor, then the walls. He looked under the carved wooden seat.

Nothing.

He inspected the twin marble leopards, prodding and poking them.

Nothing.

He turned finally to the portrait of the Master's mother, pulling aside the drapes.

The old woman looked down upon him once more, her expression of inherent malevolence unchanged.

Rangwalla shuddered, then began to examine the heavy gilt frame. He ran his fingers along the grooves. It was then that he noticed something. A line in the dust a centimetre from the edge of the painting. The line told him that the painting had been moved and had not been put back in exactly the same place. He dug his fingers under the frame and lifted the lower part of the portrait from the wall, before peering underneath.

There!

A small catch, like a lever, embedded in the wall.

Rangwalla reached up and pulled the lever.

Below the painting a section of the wainscoting swung back to reveal a gaping hole. A musty draught blew in from the opening.

Rangwalla set the painting back down, then, taking a deep breath, plunged into the darkness. Behind him the secret trapdoor swung back into place.

He waited for his eyes to adjust to the gloom.

The darkness was illuminated by tiny beams of light falling in through a succession of cut-out eyes dotted among the peacocks' tails that adorned the mansion's walls.

Crouching low he followed the cobwebbed corridor, shortly coming to an iron staircase that spiralled down to the ground floor, before abruptly ending at a doorway.

Rangwalla carefully swung back the door, and peered out.

He was at the rear of the haveli, where it abutted fields. The patter of feet moved away from him through the wheat.

He set off after the ghostly intruder, navigating through the waist-high stalks. The night swelled around him, starlight glimmering on the nodding heads of wheat.

Half an hour later he emerged into a clearing.

Before him was a narrow river, forded by a plank bridge. Beyond the bridge the trail meandered up to a village, hunkered down for the night. A bullock moved in the shadows of a peepal tree. A goat bleated. The smell of dung wafted on the breeze.

A blur of movement caught Rangwalla's eye. It was the woman, ducking into a hut on the very outskirts of the village.

Rangwalla crossed the creaking bridge, then headed towards the hut.

He hesitated outside the brick-and-thatch dwelling, and considered what he was about to do.

He could hear the sounds of movement within.

Overcoming his doubts, he pushed back the wooden door and entered the hut.

Inside, he was confronted by a scene of rural domesticity.

The woman was crouched down beside a fire-pit, blowing on hot coals, a blackened pot on the fire, a butterchurn by her side. The woman's sari was pulled back from her face and Rangwalla could see that she was probably in her early thirties, with dusky skin, and large doe eyes.

Behind the woman, on a charpoy, lay an old man, wheezing in the glow of a kerosene lantern. Rangwalla recognised him – it was the haveli's watchman, Shantaram.

The girl looked up in astonishment. Then her eyes narrowed. She snatched up a knife, and stood, facing Rangwalla. 'You followed me!' she hissed.

'Yes,' said Rangwalla. 'I want to know who you are and why you came to the haveli. What game are you playing?'

'Game?' A burst of blood darkened her cheeks. 'You think this is a game, you – you – !' She ran her eyes over Rangwalla's figure.

In the heat of the moment he had forgotten that he must seem very strange to these villagers, a eunuch from the big city, materialising in their home in the dead of night.

He lifted off his plaited wig.

'I am not a eunuch,' he said. 'My name is Rangwalla. I am a detective. I am here to find out why the Master is inviting eunuchs to his home.'

The girl hesitated, but did not lower the knife.

'Let him be, Granddaughter.'

Rangwalla turned to Shantaram, who had raised himself on the bed. The watchman coughed, a hacking, rattling sound. Sweat sparkled on his forehead. Rangwalla realised, for the first time, that the man was sick.

The watchman's eyes lingered, filled with an ineffable melancholia. Finally, he spoke: 'The Master's story is a strange one, full of sadness and horror. Are you sure you wish to hear it?'

'It is why I am here,' said Rangwalla.

'We can't trust him, Father,' hissed the girl. 'We know nothing about his real intentions. We should go to the authorities, as I have always said.'

'Perhaps this is for the best, Granddaughter,' said Shantaram. He spoke to Rangwalla: 'Listen, friend, listen, and then do what you will. It is time that the truth came out. I don't have long to live and I do not wish to go to my grave with this burden.' Firelight glinted in the old man's eyes. 'It began when the Master was young . . .'

ON THE RUN

For the first time in his life Inspector Ashwin Chopra (Retd) understood what it meant to be the hunted rather than the hunter.

A fugitive.

The word had a strange taste in his mouth. It was as if he had awoken into an alternate reality, one in which everything he knew about himself had been inverted. An upside-down world where good and evil had been turned inside out and back to front.

How in God's name had he ended up in this position?

Following the daring escape from Gouripur Jail, the Bombay Bullet Club had escorted Chopra all the way to Bhiwandi, on the outskirts of Mumbai. Here, on a deserted stretch of road, another member of the Bullet Club awaited, anxiously peering out from behind the wheel of Chopra's Tata van.

Chopra dismounted from the rear of Gerry Fernandes' motorbike.

He felt exhilarated. And yet, at the same time, there was a surreal quality to the events that had recently engulfed his life, culminating in this wild bike ride through the countryside.

He stuck out a hand. 'Thank you. I don't know how I can ever repay you.'

Fernandes grasped his hand. 'What was it you told me, Chopra? "You needed help; I did what I could. That's what friends do."'

They watched the swarm of motorcycles roar away down the road, Ganesha peering disconsolately after them as they veered around a curve and out of sight. Then Chopra loaded up the van and drove back to Sahar, and home.

On the way he dropped off Chef Lucknowwallah. 'When I employed you I didn't envisage asking you to do anything like this. This is above and beyond the call of duty.'

'You'd be surprised the things I've been asked to do, Chopra,' muttered Lucknowwallah. 'The Nawab of Oudh once asked me to baste his naked body in white chocolate. He wanted to leap out from a specially constructed cake at his son's wedding pretending to be a snowman. But the chocolate melted off him while he was in there.' The chef shuddered. 'It took me months to recover from the experience.'

They arrived at the restaurant, unnaturally quiet in the early hours, a marked contrast from the clamour and din of the daytime. Ganesha trotted into his rear compound, plopping down under the mango tree, and helping himself to a piece of fallen fruit. Poppy wiped down Irfan's dusty face, then ordered him to change into his shorts and vest. She warmed him a glass of milk, and a similar bucket for Ganesha laced with his favourite Dairy Milk chocolate.

Finally, she turned to her husband, who had been quietly sitting on the veranda, staring into space. She approached him hesitantly. Now that the surreal drama of the escape was behind them, it began to dawn on Poppy that Chopra had been through an ordeal that she could not hope to truly comprehend. She could tell this from the grim set of his mouth, the shadows around his eyes.

'Time to go home,' she said, with a forced brightness.

'I'm not going home,' said Chopra, still staring straight ahead.

Poppy's voice split the humid night air in alarm. 'What do you mean?' she protested. 'I have only just found you. If you think I am letting you out of my sight, mister, you are sorely mistaken!'

'Poppy,' said Chopra gently, 'believe me, there's nothing I would rather do than come home with you and forget this whole sordid business. But you must see that I have to finish this. And I cannot keep you with me while I do that. It is that simple.'

Poppy bit her lip. 'Have you any idea what it was like for me? Discovering that you were in that place? Locked up? I was terrified. I didn't know if I would ever see you again. But how can *you* understand? You are a man. The big macho hero. You have no idea what a wife goes through.'

'That's unfair,' said Chopra gently. 'We have always been a team. I could not be who I am without your support.' He stood, and swept his wife into an unexpected embrace. Poppy stiffened, then gradually melted into him. Finally, she looked up at him. 'Must you really go? What if your enemies are still looking for you?'

'I don't think that's likely. Rao must have kept everything off the books, if only to hide his own actions in illegally packing me off to Gouripur Jail. Of course, he couldn't have done *that* without help, possibly from those same enemies. Which means he's not likely to bring attention to the fact that I've escaped. He wouldn't wish to highlight his own failure. After all these years I know exactly how he thinks.' Chopra sighed. 'Trust me, Poppy, it's not the police or political enemies that are worrying me. No. What really bothers me is that Bijli Verma might think that I vanished with her son's ransom; or worse, botched the whole thing entirely and got Vicky killed.' Chopra did not need to add that this sat uneasily with his professional pride. Poppy knew her husband well enough.

'Why don't you go to her and explain?'

'Without the money? My explanation will sound hollow. I need to find Vicky, or at least determine what may have happened to him. I cannot go to her empty-handed.'

'Well, if you're so determined to go off into danger again, at least take me with you.'

'That would be impractical, Poppy,' said Chopra. 'And there is also Irfan to think about.'

Poppy's mouth opened to protest, but then closed again. She realised her husband was right. As much as it horrified her to know that he was going to be out there, getting into God only knew what trouble, she understood that it would be even more difficult for him if she were with him. And who would look after little Irfan? Without either of them around the boy would inevitably get into the sort of scrapes that seemed to follow him around. 'Then at least take Ganesha,' she pleaded.

Chopra hesitated, then nodded. 'Very well.'

'You're going to need some supplies,' said Poppy, drawing herself up. 'But first and foremost: a good meal. I can't imagine what they've been feeding you in that jail. You've practically wasted away. Go and wash.'

Chopra cleaned himself up as best he could in the restaurant's washroom, and then changed into the spare set of clothes he always kept in the office: a clean shirt, trousers and comfortable shoes. He stripped off his prison uniform and threw it into the pedal bin under his desk. As he dressed, he began to feel the return of normality, or at least the illusion of it.

Even that was a welcome relief.

Before leaving the office he took his spare revolver from the locked drawer of his desk and checked it, before tucking it into his trousers; he had lost his trusty Anmol at the Madh Fort when Rao had arrested him.

He returned to the veranda to find that Poppy, with Irfan's help, had laid out a meal.

Investigating the various dishes he discovered three different kinds of curry – potato and bottle gourd, spicy chicken korma, and red lentils – together with saffron rice and chapatti. The image of Poppy fixing him a meal just after she had broken him out of prison seemed ludicrous at first, but then that was Poppy all over. A lump arose in his throat as he acknowledged, once again, the great bond between them. Not for the first time he wished he had the words to express his feelings, but he had never claimed to be a poet. He liked to believe that Poppy knew, in her heart, how much he thought of her.

It was not always necessary, he felt, to spell things out.

'Here,' said Poppy as he ate, handing him her mobile phone. 'Keep this. You will need it.'

Ganesha had joined them, sitting below the veranda, watching Chopra with round eyes as he wolfed the food.

The little elephant had had a thrilling day.

Not only had he helped his beloved guardian escape from a terrible place, but now here he was with all the people he loved most in the world as they shared a midnight meal. Happiness inflated the little elephant's ears, and he trumpeted a gentle note of satisfaction.

As he ate Chopra considered his next move.

The kidnappers had taken the ransom two nights ago. According to Poppy – who slavishly followed the goings-on in Bollywood – there had been no updates to suggest that Vicky had recovered from his mystery 'illness'. Indeed, the news was agog with the delayed 'mega-shoot' on *The Mote in the Third Eye of Shiva*. The consensus was that if Vicky didn't materialise soon and finish off the cursed movie, he could kiss his fledgling career goodbye.

Chopra went over the case details.

Vicky Verma had been abducted from the dressing room beneath the stage at the Andheri Sports Stadium. His kidnapper, Ali, had made his way in through the stadium's delivery car park while the actor was onstage, incapacitated Vicky in the dressing room when he came down for his quick costume change, then nonchalantly wheeled him out bundled inside the young star's own costume chest.

Chopra had two leads to follow.

The first was the bracelet Ganesha had discovered at the scene of the kidnapping. Before his arrest, the bracelet had taken Chopra to a ramshackle home in the Mira Road district. In the home he had found a drunken old man and the woman, Aaliya Ghazi – Ali's cousin. He was not yet certain whether Aaliya was involved, or of Ali's ultimate motive in kidnapping Vicky. Could it be linked to the furore Bijli had caused with her outspoken views years ago?

Possibly.

But Chopra had always believed in following the balance of probability during an investigation, and it was his second lead, he felt, that would take him to the heart of the conspiracy. The film's producer P.K. Das, in hock to gangsters, and seeking an insurance payout by derailing his own production, seemed the most likely mastermind behind the kidnapping. Ali was merely a tool used to carry out the deed.

If Chopra wished to unravel the plot his first port of call must be the home of the feted producer.

With the impromptu meal over, he prepared to leave. Irfan had fallen asleep in his chair, and so Chopra carried him to his cot on the veranda, laying him down, and kissing him gently on the forehead. Then he led Ganesha out to the van.

Quickly, he drove Poppy home.

The guard Bahadur awoke blearily and watched as Chopra got out of the van and put his hands on his wife's shoulders. Chopra could see that Poppy was holding back tears. 'I'll be back as soon as I can.'

'If you're not, I'll find you and break both your legs,' promised Poppy groggily.

Chopra got back into the van. 'Let's get to work, boy,' he muttered, as Ganesha huddled closer to the front seats.

He switched on the van's engine and slowly edged the vehicle out from the side of the road.

HIMALAYAN STUDIOS REDUX

Chopra was led inside the palatial home of P.K. Das by a burly manservant, down into an expansive basement where he discovered the producer sitting in his private viewing theatre watching a black-and-white movie.

Das looked up as he entered. 'Isn't it a bit late for visiting, Chopra?' he said.

'This can't wait.'

Das stared at him, then returned his gaze to the screen. '*The Legend of Devdas*. The first picture I ever made,' he said. 'It was never released. The actor I had cast as Devdas got so carried away with his performance that he drank himself to death.' Devdas was the legendary tale of the jilted lover who drowned his woes in alcohol. 'I thought my career had ended before it had begun, but Raj Kapoor bailed me out, and my next picture went on to become a hit.'

Das stood and faced his visitor. His face was haggard, a deep weariness evident on his avuncular features. 'Tell me you have good news, Chopra. Tell me you have found our friend.'

'That would be difficult,' said Chopra stonily. 'Given that *your* friends have him.'

'*My* friends?' Das's eyebrows leapt in astonishment. 'What are you talking about?'

'I know that you are in debt. You took money from gangsters to finish your movie. But the gamble failed, and now they have kidnapped Vicky so that you can claim the insurance.'

Das stared at Chopra.

Then he sat down heavily, whisky spilling from the tumbler in his hand.

Finally, he spoke, his gaze hollow. 'All I've ever wanted is to make movies. My father came over from Lahore on the Frontier Mail in the thirties – just as all the greats did: Prithviraj, Dev Anand, Dilip Kumar. All he had was the clothes on his back and a dream in his eye. He joined the Zarko Circus – that's where he fell in love with Fearless Nadia, do you remember her? No? Before your time, I suppose. She was the daughter of a British army Scot posted to Bombay. After his death she toured the country as part of the Zarko, before joining Wadia Movietone, the Wadia Brothers' production house. They turned her into a star – she was tremendous in *Hunterwali*; she wore tight leather shorts and a mask, and she did all her own stunts! My father followed her into the business – he worked his way up, starting as a clapper boy. People remember him now as a great producer, but he cut his teeth on adverts. "Sweetheart Toothpaste makes your smile sweeter than sweet for your sweet."' Das chuckled. 'That was the golden age. Real actors, real plots. Brylcreemed heroes, and monsoon goddesses. Even the tantrums were better. I remember once Vyjayanthimala threw her poodle at her leading man because he kept fluffing his lines. She knocked him off the balcony of the Centaur Hotel. He fell three floors and broke both legs. But he never fluffed his lines again . . . What is Bollywood, Chopra? Show me where it is on a map. It was men like my father who made this industry.' Das rose from his seat and walked to the wall. He pushed aside a framed photo of Raj Kapoor to reveal a small wall safe.

He unlocked the safe and removed something from inside.

When he turned back he was holding a revolver.

'*The Mote in the Third Eye of Shiva* was supposed to be my magnum opus. I've won six Filmfare statuettes, but never for Best Film. I poured everything into this production, Chopra. You're right, I sold my soul to the Devil. What else could I do? The banks wouldn't give me another rupee. I saw everything I had spent a lifetime building sinking into the sand. I panicked.'

As Chopra listened, his mind raced ahead. His spare revolver had been taken from him by the security guards at the gates. Now he weighed his chances of rushing Das.

The producer stared down at the gun. 'This belonged to my friend, Sammy Sarwan. He made a number of low-budget action flicks in the eighties. Then he lost his shirt on a vanity project, *Camel Blood Feud in Rajasthan*. After the bailiffs took everything he owned, and his wife left him, he went back to the ruins of his set, sat down on the floor, and shot himself. This industry gives you the stars, but it takes its pound of flesh.' Das locked eyes with

Chopra. 'I swear to you that I – or the people I have borrowed from – have nothing to do with Vicky's kidnapping. In fact, Pyarelal and his men have been scouring the city for him. We need Vicky back to complete this picture. I've managed to gain a couple of days since his vanishing act by intimidating, bullying, and pleading with our creditors, but we are hanging on by our fingernails. If Vicky doesn't materialise by tomorrow they will call in their markers and we *all* lose. So you see, I couldn't have kidnapped him. I'm guilty of many things – arrogance, hubris – but not of *that*. I admit I was forced to discipline the boy, more than once, but I never harmed him.' He turned back to the safe. 'You're right that I took out insurance on the picture. But the problem is that insurance is only valid if you can afford to keep up the premiums.' He removed a letter, and handed it over.

Chopra scanned the red-lettered notice, picking out key sentences. FAILURE TO PAY; NULL AND VOID, and, finally, YOUR COVER HAS BEEN TERMINATED. He looked up to meet the producer's watery gaze. 'There's something else I need to know. Two days ago I went to meet Vicky's kidnappers, to deliver the ransom. But the police turned up and ruined everything. Before you showed me this insurance notice I thought that, perhaps, it was you who had put them on to me. That you knew about the exchange and tried to derail Vicky's rescue.' The question of how ACP Rao had arrived at the ransom drop had now taken on great significance for Chopra. Because if it wasn't Das or his people then it meant someone else had tipped off the cops. But who would want to sabotage the ransom exchange? And why? Whoever it was represented a hidden danger, a snake waiting in the grass, and before he could move forward he had to uncover the snake's identity.

'I admit,' said Das, 'after you came to see me my suspicions were raised, particularly when you asked me about Pyarelal and beating Vicky. So I asked Pyarelal to have you followed. He saw you go to Bijli's home, a private detective. I guessed then what I already suspected: that Vicky was missing and not ill, as she claimed. I hoped you might lead us to him. But we didn't know about any kidnapping or a ransom. Pyarelal lost you in traffic two nights ago; he's been looking for you since.' He held up the revolver. 'Find Vicky. Find him before I'm forced to use this, Chopra. My life is in your hands.'

Chopra swung the Tata Venture to a halt beside the road.

A homeless man swaddled in rags slept fitfully on a filthy potato sack, his knees curled up to his chin. Beside him a stray dog with patchy fur and prominent ribs also slept, one leg raised in the air, as if poised in a dream. A palm tree stretched up into the night above, a full moon visible between the splayed fronds.

Chopra took out the mobile phone Poppy had given him.

As he was leaving Das's home he had passed a succession of old film posters, and this had once again returned his thoughts to the mysterious woman in the poster at Aaliya Ghazi's home. Das's revelation regarding the defunct insurance policy had all but convinced Chopra of the producer's innocence. He had to look elsewhere for the true motive behind the abduction. His old policeman's instincts were screaming at him that the woman in the poster was somehow integral to the case – he had ignored them long enough.

He dialled Cyrus Dinshaw at the Goldspot Cinema. '*Queen of the Kohinoor Circus*. There was an actress in it whose name I can't remember.'

He heard Dinshaw noisily pulling old movie catalogues from his shelves and dusting them off. 'Ah, yes,' he said, eventually, 'Ayesha Azmi. Started her career with a bang, but it fizzled out in short order. There was a scandal, if I recall, all hush-hush, and then she dropped out of sight altogether.'

'What sort of scandal?'

He heard Dinshaw scratching his chin. 'I'm afraid that's stretching even my memory. Besides, she was never a big star . . . Wait a minute! It was something to do with Bijli, Bijli Verma. Yes, I remember now. That husband of hers, Jignesh, he had some sort of thing with this woman. Got her pregnant, then dropped her like a hot coal as soon as Bijli appeared on the scene. At least that was the gossip. It never made it into the press, so I never knew the exact details.'

'What happened to the woman, Ayesha?'

'No idea. She vanished from the industry.'

'And the child?'

'Probably got rid of it. I doubt she'd have been foolish enough to keep it. Not much call for a pregnant single mother as a heroine. Not in those days. What's this about, Chopra?'

'I'll tell you when I see you.'

Chopra tapped the phone against his leg. So, his intuition had proved correct. There *was* a link between Aaliya Ghazi and Bijli Verma by way of the woman in the poster, Ayesha Azmi. But how *exactly* were Ayesha, Aaliya, and Ali connected? He could hazard an educated guess, but he would need confirmation from Bijli Verma . . .

But first he had to discover who had sabotaged the ransom drop. Or perhaps the question, once again, was: who benefited if Vicky never returned?

The phone rang exactly four times before a gruff voice answered. 'Chopra? How the hell are you?' Chopra heard a second, louder voice unleashing a torrent of abuse in the background. 'Give me a second. Let me step outside.'

Ten seconds later, the voice returned. 'What time do you call this?' said Ranjan Ahuja. 'You woke up the Dragon.'

'I need your help, old friend.'

Ranjan Ahuja was the General Manager of the eastern division of Mahanagar Telephone Nigam Limited, Mumbai's principal telephone-line provider. Chopra had known Ahuja for over a decade, calling upon him when his investigations necessitated tapping the phone lines of local criminals or requisitioning call logs.

Quickly, Chopra explained what he needed.

A smoky silence drifted down the phone as Ahuja lit a cigarette. 'You know, I heard about your detective agency. I always thought you were crazy – frying pan into fire and all that. Do you know what I'm going to do when I retire? Not a damned thing. I've got a little shack down in Goa. I'm going to sit there all day drinking coconut feni and eating tiger prawns.' He launched into a hacking cough, the phlegm rattling around in his throat. 'Let me see what I can do.'

Chopra paced the dark tarmac anxiously as the minutes ticked away. Ganesha paced behind him, watching him with round eyes. 'It's okay, boy,' said Chopra, realising that he was transmitting his restlessness to his young ward. 'We're nearly there.'

His phone rang.

'Have you got a pen?' asked Ahuja.

Chopra scrabbled in his glove compartment.

'So, first, I had to wake up Mishra, the General Manager of MTNL South. I had to promise him a favour – I hope you realise he'll make my life a misery until he collects. Anyway, Mishra had one of his engineers dig out the call log for CBI headquarters on the evening you wanted, then isolate all the calls going through to Rao's unit. There weren't that many, only two between 9 p.m. and 10:45 p.m. Why 10:45? Any later and Rao wouldn't have had enough time to get from his home in south Mumbai up to Madh Fort by midnight when he arrested you. One of those two calls we can forget about – it came from out of state. The other came in at 10:33 and lasted forty-two seconds. A minute after that a call went from the unit to Rao's home.'

Ahuja paused. 'It didn't take long to trace the caller. Are you ready?'

Chopra wrote down the name and address, the pen wavering in his hand as his astonishment grew.

After Ahuja had hung up he continued to stare at the name scrawled on his notepad. 'Well,' he muttered, 'that I would not have guessed.'

A LEGAL TWIST

During his long service in the Brihanmumbai Police, Chopra had endured the company of innumerable members of the legal profession; for the most part he had found it a distasteful experience. In India, as in most parts of the world, this particular species of humanity was habitually despised, their very existence cursed. In part, this was a consequence of India's judicial apparatus, which digested with agonising slowness those victims unfortunate enough to be fed into its ever-ravenous maw – Chopra knew of one case that had been working its way through the courts since the late seventies, a bitter family feud over the will of a paterfamilias who had now been dead so long that no doubt even his shade had given up hovering over proceedings.

Over the years Chopra had routinely fenced with criminal defence advocates in the sweating interview room at the Sahar station or while sitting in the brass-railed witness dock of the Bombay High Court building in Fort. The experience invariably left him with the urge to burn his clothes and scrub himself clean with carbolic soap and a pumice stone.

Now, in his avatar as a private detective, Chopra was becoming acquainted with a new breed of lawyer: the family attorney.

Primogeniture-based land disputes, acrimonious divorces, intrafamilial industrial espionage – it seemed that many imbroglios required a private detective. And with each such case, there came the hawkish presence of the family lawyer.

As he rang the doorbell to the plush nineteenth-floor duplex apartment in the luxury Naya Bhavan tower in Cuffe Parade, Chopra steeled himself for the trial ahead.

Kantilal Lal, LL.B., advocate-at-law, opened the door, wearing comfortable slippers and dressed in a red silk robe imprinted with tigers and mythical Garuda birds. His usually immaculate widow's peak appeared to have slipped the hold of whatever unguent Lal employed to keep it in place and flopped about his forehead. A grey fuzz grizzled his chin. In his trembling fingers was a tumbler of what looked like Scotch.

All in all, Chopra reflected, Lal seemed like a man who had suddenly slipped from the edge, plummeting into personal ruin.

The change was shocking.

'Chopra?' Lal squinted at his unexpected visitor from behind wire-framed spectacles. His jaw slackened, as if he couldn't quite work out what to say next.

Eventually, he simply walked away, leaving Chopra to follow.

Lal led them through an immaculate white-marbled home. The general theme seemed to be luxuriant austerity – there were few furnishings but what was present shimmered with an air of vast expense.

Chopra expected no less.

In the perfumed suburb of Cuffe Parade wealth and style went arm in arm.

They entered a study panelled in rich oak. Bookshelves crammed with dense tomes lined the walls. A black-and-white blown-up photograph of a younger Lal with a younger Bijli Verma and a man Chopra recognised as her former husband, film producer Jignesh Verma, graced the wall behind an expansive teak desk. Legal volumes made ramparts on the corners of the desk; an anglepoise lamp threw a circle of light onto a notepad.

Lal flopped into the button-back chair behind his desk, leaving Chopra to take the seat opposite. 'A little late for house calls, isn't it?'

'Is something wrong?' Chopra asked. It was not where he had intended to begin, but the change in Lal's demeanour intrigued him.

Lal gave his visitor a red-eyed look, then swigged from his tumbler. 'Vicky Verma is dead. Bijli is inconsolable. I promised her I would get her son back. I have failed her.'

Chopra was taken aback. 'How do you know Vicky is dead?'

'It has been two days since you delivered the ransom. If they intended to return him unharmed they would have done so.'

'So you're certain the kidnappers received the ransom?' said Chopra. The edge in his tone was unmistakeable.

Lal hesitated. He blinked rapidly, emerging from the cloud of semi-drunken melancholia that appeared to have engulfed him. 'There has been no contact from them. Or, for that matter, from you. Where did you vanish to? Why didn't you call?'

'Don't you know? After all, weren't you the one who called the CBI to inform them of the exchange? Doesn't everyone think that I *stole* the ransom?' continued Chopra acidly. 'Tell me, did you know that ACP Rao was my sworn enemy, or was that pure luck?'

Lal raised a trembling hand to push back the straggly fronds of his hair. A terse silence passed. 'I had heard about you and Rao,' he admitted, eventually. 'From the High Commissioner, when he was telling us about the Koh-i-noor investigation over one of Bijli's society dinners.' His features became suddenly animated. 'It was supposed to be *me*! *I* was supposed to be the hero. I have waited thirty years for such an opportunity. Thirty years worshipping at her altar, praying that one day she would notice me. And then, finally, God listens! I was ready to make the ransom exchange, to bring Vicky back to her safe and sound. And then she would have . . . she would have . . .' Lal lapsed into silence.

Chopra was beginning to understand.

'How long have you felt this way?' he asked.

'Since the day I first met her,' said Lal. 'She was working on a film called *Anjali's Sacrifice*. The one in which she plays a prostitute forced to raise the children of her dying sister. I've seen it eighty-three times and I still think it's the best thing she ever did. I was a young lawyer back then. Her agent employed me to look over her contract.' He became animated once more. 'She was a vision, Chopra! I still remember everything about her that day, the sari she was wearing, the golden bangles, the way she smelled, the way she moved. Even the way her nose crinkled with distaste when she signed the papers.'

'And does she know how you feel?'

'I have never spoken of it. She is a goddess. I am dust beneath her feet. It has been enough for me to be close to her, to breathe in her essence.'

'How can you stand it?'

'Self-denial has its own exquisite agony.'

'But she knows, doesn't she?' persisted Chopra. 'A woman like that . . . She can tell. But she's never given a damn. She's never once acknowledged that you've been carrying a torch for her faithfully down the long, lonely years. Never once given you even the comfort of a smile, a flash of warmth. She's treated you like the faithful retainer that you are. An employee. A factotum.'

Lal looked miserable. Chopra had hit a nerve. He realised that, as he had walked through the apartment, an absence had registered in the subconscious part of his brain, an absence that now took on new meaning – the absence of others.

Lal lived alone.

With a flash of insight, he felt sure that the old lawyer had never married, had sacrificed his whole life in the forlorn hope that one day the object of his infatuation might return his slavish devotion. In his heart of hearts, the dry, ascetic advocate harboured dreams of an authentic Bollywood ending to his own love story.

'You deliberately sabotaged the ransom exchange,' Chopra said. 'How did you know the kidnappers wouldn't harm Vicky? Your plan to emerge as the hero of the hour would have come to nothing.'

'It was a gamble,' admitted Lal. 'I thought Rao would arrest you before the kidnappers revealed themselves. Then I'd be able to rearrange the exchange with you safely out of the way.'

'What if they hadn't cooperated? What if they had carried out their threat and killed Vicky because you had involved the authorities?'

'Vicky was their only bargaining chip. They would not have killed him. Even kidnappers must operate to a certain logic. At most, they might have taken another ear, or a finger, perhaps.'

'And you were prepared to let that happen?'

Lal grimaced. 'Vicky is an arrogant brat. I have watched him grow from a spoilt child into an even more spoilt adult. Whatever misfortune he is undergoing he has brought upon himself.'

Chopra had heard enough.

He stood. 'Your actions almost cost me my freedom. Do you think I brought that upon myself too?'

Lal looked up through bloodshot eyes. 'I never wanted to involve you in the first place. I advised Bijli against it, but she insisted. As for the CBI – I thought they would detain you for a while, then let you go. After all, you were a policeman, weren't you? You must know how these things work. If necessary I would have vouched for you. By then, Bijli's confidence in you would have evaporated, and I could have easily persuaded her to terminate your services.'

'You didn't anticipate they'd send me to Gouripur, though, did you?' said Chopra bitterly.

Lal's eyes widened.

He raised his tumbler, then lowered it again. 'I am sorry, truly sorry. It was not my intention to harm you. I had no idea things would go so far.'

'Your apology is insufficient,' said Chopra woodenly. 'You will have to make amends.'

'How?'

'By telling Bijli Verma the truth.'

An expression of horror overcame the lawyer. 'I cannot. She already blames me for the failure to recover her son. If I tell her this, she will banish me. Besides, what good would it do now? Vicky is gone.'

'I believe that Vicky is still alive.'

'What? Where is he?'

'I will soon find out. In the meantime, you must clear my name with Bijli.'

Lal lurched to his feet, placing both hands on the desk and glaring at Chopra, a sudden fire in his features. 'That is unthinkable,' he hissed. 'I cannot . . . cannot—'

'Live without her? You'll manage.'

'You – you –' stuttered Lal, suddenly furious.

'If you don't tell her, I will.'

Lal looked aghast. He balled his hands into fists as if he intended to fly at Chopra, but instead swayed on his feet, and then fell, with a clatter, back into his chair. His arms flopped over the sides and his head lolled back. He looked like a man drained of blood.

'There's something else,' continued Chopra relentlessly. 'I have discovered something about Jignesh Verma's past, something that may have a bearing on the kidnapping. Do you recall a young actress called Ayesha Azmi?'

Lal turned an even greyer shade of ash. 'Yes. Why?'

'Many years ago Ayesha had a child. Jignesh Verma's illegitimate daughter. Can you confirm this?'

Lal looked aghast. 'What has that—?'

'Answer the question!'

'Yes.'

'Tell me about them. What happened all those years ago?'

Lal pushed back his hair, and adjusted his spectacles. 'The trouble with being a family lawyer is that you become privy to every skeleton, every piece of dirty laundry.' He sighed. 'Thirty years ago Jignesh Verma fell in love with an actress. Her name was Ayesha Azmi, and at the time she was just beginning her career. Jignesh was already well known; *his* father had been a famed producer, and he inherited his legacy. Jignesh was a Hindu; Ayesha a Muslim. In the India of that time, even in Bollywood, this made their affair difficult. Nevertheless, Jignesh defied convention and courted her. She, in turn, was flattered to be wooed by a young man clearly destined for greatness.

'Ultimately, Ayesha fell pregnant. She begged Jignesh to marry her as he had promised. But there was a problem. Jignesh had begun work on a picture featuring another young actress, one who was setting the industry alight. Her name was Nandita Goyal – soon to be Bijli Verma.

'Jignesh was obsessed. He pursued Bijli with single-minded determination. He forgot that he had made promises to another woman, one who was carrying his child. Ayesha was distraught. She was a Muslim woman, pregnant, disowned by the father of her child. But she refused to let Jignesh ignore his responsibility, and so she pursued him; she confronted him on the set of his film; she even found her way to his home. Here she met Bijli. She felt that another woman might understand her plight. She was wrong.

'Bijli warned her to stay away. Then she gave Jignesh an ultimatum – she forced him to make a choice.

'In the end Jignesh told Ayesha that she was finished. He told her that if she ever approached him again he would use his contacts to have her imprisoned. I was the go-between he employed to carry this message.

'Ayesha, broken and afraid, contemplated suicide. But in the end she could not do it. She retreated back to her family, but they refused to help. They had never approved of her acting ambitions. In their eyes she had been punished by God for her arrogance.

'Fate is cruel to those it marks out. Ayesha took the only option available. She married.

'The man she married was the only one who would have her – a fallen woman, shunned by her family – a poor man, a habitual drunk with a violent temper.

'The child was born, a girl. And that is all I know. Shortly afterwards Ayesha vanished. Took the infant and just disappeared into the night with her no-good husband.' Lal's features gathered into a storm of angst. 'But this is ancient history. What has it to do with the kidnapping?'

'Don't you understand yet?' said Chopra. 'This kidnapping is Ayesha's revenge on Bijli Verma.'

'My God! You think *she's* behind this?'

'No. Not directly, at any rate. Ayesha recently passed away. But her daughter is very much alive. Her name is Aaliya, and I suspect she knows that she is the illegitimate child of Jignesh Verma, the man responsible for her mother's ruin. I believe that is why Vicky has been targeted.'

Lal seemed aghast. 'But – but how could she have pulled off something like this?'

'She had help,' admitted Chopra, thinking of Aaliya's cousin, Ali.

Finally, the pieces of the puzzle had fallen into place. He knew the real motive behind the kidnapping: consumed by rage following her mother's death, Aaliya Ghazi had exacted revenge on the family of the man who had betrayed Ayesha all those years ago. She had punished Bijli Verma, just as her mother had been made to suffer.

Was Vicky still alive?

That would depend on just how much rage was fuelling Aaliya's actions. In truth, Chopra feared for the actor's chances. Hacking off Vicky's earlobe hinted at a latent aggression, a genuine desire to punish. He couldn't see a scenario in which Aaliya and Ali returned Vicky willingly and unharmed.

As for Lal . . . Chopra had his answer now.

Lal had played no part in the kidnapping of Vicky Verma. It had merely presented a long-awaited opportunity to perform a heroic act for the woman he had silently adored his whole life, to finally win some acknowledgement for his devotion. Lal had staked his heart out in the desert of Bijli's affections, hoping that one day she would find her way to the succour he yearned to offer.

That day had never come, and never would.

It was curious, Chopra thought as he left the apartment, that in spite of everything Lal had done to him, he could not hate the man. Rather, he felt an enormous and undiluted pity. And he thought, as he so often had, how strange and unfathomable were the hearts of men.

CONFRONTING THE KIDNAPPERS

Chopra parked the van a short distance from the home of Aaliya Ghazi and let Ganesha out. The elephant sniffed the air with his trunk, then shuffled back into the lee of the van, peering around the front fender as Chopra jogged into the gloom.

Chopra knew that he was dealing with an adversary who was acting not through rational self-interest, but on emotions that were of greater importance than any monetary payoff. The fact that Aaliya and Ali had not released Vicky after collecting the ransom was telling. There was every chance that Vicky was now in a shallow grave somewhere.

Chopra sincerely hoped that this was not the case.

If Aaliya and Ali had any sense they would realise that murdering a man as famous as Vicky would stir up a hornets' nest. Bijli Verma would not rest until her son's killer – or killers – were found. Their best bet was to release Vicky, and vanish with the ransom.

He cautiously approached the dilapidated home.

He stepped onto the porch and peered through the flyscreen covering the windows. He held himself still, straining his ears, but could hear no movement from within.

He pushed open the sun-cracked plywood door and entered the tiny dwelling.

Instantly, he was confronted by a sense of déjà vu.

Everything appeared exactly as he had left it on his previous visit. The peeling walls, the cheap furniture, the tiny television set. And on the sofa, once again, the recumbent form of an overweight man, stretched out in the ragged slumber of the habitual drunkard.

Chopra wasted no time.

Not knowing when, or if, Aaliya would return, he took the opportunity to search the house.

It did not take long.

There were only three rooms: the living space with its tiny corner kitchen, a shower room with rusted showerhead and squat toilet, and a single bedroom.

He quickly riffled through the kitchen cupboards and the broken chest of drawers in the living room.

Nothing.

The bathroom cabinet contained only toothpaste, a single toothbrush, shampoo and soap. In the bedroom he found a steel cupboard. Inside were women's clothes, toiletries, and a number of burkas. But nothing else.

Chopra stepped back, his brow creased in thought.

Then he turned and knelt down beside the bed. Bending low, he looked underneath.

And immediately saw the flight bags.

He reached beneath the bed and pulled them out. Opening the flaps, he looked inside – the bundles of five-hundred-rupee notes were intact.

Chopra hesitated, considering his next move.

If he took the ransom with him now he would alert the kidnappers and perhaps lose the best chance he had of finding Vicky Verma, if indeed he was still alive.

He shut the bags, and pushed them back under the bed. Then he returned to the living room, where the slumbering drunk had now rolled onto his front, his face buried in the crook of the sofa, muffled snores echoing around the room. He paused, once more, in front of the poster of Ayesha Azmi. There was something about her face, about her eyes, something that arrested him, yet swam, tantalisingly, just out of reach . . . Shaking his head, he jogged back out to the van.

Aaliya arrived in a rickshaw an hour later. She left the rickshaw waiting outside, and entered the house, a slim figure in a black burka. Minutes later she returned, clutching the ransom bags.

Chopra switched on the van's ignition and followed the rick as it sped away.

The sweltering night air blew in as they moved southwards.

Even this late the roads were congested. Truly, Chopra thought, of all the contenders for the title of 'city that never sleeps' Mumbai had the most frantic claim. He supposed that the upcoming festival of Holi had something to do with it. The thought brought to him memories of Holis past, an event that Poppy celebrated with a gusto that always irritated him. But now he found himself yearning for her mischievous grin as she doused him in jets of coloured water even after he had asked her a dozen times not to.

An hour later, to Chopra's considerable surprise, the rickshaw puttered to a stop outside Sahar Hospital.

The public hospital was one of just a handful in the suburbs, the largest and most well known, a sprawling whitewashed facility that catered to the masses. Chopra was familiar with the place as this was where corpses from his own locality ended up, often for post-mortem. Indeed, his good friend Homi Contractor ran the autopsy suite . . . Why in the world had Aaliya come here?

He parked the van, left the windows down for Ganesha, then followed the young woman into the bustling hospital.

Aaliya slipped through the clattering corridors like a black-shrouded ghost, the bags swinging by her side. Eventually, she entered a crowded waiting room. Here she fell into a seat before excavating a mobile phone from beneath her burka. She made a quick, furtive call, then sat back.

Chopra squeezed into a seat in the row behind her. Beside him a droopy-eyed, middle-aged man with a makeshift bandage wound around his skull was being berated by a woman who was presumably his wife. On the seat opposite, an elderly woman squinted at him suspiciously as if, perhaps, Chopra had designs on her virtue.

Ten minutes passed and then, just as he was beginning to wonder if he should confront Aaliya . . . there he was!

Ali.

Chopra watched as the tall man spotted Aaliya, and walked over. He wore a blue hospital porter's uniform and a white skullcap.

So Ali was an employee of the hospital.

Chopra considered this.

There seemed something incongruous in a kidnapper and possible murderer working in an environment designed to save and preserve life. But during his long career Chopra had often found himself marvelling at the way the criminal mind operated. He had met many men like Ali who held completely contradictory philosophies in their heads, who could be one thing to some and a different, darker thing to others. In Chopra's experience very few people were career criminals. Many who ended up in the country's prisons had simply fallen into crime when a particular opportunity arose, when greed or lust or foolishness overtook them at a moment of weakness.

He wondered briefly why Ali had gone along with Aaliya's plan for vengeance. Was it purely for the money? Two crores, after all, was a *lot* of money, worth taking inordinate risks for. Or had Aaliya informed her cousin of the injustices Jignesh Verma had inflicted upon her mother, and thus inflamed in him an equal passion for vengeance?

Chopra considered this scenario, then flipped things back to front.

What if he had this all wrong? What if *Ali* was the real mastermind here? Perhaps Aaliya, with no one else to confide in, reeling after the death of her mother, had revealed the terrible events of the past to her cousin. Had Ali sensed an opportunity and twisted Aaliya's outrage to his own ends?

Chopra strained his ears as Ali and Aaliya Ghazi talked in terse whispers. He could sense that they were arguing, but the details eluded him.

Suddenly, Ali stood.

With a final angry shake of his head he stalked from the waiting room.

The girl sat there momentarily, her shoulders sunk in frustration. And then she stood and swept out of the room with the bags.

Chopra hesitated. Why had Ali left the ransom behind? What had the pair been arguing about?

He realised that he was forced into making a choice. Stay with the girl and the money, or follow Ali?

In the end it was no choice at all.

He strode through the swinging double doors and barrelled after Ali.

Ali moved quickly along the greenwashed corridor, then down two flights of steps to the lower basement. Here he turned right past Haematology, then left past Renal, and eventually ended up outside the mortuary.

Chopra, peering from around a corner, saw him settle into a chair in the porters' station where a fellow porter was thumbing a well-worn paperback.

The graveyard shift.

Chopra waited for fifteen minutes, during which little happened.

Ali pulled a newspaper from a rucksack and sat back to read. Occasionally, he would glance at his watch – what was he waiting for?

Chopra took out his phone and called Homi Contractor.

'Chopra?' Homi's voice snapped from the phone. He sounded tired and irritable. Homi was a gregarious and highly intelligent man, but one with a short fuse that seemed to be perpetually lit. 'It's been a long day. What can I do for you?'

'I need some information, old friend.'

Quickly, he described his mission.

'Ali?' Homi scratched his jowly chin. 'Yes, I think I know the one you mean. New man. Started a month ago. Seems competent enough. I've seen porters whose knees turn to jelly at the sight of a corpse. Of course, Rohit usually deals with the help.'

Rohit was Homi's greatly put-upon assistant in the autopsy suite.

'What's this about? Is there something I should know about him?'

Chopra hesitated. 'I think he may be mixed up in criminal activity.'

'What sort of criminal activity?'

'A kidnapping.'

'That's quite an accusation. How does a hospital porter get mixed up in a kidnapping?'

'I don't know. I just know that he's involved.'

'And who is it that he is supposed to have kidnapped?'

'Vicky Verma. The actor.' Chopra had decided that at this point it made no difference telling Homi the truth. He knew he could count on his friend's discretion.

'That oaf?' Chopra could imagine Homi's cheek twitching. Vicky Verma exemplified everything that was wrong with the modern generation in Homi's opinion. 'Are we sure we want him back? . . . Oh, very well. What can I do?'

'I need access to Ali's personnel records.'

'I don't suppose it's ethical, but then again I've never had much time for ethics when common sense was the need of the hour.'

Ten minutes later a night clerk found Chopra with the personnel file for one Sikandar Ali.

The paperwork made sparse reading.

Sikandar Ali appeared to be forty-two years old, born in the state of Maharashtra, educated to a rudimentary level, but no higher. His sketchy work history claimed that he had spent many years out of the state in Uttar Pradesh, performing a number of roles as security guard and porter. His current address, the key thing Chopra was interested in, was in Juhu. This came as a surprise. Juhu was a premier district, an expensive place to live. How could Ali afford a residence there, on a porter's salary? And the address itself seemed vaguely familiar . . .

The real mystery was what Ali was still doing here. He and Aaliya had the ransom. Why hadn't they fled? Why hadn't they released Vicky? Was Vicky already dead? Was Ali lying low to avoid attracting attention? Or was there something else Aaliya and Ali wished to achieve? Some other way in which they wished to hurt Vicky and Bijli Verma?

Try as he might, he could not get his head around Ali's mystifying actions.

Another thirty minutes passed as he lurked around the corner, watching Ali read the paper and exchange pleasantries with passing colleagues.

And then, suddenly, Ali grabbed his rucksack, and headed down the corridor.

Chopra, whose eyelids had begun to droop, ducked back just in time, pretending to examine a bulletin board swarming with leaflets.

Then he turned and plunged after him.

Outside the hospital Ali flagged down a taxi. He hurled his rucksack into the rear seats, and ducked in behind it.

Chopra raced to his van and gunned the engine.

CHASE ON THE SEA LINK

Ten minutes into the tail, Ali clearly realised that he was being followed.

The taxi suddenly stopped.

Ali leapt out, yanked the protesting driver from his seat, and bundled behind the wheel. With a screech of tyres he veered back out into traffic and hit the accelerator.

It had been a long time since Chopra's last car chase.

Many years ago he had been with Inspector Jai Kotwal from the Marol station when a white Honda had pulled up beside Kotwal's police jeep. A burly man behind the wheel had spat betel nut into the road.

Kotwal looked at the man. The man looked at Kotwal.

Time ground to a halt.

And then Kotwal yelled, 'You!'

The driver's face collapsed into panic. He roared off.

'That's Natwarlal Sen!' Kotwal had bellowed as he set off in pursuit. 'His face has been staring at me from a Wanted poster for the past four years.'

Within seconds Chopra came to a terrifying realisation.

Kotwal was a maniac.

Hunched over the wheel like a crazed bear, eyes boring into the road, Kotwal drove like a man possessed. Blasting his horn, he hurled the jeep along the congested Sahar roads, men and animals leaping out of his way, Chopra clinging grimly on for dear life.

The chase finally ended when the villain lost control of his vehicle and careened into a concrete barrier on the Western Express Highway; the resultant fireball had lit up the night sky. A week later Kotwal had been posted to the salt-desert wasteland that was the Rann of Kutch.

Chopra had never heard from him again.

Ali was an experienced driver and tore the taxi around tight corners and narrow alleyways. Chopra was thankful that it was late; he was certain that if the chase had occurred earlier, the reckless Ali might have caused serious injury to the pedestrians that usually thronged the roads.

It soon became clear that he was moving towards the lush Mumbai suburb of Bandra, home to movie stars and moguls. Once there, he weaved through the wide, tree-lined roads, bearing west.

As they moved along Swami Vivekanand Road, a sign flashed by on Chopra's right.

BANDRA–WORLI SEA LINK

1 MILE

So that was where Ali was headed.

The Bandra–Worli Sea Link – an eight-lane cable-stayed bridge that had taken a decade to construct and cost over sixteen billion rupees – shot out into the sea from the Bandra coastline, running five miles in a sinuous sweep all the way to the mid-city district of Worli. A few years earlier, the state's Chief Minister had inaugurated the bridge to a deafening fanfare; the Sea Link had shortened the journey from the city's western flank to the south by an hour. A 'marvel of modern Indian engineering', the CM had grinned, neglecting to mention the years of red tape that had dogged the project, and the rumours of bribes paid by those who had secured the construction contracts.

As Ali swept onto the Sea Link's northern viaduct, he gunned the engine.

'Hold on, boy!' Chopra muttered, and stood on the accelerator.

He had no choice now but to make a citizen's arrest. Involving himself with the police was the last thing he wanted to do, having just escaped from Gouripur Jail, but he could not afford to let Ali vanish again. There was no telling when he would resurface now he knew Chopra was on his tail. It was a gamble: arresting Ali without first finding out where he was holding Vicky Verma could place the actor's life in jeopardy – if, indeed, Vicky was not already dead.

But Chopra would have to play the hand he had been dealt.

The Tata Venture rattled alarmingly as it sped along.

The van had not been built for high-speed chases. It had been designed to ferry one man and his elephant around the city in relative comfort, though comfort was a thing far from the elephant's mind at this precise moment.

Ganesha, struggling to keep his balance, stared at the whizzing black road. His trunk was hooked around the front passenger seat as he struggled to steady himself. During the mad dash through the suburbs he had bugled a note of alarm each time the van hit a bump or veered too close to a pedestrian, folding his ears over his eyes. As they raced along the Sea Link he glanced at Chopra, as if checking to ensure that his guardian had not completely lost his mind.

And then: a stroke of good fortune.

A honking truck cut directly into the taxi's path, forcing it to veer sharply to the left, up onto the maintenance walkway, and slam into the bridge's concrete and steel railings. The bonnet was instantly crushed inwards, a gout of steam flashing up into the night sky.

Chopra whooped, and skidded the van to a halt thirty metres behind the crashed taxi.

He leapt out, just in time to see Ali stumble dazedly from the cab, glance back once, then limp off along the walkway.

'Stop!' shouted Chopra, as a passing motorist slid to a halt ahead of Ali. 'There's nowhere to run!'

Ali glanced back. At that instant the passenger door of the sedan that had stopped ahead of him opened. Ali ran straight into it, rebounded, and fell. He looked up, stunned, from the concrete, and swore at the good Samaritan in the passenger seat, who thought better of his impulse, closed the door, and ordered his partner to drive away, leaving Ali coughing in a cloud of exhaust fumes.

He rose to his feet just as Chopra caught up with him.

'It's over!' gasped Chopra. He reached for his revolver, then felt panic trickle into his bowels as he realised it wasn't there. In the excitement, he had left it in the van. 'Tell me where Vicky is. You have your money. Let him go. He doesn't deserve this. His mother doesn't deserve this.'

Ali scowled. 'Believe me, they deserve everything they get.'

'I understand your anger, Aaliya's anger. But this won't change anything. The past is the past.'

Ali's eyes widened. Finally, he spoke: 'You're a clever man, Chopra. But justice is justice, no matter when it falls.'

'You call this justice? Who made *you* "The People's Judge"?'

'*I* made me. Because in our country justice is only for the privileged. If people like Aaliya want justice they need to fashion it for themselves.'

'End this now. You don't want Vicky's blood on your hands.'

Ali narrowed his eyes. 'You have no idea of the blood on my hands.' Without warning he hurled himself forward, grabbing Chopra around the midriff and bearing him to the railings. With a monumental effort he launched him over the topmost rail.

Chopra yelled out, grabbing at his assailant. His fingers

hooked the breast pocket of Ali's hospital tunic; the pocket tore off and fluttered away as Chopra went over the parapet. Bellowing like a startled bullock, he clutched at thin air as the world cartwheeled around him . . . and then his flailing hands found the lowest rail.

Swinging out above the sluggish water flowing in the Bandra Channel, Chopra clung on for dear life.

Ali's haggard face appeared above the parapet. 'Don't worry, it's only a hundred metres to the shore,' he shouted. He turned and jogged away.

Chopra wanted to call after him, 'I can't swim,' but terror had stolen his voice. Tentacles of fire arced through his shoulders; pain flowered in his wrists.

Don't look down.

He tried to haul himself up, but failed. He tried to swing his legs up and catch the bridge's concrete underlip with his heel, but failed.

Don't look down.

He looked down.

The dark water moved below him. So *far* below him. His head swam, sweat stung his eyes, his heart thrummed like a stuttering engine . . . He felt his grip slipping—

A grey trunk reached through the railings and grasped Chopra's wrist. He felt himself being dragged up, and redoubled his efforts. With a momentous heave he gained his footing, before scrabbling back over the parapet.

He sagged against the railings in relief.

Ganesha trotted forward, concern in his eyes. 'Thank you, boy,' he mumbled, and patted the little elephant on the head . . . *Little!* It was easy to forget, he thought, that Ganesha weighed over two hundred kilos, and had the strength of a grown man.

He looked up as a truck clanked by, a man staring at him from the passenger seat with a curious expression on his face. The Sea Link had recently become Mumbai's most fashionable place to commit suicide, so much so that the state government was considering hanging a safety net beneath the bridge.

He looked along the walkway, squinting into the shimmering haze cast by the illuminated cable stays rising up the diamond-shaped concrete pylons of the bridge's central span . . . but Ali had vanished.

Chopra turned back to his van – he had to get out of here before the traffic police came to investigate.

As he passed Ali's crashed taxi, something caught his eye. On the back seat was the kidnapper's rucksack.

Chopra pulled it out.

Inside he found a change of clothes, but the clothes were expensive-looking – designer jeans, a good-quality-T-shirt, a gold watch – not the sort of thing he associated with a man like Ali. And then in a clear plastic bag he discovered something curious. Two gently curved, wedge-shaped plasticky pink objects made from some lightweight material. Mystified, he held them in his palm. What were they?

Rummaging once more in the rucksack he discovered a folded sheet of paper tucked into an inner pocket. He unfolded the sheet and scanned it:

CALL SHEET

BALAKRISHNA PRODUCTIONS PRESENTS

Love on the Amritsar Express

Call Sheet #44
Breakfast on location 7:30 AM
LIVING ROOM SET, STUDIO 16

CREW CALL
Director: Sham Goyal
Producer: Kailash Sinha
DoP: Rishi Amin

Actors on set:
Ruby Soleto
Raheem Khan
Tana Tandon
Anjuman Shah
Robin Mistry
Jaya Singh
Bina Padamsee

Chopra focused on one name, his eyes narrowing. And suddenly everything fell into place. He understood what the plasticky objects were, and he realised, too, why Ali's Juhu address had seemed so familiar . . .

Ganesha looked up at him quizzically. 'Come on, boy,' said Chopra. 'Let's go find ourselves a rat.'

A SECRET WEDDING

The Juhu apartment of Robin Mistry was well known to members of the paparazzi and the tabloid press. The scene of many a raucous bacchanal, the seventh-floor bachelor pad had gained a degree of notoriety some years previously when a fire had broken out during a party. Flames had engulfed the building and it had been a miracle that no one had been seriously hurt.

Now, as Chopra drifted the Tata van to a halt opposite Mistry's apartment complex, he saw that the cosseting influence of wealth had returned the tower to its former glory.

Chopra did not believe in coincidence.

The call sheet he had discovered in the backpack had led him here.

The sheet convinced him that Robin Mistry was involved in Vicky's disappearance, that Mistry had conspired with Aaliya Ghazi to abduct Vicky. Mistry must have discovered the story of Vicky's father abandoning Aaliya's mother, and had turned it to his own end.

For there was now a second clear motive behind Vicky's kidnapping: jealousy.

Jealousy, that oldest of human weaknesses, had consumed Mistry ever since he had been supplanted for the lead role in the biggest movie ever to be filmed in Bollywood. The wound had plainly cut deep, severing Robin and Vicky's childhood friendship.

It was not the first time Chopra had come across such a schism. He had long ago learned that friendship was a mutable endeavour; the strongest of bonds were not immune to the foibles of the human condition. Friendship was like a slipknot in a length of rope. In one direction the knot held fast, but pull it the wrong way and it unravelled in the blink of an eye.

On the eighth floor of the tower he steeled himself before a brown oak door, then rang the buzzer.

As the echoes of the blaring clarion died away he heard footsteps approach. Chopra tensed, instinctively patting the revolver tucked into the back of his trousers. This time he had come prepared.

The door swung back, and Robin Mistry was standing before him, dressed in a pair of loud Hawaiian shorts, slippers, and a T-shirt bearing the legend DO IT FOR MUMBAI. A look of frank astonishment completed the ensemble. 'Chopra!' he exclaimed. 'What are you doing here?'

Chopra drew his revolver. 'Let's talk inside.'

Mistry's jaw fell. 'Have you lost your mind?'

Chopra advanced, forcing Mistry to backpedal into the apartment.

Once inside, he kicked the door shut behind him.

Mistry continued to gape at him. 'What the hell is this about?'

Chopra fumbled in the front pocket of his shirt. He extracted the call sheet and flung it down on the coffee table. 'I took that from a man who just tried to throw me off the Bandra–Worli Sea Link. The same man who kidnapped Vicky and took the ransom.'

Mistry's gaze dropped to the call sheet.

His face reddened. Then he pulled himself together. 'As far as we are aware, *you* took the ransom. Where have you been?'

'We both know I had nothing to do with Vicky's abduction,' responded Chopra. 'But I *am* here to get to the bottom of things. Now, before we continue, tell me: is Vicky still alive?'

Mistry's expression hardened. 'You're not going to use that gun. I'm going to give you one chance to leave. After that I'm calling the cops.'

Chopra stared at him . . . Then he squeezed the trigger.

The shot reverberated around the apartment. The bullet thwocked into the sofa, a plume of stuffing spraying out onto the Persian rug below.

Mistry howled in fright, then scrabbled at his chest to see where he had been struck. When he discovered that he remained unperforated, his legs buckled beneath him, and he swooned back onto the sofa in relief.

A short, sharp scream whipped Chopra around.

A woman stood in the doorway of the bedroom, wrapped in a bedsheet, her hand lifted to her mouth in terror.

'Robin!' shrieked Poonam Panipat.

Chopra lowered his revolver, his face slack with astonishment. 'Ms Panipat,' he mumbled. 'What are *you* doing here?' As soon as the words escaped his mouth he felt foolish. It was absurdly obvious what Panipat was doing here. The bedsheet, the disarrayed hair, the lateness of the hour.

Sensing Chopra's scrutiny Panipat straightened, an angry blush stealing over her handsome features. She reached up to pat her hair into shape, then marched, straight-backed, over to Robin Mistry.

She sat down next to him and put an arm around his shoulders, then looked up defiantly at Chopra.

'The question,' she said icily, 'is what are *you* doing here? And why, precisely, are you shooting holes in our sofa?'

'*Our* sofa?' echoed Chopra, feeling lightheaded. Surely Poonam Panipat, the Queen of Bollywood, was not involved in the kidnapping of Vicky Verma? How deep did this conspiracy go?

'Did you plan this together?' he said, eventually, focusing on Mistry. 'Was this another reason for taking revenge on Vicky? Not only did he steal your dream role but he also tried to steal your lady? The rumours of an affair between them could not have been easy for you to stomach.'

'You couldn't be more wrong,' said Mistry, shaking his head. He got to his feet, pulling Panipat up beside him.

The two stood there holding hands.

'I suppose you're going to tell me it's true love,' said Chopra wearily.

'In a way,' said Mistry. He waved his free hand at Panipat. 'Allow me to introduce you to my wife.'

Chopra gaped. 'Impossible! How could you keep something like that a secret? And why?'

'Keeping it a secret was the easy part,' said Mistry. 'As for the why, that should be obvious.'

'Do you remember the first time we met?' said Panipat. 'I told you what I had gone through to get to where I am today, how hard I had to fight for the role in *Mote*. This picture will put me back on top. But this is Bollywood, Chopra. Had the producer known I was a married woman he would never have given me the part. The affair between myself and Vicky – do you remember I told you that *I* spread those rumours? Because that's the sort of thing producers want. In this business scandal sells, not domesticity.'

'So you were never having an affair with Vicky?'

'Never.'

Chopra's head was spinning. He had arrived at Mistry's apartment thinking that he had worked out the whole story. But now . . . He reached into his pocket and extracted the two plasticky objects he had discovered in Ali's rucksack. He flung them down beside the call sheet.

'It took me a little while to understand what those were,' he said. 'Cheek plumpers. Isn't that what they're called? Actors use them to change the shape of their face.'

Mistry had reddened.

'You're Ali, aren't you?'

Mistry hesitated. He flicked his eyes to Panipat, who nodded. 'Tell him.'

'Yes,' confessed Mistry.

'And it was you who entered the stadium to kidnap Vicky, disguised as Ali.'

'Yes, but—'

'Did you approach Aaliya Ghazi or did she come to you? Did *she* tell you about what happened to her mother, or did you find out some other way? You used her desire for revenge – you wanted Vicky out of the way, so you used Aaliya.' Chopra hauled in a deep breath, anger flushing through him. 'Tell me, was it you who recommended her to Vicky as a PA?'

'What?' Mistry looked startled.

'Greta Rodrigues,' said Chopra. 'She's Aaliya Ghazi, isn't she? It was the poster that did it. The poster of her mother. I'd never seen Ayesha Azmi before, I'd never seen that film, yet her face was so familiar to me. Why? And then it came to me. I *had* seen that face before. Greta. She has her mother's face. After that, things fell into place. Details that had always bothered me suddenly became clear. You see, even though Vicky was your friend and probably shared details of the concert with you, you couldn't be sure exactly when he would come down from the stage into the dressing room. Concerts like that never stick to schedule. The only way you could have known is if someone called you *at the precise moment* Vicky was in the room. And the only people there were Vicky and Greta. She told me that she stepped away when he came down, to visit the washroom. But it was to call you, wasn't it? You must have already been in the stadium by then. Waiting.'

'Yes, but—'

'Before you say another word . . . is Vicky still alive?'

Mistry hesitated, then nodded.

'Where is he?'

Mistry glanced at Panipat again. 'If you let me explain.'

Chopra raised his revolver. 'No more explanations. I want to know where Vicky is. Tell me. Or this time I won't aim for the sofa.'

Panipat stepped in front of her husband, her eyes blazing. 'If you want to shoot him you'll have to shoot me first.' She glared at Chopra defiantly. 'I took you for an intelligent man. This is not what you think. If you hear us out you will understand.'

Chopra scrutinised her features. He saw in that beautiful face only the light of truth.

He lowered his weapon. 'Very well,' he said. 'I am listening.'

As Chopra drove into the night, he dwelled on his strange meeting with Robin Mistry and Poonam Panipat. He now had all the pieces of the puzzle . . . and what a puzzle! In truth, he had worked out much of it himself. By the time he had arrived at the apartment, he had been almost certain that Robin had been working with an accomplice, someone other than Aaliya Ghazi. The CCTV images of Ali entering and leaving the stadium had all but convinced him of this . . . and now he had his confirmation, and, with it, the identity of the true mastermind behind Vicky Verma's kidnapping.

After thirty years in law enforcement he had believed there was little left to surprise him. He was wrong.

From the rear of the van Ganesha watched him with a quizzical eye. The little elephant knew that something had changed since Chopra had returned from the apartment complex. Over the past months he had become intimately attuned to his guardian's moods – he recognised the set of Chopra's shoulders, the expression of clarity and determination. His guardian was a man on a mission.

He wondered where they were headed now, and, more importantly, whether there would be any food there.

FILM CITY SHOWDOWN

The road blurred beneath the tyres of the Tata Venture as Chopra drove north, back towards the suburbs. It was the dead of night but the city continued as if the distinction between night and day was irrelevant. Mumbai, Chopra had long ago realised, was never still. It wasn't so much that it didn't sleep; it was more that sleep, confronted each evening by the frenetic pandemonium before it, simply fled from the city. Chopra had become used to the sights and sounds of the night. A vast night-time economy – straddling both sides of the law – pulsed in the darkness around him: the office cleaners and sanitation trucks, the night porters and dragomen, the barkeeps sweeping bleary drunks off rush-matted floors into the backs of waiting rickshaws, the sewage workers wading waist-deep through the great river of excrement that oozed beneath the city's streets, the smiling pimps and drug pedlars waiting for tourists in darkened doorways . . . As he barrelled through the sodium haze of the Western Express Highway, another mote in the great river of cars, trucks, ricks, and motorbikes that moved through the guts of the city, he couldn't help but feel connected to that omnipresent reservoir of humanity that marked Mumbai as the most exhilarating place on the subcontinent.

At the gates to Film City Chopra leaned out of the truck towards the night guard. He jerked a thumb at Ganesha. 'I need to drop him off to Studio 16. If the producer doesn't find him there first thing in the morning someone will lose their job.'

The guards, used to shooting crews moving in and out of the five-hundred-acre plot at all times of the day and night, shrugged and waved him through. Elephants and irate producers – there was nothing new in Film City about that.

Chopra drove swiftly along the poorly lit roads that curved through the vast site.

When he arrived at the studio he discovered a drab cinder-block building with a trellis of grey-painted columns affixed to the front like the bars of a cell. Lattice-worked windows were embedded high up, and a flight of well-worn and pitted steps led up to an arched doorway. A broad smear of off-yellow marred the building's whitewash where the façade met the flat roof, the result of rain dripping from the guttering. Gnarled banyan trees crowded around the studio on all sides, from which the hoots and gibbers of langurs and night birds could be heard.

Chopra parked the van in the gravel car park, let Ganesha out, then approached the eerily silent building, the little elephant drawing anxiously closer beside him. Light spilled from the doorway, but Chopra could hear no noises to suggest shooting was going on. In truth he did not expect there to be anyone in the building except the mastermind behind the kidnapping. The confession – of sorts – provided by Poonam Panipat and Robin Mistry had ended by revealing where he might find his ultimate quarry.

And now Chopra was here.

Inside, the studio was magnificent. Extending two floors in height, the set mimicked the interior of a sumptuous Delhi mansion, with marble flooring, expensive sofas, and a grand staircase curving up to an ornately balustraded upper floor, with a glittering chandelier overhead.

Around the edges of the set, film equipment stood in silent slumber, patiently waiting to be reanimated. A dolly track ran from the shadows to the centre of the marble floor, the dolly lurking at one end of the track like a giant beetle. A crane loomed beside the dolly, the boom arm reaching out above the sofas, a digital motion camera fixed to the end. The set was lit by a ring of studio lights. Mounted on their tall stands, the bulb-beds surrounded by reflectors, they looked, to Chopra, like a row of mechanical flowers.

His penetrating gaze took in the silent set, and then the darkened doorway to one side that led off into the rear of the studio, a warren of make-up and changing rooms.

Ganesha shuffled beside him, releasing a soft snort of nervousness.

'There's nothing to be afraid of, boy,' muttered Chopra.

He moved towards the shadowed doorway, but was halted by the sound of feet approaching.

And then Ali walked out onto the set.

He saw Chopra, and his expression widened into a grimace of surprise.

'You don't give up, do you?' he growled.

'It's over,' said Chopra calmly. 'I know everything. It's time for you to return Vicky to his mother.'

Ali's face slackened in astonishment. His mouth worked, bouncing his red beard up and down, but nothing came out. Finally he said: 'Who told you?'

'Robin,' said Chopra. 'And Poonam. I also spoke to Lal.'

'Lal? He doesn't have anything to do with this.'

'No,' said Chopra. 'But he was there thirty years ago when this story began.'

Ali shook his head angrily. 'Story? Is that what you call it? Hah! If it's a story then it's nothing less than a tragedy.'

Chopra was prevented from replying by the putt-putt of a rickshaw pulling up outside. A narrow beam of light swept the entrance. There was a short exchange of voices, then the rick pulled away again.

As silence returned, footsteps approached the doorway.

And then the burka-clad figure of Aaliya Ghazi swept into the room, clutching the flight bags that held the ransom.

Spotting Chopra she ground to an abrupt halt. Her veiled head swung from him to Ali. Finally, she set down the bags.

'You can take off the burka,' said Chopra. 'There's no need for it any more.'

Aaliya hesitated, then pulled back the veil, revealing the face Chopra had seen days earlier in the offices of Vicky Verma's agent – the face of Greta Rodrigues.

Aaliya walked over to stand beside Ali. 'I got a call from Poonam. They said you would be here. And him, too. I thought you might be in danger.'

'I couldn't have found him without their help,' admitted Chopra. 'But he's in no danger from me. I simply want the truth.'

'Truth?' said Ali bitterly. 'The truth is a dirty word in our country. Haven't you heard?'

'Why don't you tell me your side of the story?'

'I thought you already knew everything.'

'I would like to hear it from you,' said Chopra. 'Or rather I would like to hear it from Vicky. The beard is distracting,' he added.

Ali seemed about to retort, but then Aaliya placed a hand on his arm. He looked down at the girl, who merely nodded, sadly.

Ali straightened, his shoulders suddenly taking on a new breadth. Reaching up he pulled off his skullcap, and with it the wig of short red hair underneath. Then his hands moved over his face. The beard came off. A prosthetic nose bridge went next. He reached into his mouth and out came cheek plumpers, and a dental bridge. Lastly he peeled off his red eyebrows, before running a hand through his dark hair.

Vicky Verma faced Chopra, an expression of defiance animating his handsome features.

'How much do you know?'

'I know that your father abandoned Aaliya's mother when Bijli crossed his path. I know that Aaliya's mother vanished into obscurity with her unwanted child – your half-sister.'

'She didn't vanish,' said Vicky vehemently. 'She was hounded out of the neighbourhood in which she had grown up. A tainted woman. Her circumstances forced her to marry a lowlife, a worthless drunk who wanted nothing to do with her child once she was born. They moved to Mira Road where Ayesha raised the girl alone – she worked as a cleaner, and later, as a seamstress. Thanks to my father she could no longer work in the industry that had beguiled her with its bright lights. A weaker person might have succumbed to bitterness, but Ayesha taught her daughter to be, first and foremost, a good person: intelligent, generous, kind.

'The girl did well in school, and eventually became a teacher. Years passed, and then, one day her world was turned upside-down. Her mother was struck down by cancer. Days before her death, Ayesha called her daughter to her bedside. She clutched her hand, and looked at her through sunken eyes. And she told her that her life had been a lie. The man she believed to be her father was not. Her real father was famed film producer Jignesh Verma; her half-brother was film star Vicky Verma.

'Devastated and truly alone for the first time in her life, Aaliya considered the future. The man she had called her father her whole life – a man she had hated as long as she had known him – was a drunk who meandered through the world in an inebriated haze. Her real father was gone

– Jignesh Verma had passed away, never having looked back to discover the fate of the woman and child he had forsaken. The only blood relative she had in the world was Vicky Verma – who had no knowledge of her existence.

'She thought long and hard before acting.

'And then, finally, she came to see me. Posing as a journalist, she secured an interview with me, where she told me, in a matter-of-fact way, the truth about my father, her mother, and herself. The sister I never knew I had.'

Vicky paused, a shadow passing over his face. 'Overnight, my world changed, and my perception of my place in it. I struggled to understand how my parents could have done this – I had placed my father on a pedestal, and to have him torn down was almost more than I could bear.

'I am ashamed to say that I responded, at first, with anger. I demanded proof; I demanded to know what she wanted from me. Was she trying to blackmail me? But Aaliya just smiled sadly at me. "I just wanted you to know," she said.

'It took me a month to realise I couldn't go back to the life I had known. It took me another month to summon up the courage to go and see her. And thus I began to learn about the sister I had never had.

'Three months later I made the decision to make amends for my father's crime. I would set things right. A young man's hubris, perhaps, but I knew I could not go on without attempting to reverse the harm that had been done. The simple, shameful fact was that half of everything that I and my mother took for granted – wealth, fame, respect – belonged to my half-sister.

'But I knew that I would never get my mother to agree. Bijli would never acknowledge Aaliya, would never share my father's wealth with his illegitimate child. And because my mother controlled that money with an iron fist I knew I would have to find another way.

'It took me a long time to come up with a plan.

'In the end I decided that I must turn my mother's patent devotion to me to my advantage.'

'And so you faked your own kidnapping,' said Chopra.

'Yes.' Vicky grimaced. 'The first step was to set up the crime. I had to think of it as a film production, and I needed a crew. I enlisted Robin Mistry and his new wife Poonam Panipat, my co-star. I knew I could trust them because I was one of just a handful of close friends that were aware of their secret marriage. Under my instruction Poonam wrote a series of threatening letters to me. They would help establish the credibility of the kidnapping – I knew my mother would be very difficult to convince. Ultimately, it was my intention that Robin be entrusted with the ransom drop. But you put paid to that part of the plan.' Vicky grimaced again. 'The main hurdle was the kidnapping itself. It had to look real. That's why it had to happen in a public place – like I said, I knew my mother would not be easy to convince – and so I decided that the concert at the Andheri Sports Stadium would provide the perfect opportunity. Coming as it did before the big shoot on *Mote,* all eyes would be on me. That's when I decided to bring Aaliya in as my new PA, Greta Rodrigues. I needed a witness in the changing room, you see – none of my usual friends would have been any good; my mother would have smelled a rat.'

'And that's also when you decided that there would be two Alis, isn't it?' said Chopra.

Vicky raised an eyebrow. 'I suppose Robin told you that.'

'He confirmed the who. But I'd already worked out that there were two of you. I examined the CCTV images of Ali entering and leaving through the rear door of the stadium. It's quite a low door, and something about the doorframe kept bothering me . . . and then I realised it wasn't the doorframe. It was Ali's height *in relation to* the doorframe. It was slightly different coming than going. The untrained eye might have missed it, but I've been a cop for thirty years. Robin is a little taller than you, isn't he?'

'Only by three inches,' muttered Vicky.

'You had Robin come in disguised as Ali so he would be captured on the CCTV camera at the rear entrance while you were still up onstage. Once inside, Robin, his part of the plan complete, changed out of his get-up in a washroom, and snuck out with the crowds at the end of the concert. Then, when you came down into the room below the stage, you changed into Ali, and walked out with the costume chest, right?'

'Yes.'

Chopra turned to Aaliya. 'One thing I don't understand. Why did *you* go along with this? Vicky claims you have no material interest in him. So why?'

Aaliya hesitated. 'At first I refused. In fact, I tried to talk him out of it. You are right: I have no interest in my father's wealth, and I didn't want Vicky to get into trouble. I was happy simply to know that I had a brother who accepted me as his sister. I was happy to know that I was not alone in the world. But Vicky wore me down. I realised that with or without my help he was determined to carry out his plan. I thought that I could keep an eye on him, perhaps convince him to see reason and abandon his scheme before it went too far. Unfortunately, I did not succeed.'

'But we did succeed, sister!' said Vicky defiantly. He took up the story. 'On the night of the kidnapping the plan unfolded better than I could have hoped.

'At the end of the performance, when I fell through the trapdoor as part of the "vanishing Vickys" sequence, instead of coming back onstage, I changed, as you say, into the guise of Ali. I threw some of my own blood – which I'd drawn earlier – into the alcove, then hauled the chest onto a porter's hand truck, and exited the stadium. I thought that once the police came to investigate they would discover the blood. That – added to the letters, and Aaliya's, or I should say Greta's, testimony about a strange porter hauling off my costume chest, combined with the CCTV footage of "Ali" – should have been enough to convince my mother that I had genuinely been kidnapped.'

'And the whole Ali disguise,' said Chopra, 'that was deliberate, wasn't it? You knew that when your mother heard about the "bearded man in a Muslim prayer cap" her thoughts would go instantly to the threats she had been subjected to in the past.'

'Yes,' admitted Vicky. 'I knew she would think that crazy idiot was making good on his promises of revenge. At the very least it would muddy the waters. Of course, I didn't expect her to keep the police out of it, and to bring you in instead. But when Aaliya told me about you after you interviewed her as Greta I realised that the plan would still work – in fact, it was even better! Now, there was a chance of pulling the whole thing off without raising a fuss in the media. That was the one aspect of the plan I couldn't control.

'I knew that to begin with my reputation would work against me; that everyone would think I had simply pulled another of my vanishing acts. I had to force my mother to the point where she truly believed my life was in jeopardy. After that it would be a simple matter to arrange a ransom exchange, and then "Vicky" could return.

'Of course, I couldn't anticipate everything. For instance, I didn't anticipate that you would actually track me down to Aaliya's home – how did you do that anyway?'

'Your bracelet,' said Chopra. 'You left it in the costume room below the stage.'

Vicky nodded. 'I noticed it was missing the day after my "kidnapping"; I suspected I had lost it that night but I wasn't sure where. I suppose I should never have worn it, but Aaliya gave it to me and I put it on for good luck.'

'What about the photograph you sent to your mother with the ransom note?' said Chopra. 'You looked like you'd taken a fearful beating.'

'The magic of make-up, Chopra. It's one of the reasons I've been coming here. Robin got me access to a make-up room around the back. And, just so's you know, the gun I pulled on you at the Madh Fort wasn't real. It was a prop.'

'And the ear,' said Chopra. 'Let me guess: from the morgue?'

Vicky pulled a rueful face. 'The ear was one of the reasons I became Ali, hospital porter, in the first place. The ear was the finishing touch to my production, necessary to convince my mother that my life was in genuine danger. It belonged to an unidentified man whose body was scheduled for cremation.'

'You desecrated his body,' said Chopra sternly.

Vicky had the decency to blush. 'Yes, and for that I am truly sorry.'

'What exactly did you plan to do with the money?' asked Chopra, changing tack.

Vicky exchanged glances with Aaliya.

'We haven't worked that out yet. I wanted to set Aaliya up, but she won't hear of it. She wants me to return the money. We've been arguing about it.'

Chopra was silent a moment, recalling the argument he had witnessed in the Sahar Hospital. 'I don't understand why you didn't return as soon as you had the cash. Why did you keep up the charade? Your film is on the verge of collapse. A lot of people's lives will be affected, some ruined. Your career, the career of your co-stars, are all on the line.'

It was the actor's turn to hesitate. 'Yes, I thought about that. I talked the whole thing over with Poonam – she had worked so hard to get the role in *Mote* I felt terrible jeopardising her comeback. But she told me to do what I had to. She rose up from a very poor background; in her early career she was taken advantage of. Ayesha and Aaliya's story struck her deeply. She and Robin insisted on helping, no matter what the fallout was. I am truly in their debt.'

'But why not stop as soon as you had the money?' persisted Chopra. 'Why risk the whole movie going up in smoke?'

'The truth? It was because I *wanted* my mother to suffer. I wanted her to feel some of the pain that Aaliya's mother felt when my father abandoned her. And I needed time to think. You may not believe this, but once I got inside Ali's skin I felt myself changing. It was no longer a performance. I was living the life of an ordinary man, helping out at the hospital, seeing the world through the eyes of the poorest people in our society. It sobered me up, I don't mind telling you. For the first time I felt as if I was making a *real* difference in people's lives. I wasn't sure – I'm still not sure – that I want to go back to my mother and the life she's laid out for me. I'm not sure I want to be movie star Vicky Verma any more.'

'A lot of people are relying on you,' said Chopra. 'Many people will suffer if you don't return to finish *The Mote in the Third Eye of Shiva*. Not just your mother.'

'You're right, of course,' Vicky sighed. 'And God knows I want to confront her with the truth, to have it out with her. I want to see her face when I tell her what I've done. I need to know that she feels some remorse for ruining two lives.'

Chopra observed the boy's defiant expression, reflecting once again on the endless ability of human beings to surprise him. Whatever happened now, one thing was certain: Vicky Verma would never be the same vain, arrogant young man he had been just a few short months ago.

If any good had come from this sorry episode, then it was that.

A CRIME FROM THE PAST

Rangwalla stood before the eunuchs in the breakfast hall. He glanced at the clock on the wall. He had timed his morning's entrance precisely. One by one the eunuchs fell silent, perhaps sensing that something was amiss.

'Aren't you going to eat, dear?' said Parvati, eventually. 'We must keep up our strength.'

'I'm afraid it is time to bring this charade to an end,' said Rangwalla. 'It is time for truth.'

'Truth?' Mamta frowned. 'Whatever do you mean?'

'It is time for me to introduce you to our ghost.'

'Hai, Ram!' squeaked Rupa. 'Have you gone mad?'

Rangwalla glanced up at the clock again . . . Any moment now . . . Just then it chimed the hour, and the doors to the breakfast room swung back.

Munshi Premchand entered, followed by the watchman, Shantaram. Premchand tapped his walking stick with annoyance on the parquet floor. 'What is the meaning of this? Why did you wish to see me? We're not due to begin for another hour, and I am a busy man.'

Rangwalla held up a finger. 'Just one moment, please.'

A minute passed during which everyone looked at each other in bewilderment, and then the door opened again. This time a woman entered – the woman Rangwalla had trailed to the village the night before.

'The ghost!' wailed Rupa, rising to her feet. She swooned dramatically, falling backwards into Mamta's lap.

'Stop overacting, you fool,' said Mamta crossly, and pushed the eunuch onto the floor. Rupa's head quickly reappeared, peeking above the table.

'This is no ghost,' explained Rangwalla. 'Though, I'll admit, she *is* the woman who has been singing in the haveli at night. Her name is Darshana.'

'What is the meaning of this?' asked Premchand. 'What is this girl doing here?'

'She is here to help me tell a story.'

'A story?' echoed Parvati. 'What story?'

'The story of the Master and his mother.'

Premchand scowled and seemed about to say something, but then the watchman, Shantaram, placed a hand on his arm. The two men exchanged a long look, and then Premchand subsided.

Rangwalla looked at Darshana, and nodded.

'Once upon a time,' began the young woman, 'there was a thakur – a landowner – named Ranveer Pratap Rathore. As landowners go he wasn't a bad man. He was tough, but generally regarded as being good at heart. He drank too much and chased women, but which landowner didn't?

'And then, one day, Rathore married.

'The woman he married was young, and came from a wealthy family in another state. She thought of herself as a princess, and in some ways she was. The woman – Thakurani Jaya Rathore – soon proved to be the antithesis of her husband. She was a hard, cold woman, wedded to tradition. A streak of cruelty distinguished her, quickly alienating the local villagers.

'In time the union was blessed by a son. The boy – named Suraj Pratap – was an instant disappointment to his mother, a cripple, with a crooked leg and a retiring disposition. Unable to mask her dismay the Mistress treated the boy with coldness from the day of his birth. If the boy found any warmth at all it was from his father, but this was not destined to last.

'Thakur Rathore died when his son was only three years old, the circumstances of his death shrouded in controversy. The police report stated that he fell from the haveli's roof terrace, breaking his neck. At the time only he and the Mistress had been up on the terrace. The report ruled that his death was an accident, but it was later discovered that the Thakur had been consorting with a woman from a neighbouring village, a rich widow. There was even talk that he had expressed a desire to take another wife.

'Whatever the truth, the fact is that, from that point forward, the Mistress took charge of the Rathore estate. She ruled with an iron fist, tripling the land tithes, and forcing many of the locals to the edge of starvation. She hired a gang of thugs – voices raised in protest against her were swiftly silenced.

'As the years passed, the Master grew up learning to tread warily around his mother. He was forbidden to leave the haveli, forbidden to keep friends. The Mistress had no desire for her shame to be exhibited before others, the shame of a cripple for a son. His schooling was undertaken by a series of tutors personally approved by her. In this manner the Master grew to sixteen. And then something happened that changed his life for ever.

'He fell in love.

'It happened, as these things do, in the blink of an eye. One day, the Master wandered into the orchard at the rear of the haveli, a place where he had spent many solitary hours. But instead of being alone with the peacocks and mango trees as he usually was he saw that a strange girl was seated against the well, reading. He shrank back and watched her. Eventually, the girl told him to come out. She didn't like being spied on.

'Her name was Kalpana, and she was the watchman Shantaram's daughter, newly employed as a maid in the haveli.

'She was everything the Master was not: bold, mischievous, outspoken. In time a friendship developed. Each day the Master would arrive in the orchard to find Kalpana reading beside the well. Each day she would mock him: his shyness, his stutter, his constellation of fears. But one thing she never mocked: his crippled leg. That, she told him, was God's design. And who were mere mortals to mock God?

'Friendship became love; the first true love the Master had ever known.

'Two years passed in this secret friendship, until, one day, Kalpana said, "My father wishes to marry me to Alok. He is a blacksmith. He is handsome and strong; he has a livelihood. What do you think?"

'The Master was stricken, but he mumbled, with downcast eyes, "He would make a good husband for you."

'She stared at him, then shook her head. "You are an idiot."

'In the end they married. The Master knew he could never hope to secure his mother's approval for such a match. He knew she wanted him wedded to a highborn woman, to add to the estate's wealth. And so they married in secret, in a temple in the woods, professing their vows to one another with only Kalpana's elder brother in attendance.

'They lived as if in a fairy tale. Married in each other's eyes, but not in the eyes of the law or those around them. Their trysts in the orchard, surrounded by peacocks, became the focal point of their lives. Inside the haveli they studiously ignored one another.

'But Time does not play handmaiden to the whims of men, and eventually the inevitable came to pass.

'Kalpana became pregnant.

'In the village, scandal brewed, but the girl would not reveal the father's identity, not even when, months later, the child – a boy – was born.

'Inevitably, some guessed the father's name, but a conspiracy of silence enfolded the lovers. For no one wished word of the affair to reach the ears of the Mistress. The villagers knew that her wrath would be unimaginable, and that her fury would fall not only upon the girl, but also upon the village.

'But secrets are like worms inside an apple. One day they will eat their way into the light.

'When the Mistress found out, it is said she became silent, unmoving for hours. Finally, she summoned her son.

'Confronted with his mother's knowledge, the Master, for the first time in his life, spoke to her with courage. Leaning on his cane, he spoke of love and happiness. He begged to be allowed to live the life of his desires. He believed – he *hoped* – that his mother would understand.

'He was wrong.

'The Mistress imprisoned her son in the haveli. Then she sent her thugs to find the girl.

'The next day Kalpana's elder brother was discovered by locals in a forest clearing. Dead by knife and fire. Of the girl and her infant son there was no sign. The rumour was later circulated that bandits had surprised them, that the brother had died defending his sister, and that Kalpana and her child had been carried off by the dacoits.

'This was not the truth.

'The Mistress's punishment, you see, was not yet complete.' Darshana stopped, and looked at Rangwalla.

'Please follow me,' said the former policeman. He turned and headed towards the doors of the breakfast room.

Rangwalla wound through the haveli, heading down.

Finally, he reached the lowest level, arriving at a wooden door studded with iron rivets.

He waited while Shantaram unlocked the door. Then he lifted a wax torch from a cresset beside the door, and lit it.

They all trooped into the room, a dank and musty cellar, with grey flagstones underfoot and walls of seeping brickwork. The air smelled of repressed memories, and in the shadows it seemed they could hear the papery whispers of the past.

'What are we doing here?' whispered Rupa.

Rangwalla walked to the far wall of the cellar, his torch casting a wobbling circle of light around him. Then he turned and faced them. 'Shantaram?'

The watchman hobbled forward, removed the sling from his shoulder, and unwrapped the bundle to reveal two pickaxes.

'Mamta, I need your help.'

'What are we supposed to be doing?' said the big eunuch stepping forward.

'Breaking down this wall.'

Rangwalla handed the torch to Shantaram, hefted the pickaxe, then, with a grunt, swung at the wall. The pickaxe embedded itself in the crumbling stone, showering chips in all directions. Rangwalla heaved, pulling out a trio of rotted bricks. Rolling her eyes, Mamta joined him, and together they hacked and bludgeoned away at the wall.

Minutes later, Rangwalla stepped back, passing a forearm over his dust-covered brow. He took the torch and held it up to the gaping hole now visible in the wall.

A gasp echoed around the room.

Leering from the hole, at about head height, was a human skull, with the clavicles visible below the sagging lower mandible. A frayed rope wound loosely around the cervical vertebrae, securing the skeleton to a wooden post.

'Who is that?' whispered Rupa, trembling in the flickering torchlight.

'The Mistress was not content with simply murdering her son's bride,' explained Rangwalla. 'She had the Master brought down here, and she made him watch as Kalpana was entombed alive.'

The eunuchs shivered. Rangwalla heard Kavita crying.

'But that is too cruel!' Rupa gasped. 'How could the Master have borne it?'

'Why don't we ask him?' said Rangwalla.

The eunuchs looked at him in confusion . . . And then it dawned on them. They followed Rangwalla's gaze . . . to where Premchand had straightened from his habitual stoop. Suddenly, his features realigned themselves. The perpetual scowl was replaced by an expression of indescribable sadness. His hands gripped his cane as he stared into the distant past.

'You cannot imagine,' he began, 'what it means to look on as everything you ever wished for is extinguished before your eyes. While you stand there, powerless to do anything about it. And afterwards, bloodying my fists against the walls of my own cell, knowing that the love of my life was slowly suffocating to death in her lightless tomb.

'I haven't set foot down here since that day. I could not. Yet neither could I bring myself to disinter my beloved and cremate her, as I knew I must. I wanted to preserve her as I had last seen her, right here in this room. I wanted that moment – the last time we had looked into each other's eyes and professed our love – to last for ever.'

He fell silent, the memory of that terrible event stifling his words.

'But the tale does not end there,' continued Rangwalla gently. 'The Master was a broken man. He had been a recluse since childhood, now he became doubly so. He never again ventured beyond the walls of the haveli. He never again struck up a friendship with another human being.

'Years passed. And then the Mistress died.

'But the routines of his life had become so ingrained in the Master that he could not break free from the invisible chains that bound him. He haunted the haveli, never venturing far from his dead wife.' Rangwalla paused. 'But one mystery remained. What had happened to the child? The infant son whose death had been ordered by the Mistress?

'The Mistress had given the child to her munshi – you see, there *was* a real Premchand once – and ordered the child to be disposed of. But the munshi, loyal in all matters to his mistress, could not bring himself to curse his own soul by murdering an infant. And so he did the next best thing. He travelled to the city, to Mumbai, and he gave the child to a community from where he knew there could be no return, a community shunned by all others.

'He gave the boy to the eunuchs.'

Another gasp echoed around the cellar. 'Hai Ram!' whispered Rupa.

'The Master, of course, did not know this. He grew old, continuing to believe that his son was dead.

'And then, one day, everything changed. On his deathbed, the munshi, the real Premchand, wishing to atone for his crime, revealed to Shantaram – the child's grandfather – the truth. Unable to conceal this truth from the Master, Shantaram repeated the story to the man who had once been his son-in-law, and who he had continued to loyally watch over since the death of his daughter.

'And so began the Master's quest.

'From the beginning he suspected that his task was hopeless. To find the child who had been fed into the monster that was Mumbai more than thirty years earlier – assuming the child was even still alive. Yet he had to try. He owed that much to his beloved Kalpana.

'But his ways were too deeply ingrained. The prospect of setting foot outside the haveli filled him with dread. Yet neither did he trust anyone else to look for his lost child. And so he decided that if he could not go to the eunuchs of Mumbai, then they must come to him. But he did not wish his mission to be openly known – for he had no idea how his son would react upon discovering the truth – and so he began to invite eunuchs to the haveli, to observe them as they completed meaningless tasks. He felt certain that he would know if one of them was his own flesh and blood.

'It was an impossible quest, yet what choice did he have? For, like so many of us, the past had him in its clutches. He could not live or die in peace until he had his answer.'

A grim silence filled the stone vault.

'But how does the ghost come into it?' asked Parvati eventually.

'As you can see, she is no ghost,' said Rangwalla, pointing at Darshana. 'She is the child of Kalpana's elder brother, the one murdered by the Mistress's thugs.'

'But why were you singing in the haveli?' asked Parvati.

Darshana glanced at her grandfather Shantaram. 'Because I was angry. Ever since I was a child I had been told that my father had died in a terrible accident. I was told nothing about my aunt at all, except that she left the village when I was an infant. It was only when my mother fell gravely ill a few years ago that she finally told me what had happened to my father, and my aunt. I was furious, furious that everyone had lied to me. I wanted to go to the authorities. I wanted a proper police investigation into my father's death. But my grandfather stopped me. He was concerned about the Master. I couldn't understand his loyalty. As far as I was concerned the Master was complicit in my father's death. I went to the haveli and confronted him. I said many things; I even accused him of standing by while his wife, my aunt, was murdered in front of his eyes. He was furious, and banned me from the haveli.

'And then, when the real Premchand passed away and revealed the fact of the Master's lost child, I saw the opportunity for the truth to finally come out into the open. I didn't agree with my grandfather that we should allow the Master to do things his way. I wanted to go to Mumbai to search openly for my cousin, the Master's son. Only by finding him and restoring him to his rightful position can some of the evil inflicted upon my family be undone.'

'And so you pretended to be a ghost?'

'I never said I was a ghost,' snapped the girl. 'I simply couldn't sit by while this charade went on. And so I snuck into the mansion. I thought if I created enough of a disturbance you would run away, and eventually the Master would be forced to abandon his silly plan, and bring in the authorities as I wished.'

'But why didn't you just tell us the truth?'

She sighed. 'I thought about it. But my grandfather was dead set against it. He's all I have left. I love him dearly and would not have hurt him for the world.'

'So what happens now?' asked Mamta.

'I will keep looking,' said the Master sadly.

'Your task is hopeless,' said Parvati gently. 'At least in the way that you're going about it. Have you any idea how many eunuchs there are in Mumbai? Assuming your son is even still alive and in the city. It will take years. You could advertise, I suppose, make a big production of it, but then every chancer and crackpot in the city will come crawling out of the woodwork. And besides, how could you ever be certain? How will you know if a particular eunuch is your child?'

'I will know,' said the Master stubbornly.

'There is a better way,' said Parvati. '*We* will search for you. The eunuchs of Mumbai are like a hive of bees. Nothing happens in our community without us knowing about it. And we keep records. Not in dusty ledgers, but here—' She tapped the side of her head. 'Our oral tradition goes back centuries. If your son is alive we will find him.'

The Master looked at the eunuch with astonishment. 'Why? Why would you help me?'

Parvati's pumpkin-like face split into a smile. 'Because it is the right thing to do.'

THE FESTIVAL OF COLOURS

The Holi festivities were well underway when Chopra and Poppy left the restaurant and headed through the thronged streets towards Film City. Around them, the city was a carnival of colour. For one day, the gods had granted the residents of the subcontinent's most vibrant metropolis the licence to paint the town red. And green . . . and yellow . . . and every other colour under the sun.

As the Tata van weaved its way past knots of celebrants, Poppy looked out with sparkling eyes.

Holi was her favourite festival; something about the childlike gaiety that it inspired in even the most staid of her fellow Mumbaikers transported her back to her carefree youth, in the little village of Jarul where both she and Chopra had grown up. Even there Holi had brought people together – people of all faiths and castes – for Holi was the one Indian festival that transcended the barriers that so often kept people apart.

She glanced into the rear of the van where Irfan and Ganesha had their faces glued to the windows, wistfully observing the merriment.

Suddenly, a broad swathe of orange colour smacked against the windows, causing the pair of them to leap back with delight.

Poppy smiled. Holi! Street urchins with bands of red smeared across their foreheads like holy ash. Balloons full of water arcing over the streets to unerringly find their targets. Roads puddled with vibrant colour. Even the city's animal population was not spared – cows, goats, dogs, and pigs wandered about in bemused consternation, their faces painted like Pandava princes from the Kurukshetra War.

And on the balconies, the rich celebrated in their own style, with urbane Holi parties, canapés, and white-suited brass bands.

They arrived at Film City where Chopra drove them to the set of *The Mote in the Third Eye of Shiva*.

Parking the van, he let Ganesha and Irfan out, then turned just as Vicky Verma, resplendent in the costume of a Mughal prince, bore down on them. He was accompanied by his sister Aaliya Ghazi, who was wearing a bright yellow blouse, blue jeans, and a red headscarf. She smiled as she reached out to tickle the top of Ganesha's head. The little elephant responded by shyly tapping her cheeks with his trunk.

'Chopra!' beamed Vicky. 'So glad you could come!' The actor's arm flashed from behind his back in a blur.

Whump!

Chopra looked down at his pristine white shirt, freshly laundered that very morning. An enormous pancake of mustard yellow marked the front.

'Happy Holi!' laughed Vicky.

Oh dear, thought Poppy. Her husband had always been one of the few curmudgeons who preferred to stay aloof when the annual 'madness' of Holi gripped the city. For one alarming moment, as she observed his grim expression, she thought that he might explode . . . but then he winched forth a smile. 'And a happy Holi to you too, Vicky.'

They moved to a table on the edge of the set. The cast of thousands milled around on all sides, waiting for the director to summon them for the big shoot.

As they sipped glasses of watermelon juice, Chopra asked the actor how things were at home.

'It's been a real shock for my mother,' admitted Vicky. 'But she's taken it better than I had hoped.'

Chopra recalled the meeting with Bijli Verma, immediately after he had tracked Vicky to his hideout in Film City. He had advised the young actor to confront his mother that very night – and to take his half-sister with him . . .

Chopra had expected the encounter to be difficult and he was not disappointed: dredging up the past and forcing those who had behaved badly to confront the consequences of their actions often was. At first Bijli was overwhelmed with relief to be reunited with her son and to discover that he was unharmed. And then the truth came out and she slumped, stunned, onto the sofa of her Malabar Hill apartment, listening glassy-eyed as Vicky poured forth the whole sordid story.

And finally came the rage.

The name Ayesha Azmi – her bitter rival all those years ago – acted as a magic incantation. For a moment Chopra saw the old fire, the fire that had once made her the doyenne of Bollywood, feared by directors and paramours alike. At one point he thought Bijli would actually strike her son.

He stepped between them. 'The past has a way of catching up with the best of us,' he said, holding fast against the tide of fury pouring from Bijli. 'You and your late husband may not have committed any offence in the eyes of the law, but what you did was nevertheless a crime. A crime of the soul. Your son has attempted to make amends for that crime. Perhaps the manner in which he has gone about it is questionable. But he has done what *you* should have a long time ago.' Chopra paused. '"Anger and intolerance are the enemies of understanding." Gandhi said that. It is time to make things right, Bijli.'

Bijli's furious eyes scanned his face . . . and then the rage drained away.

He watched as she stepped up to the girl.

A silence fell as the former starlet scrutinised Aaliya. 'You look like your mother,' she said finally. 'She was very beautiful.' She sighed. 'I always knew you would come, one day. To be honest I often wondered how you would turn out . . . It's no good looking at me like that. I have never claimed to be a saint. Besides, what else could I have done? Should I have just given him up? He made his choice. He chose *me*. I loved him, don't you see?' Chopra had the feeling Bijli was talking to herself. 'I was young. Immature . . . No. That's not true. I knew what I was doing. I knew what I wanted and I wasn't prepared to let anything stand in my way. And once I made that decision, once I stepped onto that path, how could I turn back? Some skeletons are supposed to stay buried.' Finally, her face crumpled. 'I thought of her, so many times. I thought of you. Out there in the darkness I left behind.' Tears glistened on her cheeks, but she did not raise a hand to wipe them away.

'So what now?' she finally said, looking up at Vicky. 'Are you still my son?'

For a long moment Vicky was silent. Chopra knew that the actor still retained a deep anger towards his mother. He felt betrayed in a way that few others could comprehend. On the way to Bijli's apartment he had again said that he'd wanted to punish his mother, to make her feel the pain of loss, just as Aaliya's mother had once suffered. But there was something else too. The revelation of his mother's actions had forced Vicky to look into the mirror. And in that mirror he had seen a reflection he did not much like. His own cavalier attitude towards the legions of women who adored him; the ease with which he took advantage of their affections when it suited him. He felt ashamed of the man he was turning into.

'I don't want to become my father, Chopra,' he said.

Chopra had patted him on the shoulder. 'Life forces us to re-evaluate at every step. This whole episode has given you the opportunity to change. The rest is up to you.'

'I will always be your son,' said Vicky finally. 'The question is, can you be the mother that I want you to be? A mother I can be proud of?'

Bijli looked into the distance. 'The truth is: I don't know. I am old, like wood. And wood doesn't bend.'

'Will you try?'

She looked at Chopra, who nodded gently.

'Yes,' said Bijli Verma. 'I will try.'

Returning to the present, Chopra remarked, 'These things take time. I am sure your mother will come around.'

'If she does it will be all Aaliya's doing,' said Vicky, nodding at his sister. 'She is determined to win my mother over.'

Aaliya smiled. Her pretty face shone. 'She is my mother too now. The only one I have left.'

'It's lucky you have the patience of a saint,' chuckled Vicky. 'Some of the barbs my mother lets fly . . . Anyone else would have run off by now.'

'Oh, she's not as bad as all that,' said Aaliya. 'To be honest, I think she quite likes having a daughter around. Apparently, you were a bit of a brat.'

The pair laughed again.

Chopra felt a resounding happiness engulf him.

He could not have hoped for a better resolution to what had at first seemed a grim case. In the past few days the newspapers had had a field day with the story: FORMER FILM PRODUCER'S ABANDONED LOVE CHILD; VICKY VERMA'S SECRET SISTER; BIJLI VERMA WRECKS HOME OF PREGNANT RIVAL.

The details of the 'kidnapping', however, had been kept out of the media – Chopra had felt that little was to be gained by making a public issue out of Vicky's badly judged attempt to rectify the past.

Besides, was it really a crime to kidnap yourself?

Instead, Chopra had encouraged Vicky to give the press the story that mattered: the story of his sister.

And that is exactly what he had done.

With the country's eyes upon him he had publicly declared his kinship to Aaliya Ghazi, informing a packed news conference that as far as he was concerned Aaliya *was* his real sister. He confirmed that should she wish it, she was free to adopt their father's name – though Aaliya had politely declined – and that his sister was entitled to her share of their father's estate.

The press conference had done wonders for his reputation. His transformation from Bollywood brat to compassionate sibling had won him a whole new legion of fans. Chopra had even overheard the usually hawkish Mrs Subramanium, the head of the management committee of the apartment complex where he and Poppy lived, remarking: 'What a sensible young man.' High praise indeed from a woman who had once accused Gandhi of being little more than a 'badly dressed rabble-rouser'.

Nor was Mrs Subramanium the only one to have mellowed.

Chopra had been surprised to discover that the lawyer Lal had not been dismissed by Bijli following his admission that he had sabotaged the ransom drop. Explaining his reasons with a stiff-backed formality – and gaining some measure of relief by finally confessing his lifelong devotion – he had proffered his resignation. Which Bijli had declined, to universal astonishment.

Perhaps Aaliya was right. Perhaps Bijli wasn't 'as bad as all that'.

Privately, Chopra thought that Bijli, having been forgiven for such a grievous error of her own, was now willing to show more compassion for the mistakes of others. And as for Lal . . . the man had almost cost Chopra his freedom. But it had not been his intent. Could Chopra really hold a grudge?

In this respect reel life, he reflected, was different to *real* life. In Bollywood there were no shades of grey: heroes were whiter than white; villains were irredeemably bad. But men and women like Lal, Das, and Bijli herself, did not live up to these tropes in the cold light of reality. He thought of the producer, rescued at the last minute from ruin. Was Das truly a thug, as Panipat had labelled him? Chopra could not be sure. Das, like so many in the industry, was an enigma, a reflection of the smoke-and-mirrors nature of Bollywood.

He realised that Poppy was looking at him. His wife, radiant as ever in a multi-hued Holi sari, was a sucker for a happy ending. She was also a tremendous fan of Vicky

Verma, and had bent Chopra's ear to get her an audience. Well, here they were . . .

He coughed. 'Vicky, I wonder if I could trouble you for something?'

Vicky smiled. 'Don't worry, Chopra. A cheque is on its way to you. With a substantial bonus, I should add. You have certainly earned it.'

Chopra shook his head. 'That's not what I meant.' He pulled a photograph of Vicky from his pocket. 'I, er, I'd like your autograph. It's not for me,' he added hurriedly. 'It's for my wife.'

'Of course it is,' said Vicky, grinning. He looked over at Poppy and winked.

'It really is,' said Chopra. 'Tell him, Poppy.'

'Oh, don't be bashful,' said Poppy mischievously. 'He's your number-one fan.'

Chopra coloured.

Behind them, Ganesha gave a little bugle.

'All right. Number two, then,' smiled Poppy. 'Little Ganesha never misses one of your movies. It's a shame *he* can't ask for an autograph.'

'Perhaps I can go one better,' said Vicky. 'Come with me. I need to see a man about an elephant.'

THE MASTER COMES FULL CIRCLE

At about the same time that Inspector Chopra (Retd) was visiting Film City, former sub-inspector Rangwalla was making an important visit of his own. Having returned from the haveli of the Master – Thakur Suraj Pratap – Rangwalla had found his usual routine disturbed.

He discovered that he could not let go of this odd case.

There was little doubt that the Master was a strange duck, but was it any wonder? The man had suffered terribly in life; fate had dealt him the worst of hands. The horrors that had been inflicted on him – the murder of the woman he had loved, the abduction of his infant child – would have laid low even the most resilient of men, let alone a boy browbeaten from birth by a domineering and black-hearted mother.

Yet now, finally, he had been released from the shackles of his past.

The secrets that had held him in chains had been blown to the four winds. Past had caught up with present, and the only thing that mattered to him was finding the child he had so long believed lost.

And in this Rangwalla was determined to help.

It was not an easy choice. His time with the eunuchs had challenged and subverted his most basic assumptions about the transgender community of Mumbai. He found that he could no longer rewire the circuits of his brain to think of them as he had once done. He imagined how it might feel to be sundered from his own family. It seemed to him that the emotions that churned inside the human heart were the same no matter who you were, eunuch or otherwise. To make this journey, however, Rangwalla knew that he had a lifetime of unlearning to do, a daily battle to wage against the smog of reflexive attitudes that darkened the very air of Mumbai. Then again, didn't they say that every journey had to start somewhere?

Rangwalla stepped out from the passenger seat of the classic 1950s Chevrolet Fleetmaster.

It was another stiflingly hot day.

Further along the street he could hear the din of Holi celebrations.

He waited as the driver opened the rear door of the cream sedan. The venerable automobile had only just been removed from storage – it had belonged to the Master's mother – cleaned and polished, and tuned into full working order, in preparation for this momentous trip.

And now they were here.

From the rear came a voice. 'Here?' asked Thakur Suraj Pratap.

'Yes,' said Rangwalla. 'Here.'

Silence, then: 'I don't think I can.'

Rangwalla reached in. 'Thirty years is a long time to wait.'

Thakur Pratap grasped Rangwalla's hand and allowed himself to be helped from the Fleetmaster.

Then he looked up at the façade of the Red Fort.

'He's here!' sang a voice from the first floor. Rangwalla looked up and saw Parvati's familiar face. 'Halloo!' she waved enthusiastically.

Minutes later, eunuchs crowded around the little company, showering the bewildered Pratap with greetings and good wishes.

'So glad you could make it,' said Mamta.

'You look much better in this get-up,' observed Rupa. 'I never did like the munshi look.'

'Come,' said Kavita shyly. 'You honoured us in your home. Now let us welcome you to ours.'

Gradually, they were borne along by the gaggle of excited eunuchs into the interior of the Red Fort.

They stopped before a bead curtain. 'Are you ready?' asked Rangwalla.

Thakur Pratap blinked. 'No,' he said hoarsely.

'Then you are as ready as you will ever be.'

They ducked through the bead curtain into the Queen of Mysore's chambers. The room was as Rangwalla remembered it: red lit, with the curtains drawn, the smell of incense, hashish, and lotus blossom thickening the air.

The Queen of Mysore sat on her raised divan, toking furiously on her hookah. Once again, she was finely dressed in a sequinned gaghra-choli, her jewellery even more ostentatious than when Rangwalla had last seen her.

Even the Queen had made a special effort for the occasion.

Beside her was her young assistant; standing to one side was Anarkali, biting her lip in anxiety.

'Welcome,' said the Queen, eventually.

A strange silence descended on the company, holding them all in a sort of electrified paralysis. No one dared disturb the moment.

Rangwalla knew that they were here thanks to the tireless efforts of the eunuchs who had returned with him from the Master's haveli, in particular Parvati and Mamta. They had sent emissaries to every eunuch dera in the city, tapping into that vast reservoir of memory that the eunuchs held within their community, and which was passed down from generation to generation in their great oral histories.

In short order they had discovered that some thirty years previously a boy-child had indeed been handed to a eunuch dera in the southern half of the city by a man who resembled the old munshi of the Master's estate.

Then had begun the process of tracking that ill-fated child's journey to adulthood.

It appeared that the boy had been castrated as per the rituals of the eunuchs and initiated into their community. He – now *she* – had been cared for by an elder eunuch, but, when that guardian had passed on, had been left to the whims of fate.

She had grown up angry and wild, swept along by her own internal fires.

In time the firebrand had risen within her community; she had fought and suffered, but she had prevailed.

And now, it seemed, history had come full circle.

The past was about to meet the present.

Rangwalla broke the spell. He moved forward to stand before the Queen of Mysore. 'Thakur Suraj Pratap, permit me to introduce you to your . . . daughter.'

Rangwalla held out a hand towards the Queen.

A tremble of emotion passed over the Queen's features.

Thakur Pratap moved forward. Rangwalla could see tears standing in the old man's eyes. 'Daughter,' he breathed. 'My daughter.' He moved closer until he stood directly before the dais, his gaze locked on the Queen of Mysore.

'You have your mother's eyes,' he eventually said.

The Queen bowed her head. 'Get out!' she growled. 'Everyone get out!'

Rangwalla knew that she did not wish her tears to be seen. He could not imagine what was going on inside her; the dark wraiths that had been unleashed from the deepest pit of her memories.

A childhood lost and scattered to the winds.

A life stolen.

Her shoulders shook as she wept.

He looked up and saw that no one had moved.

Finally, Thakur Pratap reached out with a trembling hand and placed it on the Queen's shoulder. 'Do not be troubled,' he said. 'Daughter.'

And at last the Queen of Mysore raised her head. Tears glistened on her cheeks. 'Daughter?' she said, hoarsely.

Thakur Pratap nodded. 'Daughter,' he confirmed.

Rangwalla felt something he had rarely known: the blazing sun of a moral rightness.

In spite of the best efforts of men to crush the spirits of their brethren, hope and goodness still flowered. The eunuchs, earthy-spirited, with basic human goodness in their bones, had risen time and time again, had prevailed in the face of relentless adversity.

And one day, he was now certain, they would gain the emancipation they so richly deserved.

THE FINAL TAKE

Scene Ninety-three. Exterior. Bank of the Yamuna River. Day.

(LIGHTS! CAMERA! ACTION!)

Fade in:

Mist boiled from the surface of the river, rolling over the ghostly silhouette of the Taj Mahal as a solitary bugler greeted the dawn. Crows lifted from the water's edge, cawing in indignation, as the prow of an imperial barge parted the streams of mist and glided towards the riverbank. At the last second courtiers in Mughal finery leapt from the barge's bow, and tethered the longboat to mooring posts.

The barge discharged its passengers – a platoon of armed warriors in cavalry battledress: chain mail, golden breastplates and pointed helmets – closely followed by their steeds, also resplendent in riveted chain mail. Behind the cavalrymen came a group of chattering religious clerics, dressed in white. Finally, flanked on either side by his personal bodyguard, came Prince Shah Saleem, anointed heir to Emperor Shah Jahan, atop his magnificent white stallion, Buharrim.

In one graceful movement the stallion leapt from the boat to the shore, then at the subtle urging of the prince's heels, raced ahead onto the plateau that lay before the Taj.

Cries of alarm followed the prince, and then his cavalrymen gave chase, even as princely laughter fluttered back towards them on the gentle wind.

Prince Saleem raced on towards a copse of trees cresting the rise of a shallow hill. The dawn air invigorated him, filling him with optimism. He could smell the coming battle, and he was not afraid. In the distance smoke rose from the fires of the encamped armies, all the way out to the nearby town of Agra, which had been besieged by enemy forces. He knew that death stalked him out there. Perhaps, tonight, when the final battle began, it would hunt him down.

But that was beyond his control.

For now all that mattered was that he was here, alive, and ready for war.

He wheeled his stallion around, and looked back at the Taj Mahal.

The great monument had only recently been completed. His father's chief architect had planned a surrounding wall and formal gardens, but for now the Taj stood alone on the river's edge, open to the four winds on its lonely plain, the plain that today would serve as the battleground for the final clash between the forces ranged against the emperor.

It would be the greatest battle in history, thought the prince.

And he would be in the very thick of it.

A noise spun him around.

He saw a shadow moving in the copse of trees.

'Who goes there?' he shouted.

No reply came.

Drawing his curved sword – his father's sword, with its ruby-encrusted gold hilt, which he had named Alamgir or 'World-Seizer' – the prince dismounted, then moved on foot towards the trees. Behind him the thunder of hooves drew nearer as his soldiers approached.

'Who goes there?' shouted the prince again.

And then a short, squat shape appeared from between the trees. It saw the prince, then turned in alarm and limped back into the darkness.

The prince jogged behind the creature and into the copse.

In a clearing, the prince saw an elephant lying on its side in a mulch of churned grass and leaves. The great beast had been mortally wounded – blood seeped from a constellation of wounds on its flank. The grey hide rose and fell in laboured breathing, the eyes glassy. Death was only moments away.

The infant elephant he had followed into the copse was now hunkered close to its mother, caressing her face with its trunk.

Prince Saleem understood that this was an omen. He did not know yet if the omen was good or bad.

He moved towards the young elephant – a bull – who limped backwards, away from him.

Saleem saw that an arrow protruded from the beast's right foreleg. 'Steady there, boy,' he said. 'Let me help you.'

He knelt down beside the beast, and looked into its eyes. A bright intelligence looked back at him. The calf lifted its foreleg, and twirled its trunk.

'I understand,' said the prince.

He took hold of the arrow's shaft. 'This is going to hurt,' he said. Then, with one sharp tug, he pulled the arrow from the elephant's hide.

The little calf trumpeted in pain, ears flapping in alarm. His eyes fluttered, and he limped back and forth. Finally, he calmed himself, and stood, eyes downcast, trunk hanging between his legs, staring forlornly at his dying mother.

('Isn't he good?' breathed Poppy, watching with Chopra from behind the director's camera.

'He needs to be careful not to ham it up,' smiled Chopra. A swell of pride puffed out his chest as he watched Ganesha in the minor role Vicky had engineered for him. 'There are enough hams out there already,' he added, under his breath. But he was, nevertheless, glad that he had accepted the gesture.

'It's the least I can do after throwing you off the Sea Link bridge,' Vicky had said. 'It never occurred to me that you might not be able to swim.')

'Do not be sad, little one,' said the prince. 'Death comes to us all. Man and beast, prince and pauper. Who knows? Perhaps tonight I will join your mother in the afterlife. If that is God's will, then so be it. War plays no favourites.' The prince sighed, striking a pose, as he delivered his soliloquy. 'Perhaps the time of princes is at an end.'

He raised his eyes to the heavens, his expression wistful.

('Doesn't he look dashing?' murmured Poppy. 'I am sure it will be a hit.'

'If it isn't, a lot of people are going to lose their shirts,' said Chopra.)

Prince Saleem turned back to the calf. 'Go,' he declaimed. 'Go, before the battle comes. If any of us deserve to survive the coming night then it is you, my little friend. You are a symbol of the innocence we have lost. Go, now, your prince commands you. And perhaps, one day, if I live to tell the tale, we will meet again.'

Little Ganesha looked up at the prince, then turned and limped to the edge of the clearing.

At the last second, he glanced back, hesitating for one brief second, fixing the prince with a look of heartrending sorrow, before turning and melting into the shadows.

'CUT! CUT! CUT!' bellowed the director, B.P. Agarwal, brandishing his megaphone.

Immediately, the gathered cast and crew relaxed. Vicky's co-stars slapped him on the shoulder and congratulated him on a great performance.

Agarwal glanced over at Poppy and Chopra. 'That elephant is a natural,' he declared. 'You should consider a career in the pictures.'

Chopra stood. 'He has a career already.'

'But he could be a movie star,' said Poppy, her eyes shining with possibility.

Chopra smiled. 'Perhaps,' he said. 'But for now, he is a private detective, and a damned good one at that.'

GLOSSARY

Alghoza – a pair of flutes joined together and played simultaneously

Astrakhan – hat with dark curly fleece of young karakul lambs from central Asia

Betel nut – areca nut, often chewed and the resultant fluid spat out

Dhoti – traditional men's garment wrapped around legs and knotted at the waist

Dupatta – long scarf made from light fabric

Goonda – thug or bully

Hookah – instrument for vaporizing and smoking flavored tobacco

Jaggery – cane sugar

Kabaddi – a traditional form of Indian wrestling

Kurta – loose collarless shirt worn usually with a salwar or pajama.

Lathi – a stick / baton

Maya – that which is not (i.e. illusion)

Parotta – a layered flatbread

Pajama – a pair of loose trousers tied by a drawstring around the waist

Peepal – sacred fig tree

Ram ram – a common Hindi greeting meaning hello.

Rangoli – decorative patterns created using colored rice, flour, sand or flower petals

Salwar – a pair of light, loose, pleated trousers, usually tapering to a tight fit around the ankles, worn by women with a kameez or long shirt

Shree – polite form of address equivalent to the English "Mr."

Sundari – double-reed wind instrument

Thaali – steel platter with individual sections to serve a variety of dishes.

ACKNOWLEDGEMENTS

The best encouragement any writer can receive is to hear the words "you're getting better". So thank you, first and foremost, to my agent Euan Thorneycroft at A.M. Heath and to my indefatigable editor Ruth Tross at Mullholland. If I was adrift in the ocean in a small boat, I'd want them both there . . . just so we could go over the final manuscript one more time.

Once again a big thank you to Kerry Hood at Hodder, who continues to promote these books with gilt-edged zeal, and her assistant Rosie Stephen.

I am grateful too to others who helped improve the original manuscript. Thomas Abraham and Poulomi Chatterjee at Hachette India; Amber Burlinson, copy-editor, and Justine Taylor, in the role of proofreader.

I would also like to thank Ruth's team at Mullholland, Naomi Berwin in marketing, Laura Oliver in production, Dom Gribben in audiobooks, and assistant editor Cicely Aspinall. In the US thanks go to Devi Pillai (who will be missed as she moves on to pastures new), Ellen Wright, Laura Fitzgerald and Lindsey Hall, and also Jason Bartholomew at Hodder. Similar thanks go to Euan's assistant Pippa McCarthy, and the others at A.M. Heath working tirelessly behind the scenes.

Another wonderful cover to add to those in the series – fast becoming artistic pieces in their own right – and kudos for this one goes to Sarah Christie and Anna Woodbine.

Lastly, much gratitude is due to Jonathan Kinnersley at The Agency and the great people at Cinestaan Films – Rohit Khattar, Deborah Sathe and Tessa Inkelaar – for agreeing a film option deal for book one in the series. And yes, I am ridiculously excited at the prospect of Chopra and Ganesha ending up on the silver screen. After all, no one is immune to the magic of Bollywood, not even fictional baby elephants and their creators.

ABOUT THE AUTHOR

Vaseem Khan first saw an elephant lumbering down the middle of the road in 1997 when he arrived in India to work as a management consultant. It was the most unusual thing he had ever encountered and served as the inspiration for the Baby Ganesh Agency series.

He returned to the UK in 2006 and now works at University College London for the Department of Security and Crime Science where he is astonished on a daily basis by the way modern science is being employed to tackle crime. Elephants are third on his list of passions, first and second being great literature and cricket, not always in that order.

For more information about the world of the book (plus pictures of baby elephants!) please visit vaseemkhan.com.